The
SWORDS
of
SILENCE

Harper*Inspire*, an imprint of
HarperCollins Christian Publishing
1 London Bridge Street
London SE1 9GF

www.harpercollins.co.uk

First published by HarperCollins 2019.

A catalogue record for this book is available from the British Library

ISBN: 9780310101307 (TPB)
ISBN: 9780310101277 (ebook)
ISBN: 9780310101369 (Audio)

The novel is entirely a work of fiction. The names, characters and
incidents portrayed in it, while at times based on historical figures, are
the work of the author's imagination.

Set in Crimson Text by e-Digital Design

Printed and bound in the UK by CPI Group (UK) Ltd,
Croydon CR0 4YY

Scripture quotes are taken from the Authorized King James Version
(KJV) and the New International Version (NIV) of the Bible.
Used by permission.

'The Christian Century in Japan 1549-1650' by C.R. Boxer
(*The Christian Century in Japan 1549-1650*, 1994) is reprinted here
by kind permission of Carcanet Press Limited, Manchester, UK.

MIX

Paper from responsible sources

FSC

FSC™ C007454

SHAUN CURRY

The SWORDS *of* SILENCE

THE SWORDS OF FIRE TRILOGY:
BOOK ONE

INSPIRE

About the Author

Shaun Curry has been fascinated by Japan from an early age. He went on to study and work in Tokyo, where he developed a passion for the country, its culture and history.

His research on feudal Japanese history has informed not only his fiction, but also numerous articles, and has led him to be featured as a guest on BBC Radio. A British and Canadian national, he now lives and writes in London.

Dedication

Between 1614 and 1643, Japan's Shogun and his regime executed almost 5,000 Christian martyrs.

At the broadest level, I would like to dedicate this book and the entire *Swords of Fire* trilogy to all the courageous martyrs and missionaries of Japan, then and now.

On a more personal level, I would like to dedicate this book to the loving memory of Kimberley Ann Wilshire, who set me on a path of self-discovery and re-awakening.

PROLOGUE

20 June 1626
Nagasaki City, District of Nagasaki, Kyushu

Provincial Francisco Pacheco staggered ahead of a sombre procession of prisoners. Behind him, a dozen or so souls, pale and gaunt, their clothes filthy and many worn to rags, moved, each step agony. The beatings driving them forward had been hourly. Or was it every few minutes? Pacheco could no longer clearly recall. It had gone on for so long now. A chorus of soft groans accompanied their lurching footsteps along the dusty road through the streets of Nagasaki, but few had the strength or the will left to even plead for mercy, had they been able to spit out the rags stuffed in their mouths.

The day was overcast, threatening rain, and a chill, late-afternoon breeze brushed against them from behind, rustling the occasional pennants on the *mochi yari,* the hand spears of the samurai and foot soldiers guarding the condemned. An acrid smell of stale blood, sweat, human evacuation and horses permeated the air.

For Pacheco and his flock it was a death march of broken people, their bodies beaten, bruised, blood-streaked, and covered in ulcerous wounds. When they had been confined in sewer-like prisons, Governor Kawachi had administered multiple beatings prior to their execution.

The prisoners included the most prominent and influential Christians and their aides.

The townspeople, whether secretly Christian or not, lined the streets and watched quietly, the horror of the slowly winding parade too much for some, and they looked away or covered the eyes of the children huddling beside them.

The metallic taste of stale blood persisted in Pacheco's mouth. He was the highest-ranking Catholic in Japan, a Provincial Superior in the Society of Jesus. The authorities had captured and arrested the seventy-year-old Portuguese priest a year earlier in Kuchinotsu at the southern tip of the Shimabara Peninsula. He had been held in Omura Prison ever since, counting the days to his execution.

That hour was now upon him.

* * *

Governor Kawachi was a hard, stocky man who believed in a personal regime of daily icy baths, and rigid obedience from his retainers. He stood amid a group of aides and sneered victoriously as the procession slowly wound past him. He had instructed his officials to shave the prisoners' heads and paint their scalps bright red to single them out and highlight their impending execution.

One final touch. He had ordered that rags be shoved into their mouths so they could not speak and inspire others during their death march. Christians in particular who witnessed the display had to be warned and paralysed with fear at the thought of disobeying his orders.

The Governor recalled the last public execution, three years earlier. Most of the Christians had faced their deaths with resolve, even rapturous joy. Not this time. None of these people would be vocal martyrs as they died. As the condemned passed him, Kawachi felt satisfaction at this visceral demonstration of his authority and power.

Ever since his appointment as the new governor, Kawachi had anticipated this day. The death march through the streets of Nagasaki, with Provincial Pacheco at its head, consisted of two European priests, five lay Portuguese prisoners, including a fourteen-year-old boy, and two ships' captains. Their crime: aiding Japanese Christians. The final shaven-headed victims comprised Japanese individuals who had sheltered priests.

The prisoners were tied to each other by a rope around their necks to keep them in line. Officials spat contemptuously in their faces as they dragged them through the streets like animals condemned to an abattoir. Kawachi's soldiers jeered as they brandished their whips and sticks, scolding and hitting the prisoners for unknown infractions whenever they felt inclined. Samurai steel pinched and sliced skin and muscle made tender by the lash. Blood dripped into the dust at their feet. The Governor had insisted his men must show the utmost contempt to the men and the boy as they trudged, humiliated, to their fate through the mostly quiet crowd that lined their route.

The procession drew to a halt and the Governor's men shoved the condemned into a secured area where execution stakes awaited them. As the afternoon light began to fade, a flickering torch flame cast the only light as officials readied the execution posts.

Governor Kawachi had expected more resistance but the prisoners, particularly Pacheco, showed a submissive acceptance that Kawachi found enraging. He had forbidden the public from entering the fenced execution zone. He caressed his wooden clipboard, displaying the names of each of his victims, then moved it away from his expensive navy-blue silk kimono. He drew satisfaction from his choice of execution method. Since the Christian holocaust in his country had begun, officials had learned to calculate the victim's exact distance from the fire to ensure the most drawn-out death by incineration.

Head erect and shoulders back, Provincial Pacheco paid little attention to any of the officials. He took a deep breath and gathered his remaining strength, hobbling as best he could past the Governor and Deputy-Lieutenant Suetsugu without a glance in their direction as he led his fellow prisoners towards the stakes. Stacks of dried wood lay three feet from each execution station which themselves had a small mound of kindling at the base of each.

Both Pacheco and Kawachi knew that just as Soldiers of the Sword were venerated in Japan, so too were Soldiers of the Cross. In the eyes of Japanese Christians, the Ways of the Cross echoed the service and ways of the samurai in honour and discipline. How Pacheco comported himself now would be crucial to rejecting Kawachi's cruel effort to crush their spirit. All eyes would be upon him, and Pacheco struggled to hold on to that thought.

Kawachi grunted with satisfaction as he smelled the scent of the burning wooden torch. Yet despite all he had achieved, frustration gathered within him. None in the procession had resisted the scourging. The Christians' resolve tore at his satisfaction, and he understood that what he and his men were seeing was true courage – what was now being called *Bushido*. He secretly feared it might infect his men in some way and the thought enraged him. He watched his men move forward and scan the condemned for signs of fear. Some wriggled and twisted at their tight bonds, but only the frailest and youngest of the Christians uttered involuntary whimpers through their gags. Even so, they first fixed their eyes on Pacheco, and seeing his stoic resolution then turned to face their tormentors with quiet determination. Kawachi noticed one or two of his men flinch slightly from their gaze, and clenched his fist at his side.

The Deputy-Lieutenant bellowed an order. The officials bound their victims roughly to the wooden stakes. The Governor's men circled the prisoners and inspected each knot and rope. There would be no mistakes today. No survivors.

Kawachi strode up to Pacheco. The Governor's eyes squinted with hate, and he spat in the priest's face. Pacheco maintained his composure, and appeared to be mumbling to himself. He stared ahead.

Deputy-Lieutenant Suetsugu then approached the Governor. Kawachi took a torch from a soldier near him and handed it to Suetsugu, who bowed and ignited the kindling in front of Father Pacheco.

'You are criminals of the Empire. You will all die with shame!' Suetsugu shouted. He had been a Christian once himself, so it was imperative he showed how much he truly despised the faith now, and protected his coveted position as Nagasaki's Deputy-Lieutenant. He lit the remaining wood piles, grunting with satisfaction as he heard the crackle of flames catch at each execution station.

Governor Kawachi approached the human torches. Above their muffled cries he shouted: 'Our lands have been infected with vermin like you since you brought this Christian nonsense to our shores. You have violated the Shogun's laws and this regime will not tolerate your religion. May your deaths be a warning to any who dares embrace this useless faith!'

The flames caught hold, roaring louder as the prisoners' involuntary cries grew louder in response.

Kawachi stared at Pacheco as the flames licked at the priest's waist and he spat on the ground with disgust. The Governor had hoped for begging, pleading, perhaps cries for mercy, but this stubborn defiance was intolerable. He stepped back, shaking his head with annoyance.

Thick and muggy air made the soldiers cough and tug at their armour. The flames spat at the Governor's men, several of whom took a step back. The Governor and the Deputy-Lieutenant also retreated, shielding their faces from the flames' growing fury.

Father Pacheco managed to spit out the rag lodged in his mouth. 'Brothers in faith,' he shouted in a voice wracked with pain, 'the Holy Spirit is with us! Despair not!'

'What's happening?' Kawachi yelled.

His subordinates looked bewildered and shrank back from his temper. He pointed a finger at Father Pacheco. 'Imbeciles! How has he lost his gag?'

'I'm not sure,' Suetsugu said. Panic washed over his face.

'Shove it back in. Now!' Kawachi roared over the sound of the fire. The soldiers looked at each other wildly, hoping another would obey the Governor, but no one stepped forward.

'It's too late, Governor!' Suetsugu yelled.

Kawachi watched an anguished moan of pain escape from the priest as the flames blackened his face. It gave the Governor a moment's satisfaction.

Pacheco cried out to anyone who could still hear him, 'Take comfort! These men can do no more harm than God allows. They know not what they do.'

Someone cried, 'Amen!' Another gave a muffled scream.

'Silence them!' the Governor yelled.

'It's too late. The fire is too strong to approach,' Suetsugu said.

Despite coughing and burning, Pacheco cried, 'The Lord is with me still,' until his voice reduced to unintelligible grunts of pain. Kawachi watched the priest's eyes bulge as his face slowly blistered and melted.

A number of the officials turned away, bent over and vomited at the smell and horror of the moment. Kawachi approached them with a disdainful snort. His hostile glare took them all in, in turn. He pointed to the now silent fires raging behind him. 'I want *all* their ashes shovelled into sacks – nothing will remain. Then I want those ashes scattered in the deep sea.'

'Yes, Governor.'

'Before you return, I want every man to bathe twice, at length, before touching shore.'

'Bathe twice, Governor?'

'Not one ash will remain. Nothing from their bodies will endure. Japan will forget this vermin ever existed! Do I make myself clear?'

'*Hai*, Governor!' they replied in unison.

CHAPTER ONE

21 May 1626. One month earlier
Arima, Shimabara Peninsula, Kyushu

'Shigemasa is coming! Shigemasa is coming!' shouted a farmer. His eyes bulged as he burst into Father Joaquim's quarters.

Onaga birds squawked and scattered to the skies before the rattle of hardened leather and metal armour, as hundreds of horses approached in the distance down a well-worn path at a steady, military pace.

Had the village's early warning system – a child on the far edge of the forest, whose waving arms had been seen by another youth at the near edge – given them enough notice?

The villagers had just minutes, so they mobilized quickly as they'd done numerous times before. Several lifted floor planks exposing secret spaces, some just large enough to hide forbidden items such as bibles and crucifixes, others big enough to conceal bigger secrets, like foreign Christians, including Catechist Miguel, Catechist Tonia, and Father Joaquim. The priest was already in a concealed room cleaning a small basin with which he conducted baptisms. He tossed it to the side, lifted a muddied plank of wood, and hid himself underground. Joaquim closed his eyes, lay quietly, and muttered a fervent prayer. They could not find him here. They *would* not find him here. The Lord would protect his servants and keep them safe. Since Christianity had been officially banned more than a decade before, life had become more dangerous for the faithful.

Father Joaquim thought back to what had brought him to this location. How could he forget that night?

He could still hear the screams of his mother – a woman abandoned by an absent and drunken husband, left to care for three children under ten and Joaquim, a mere sixteen-year-old.

To this day Joaquim questioned how the man had found his way into their house. When the intruder pulled a knife on them, he did what any son would have done. Perhaps he had underestimated his own strength. All that mattered had been keeping his family alive. In a frantic and chaotic struggle, he'd managed to claim the knife from the man and thrust his arm around the man's neck, pulling hard and not letting go until he felt the man fall limp. It only took a few minutes, but to Joaquim it had seemed like hours.

He'd killed him. Strangled him. A man almost twice his weight.

Even the authorities had agreed it was self-defence, but the memory and the guilt had followed him each day like a stray dog.

Perhaps that's why it had been easy to enrol, a few months later, in the College of Jesus at the University at Coimbra. Eventually he'd been sent to Japan with the Society of Jesus. And it was here that Father Joaquim had found a symbiotic home in Master Yamaguchi's village, where he proselytized the Word of God and, in return, learned the Way of the Sword.

Arima was located on the Shimabara Peninsula in the old province of Hizen, on the island of Kyushu, Japan's southernmost island. All the villages in Arima feared Lord Shigemasa. But those in this village had a special reason to fear the approaching Daimyo and his samurai.

* * *

Daimyo Matsukura Shigemasa surveyed the village in the distance. He was a large man with a battle-scarred face, and could command obedience with a simple stare. He straightened his helmet that brandished jutting horn-like ornamentations. Like other days when he'd conducted surprise visits, today he'd chosen to wear traditional battle dress, painted in his official colours of black and red. His body armour included a metal breastplate lacquered to give a smooth finish, coupled with layers of protective metal plates.

He passed the rice paddies and arrived at the upper edge of the village. 'Where is Yamaguchi-san?' he shouted.

'He's resting, Lord Shigemasa,' a peasant replied.

'Find him.' Shigemasa glared at the man bowing before him.

Another man darted away and ran down a narrow path.

The Daimyo roared at the bowed heads before him, 'I have heard reports of Christians hiding in Arima. Are you hiding any of the vermin here?'

'No, Lord Shigemasa. There are none here,' someone answered. 'We are a Buddhist community, Lord.'

'So you say.' Shigemasa scanned the peasants kneeling before him. Several dared to glance up at him. 'I will have the pleasure of torturing and killing any Christians found on my lands … including those who aid or conceal them.'

'Yes, Lord, we understand.'

'Do you? We will see.' Shigemasa motioned for his soldiers to search the village.

Several samurai dismounted from their horses, heaving villagers out of their way as they walked towards the dwellings. They approached the first home and a bulky samurai kicked the door open. The door spun backwards on frail hinges as he charged into the shack. The hut owners, standing near the front door, gasped at the blatant disrespect. Not only did the samurai neglect to bow before entering, as was the custom, but they stormed from house to house, their swords raised and ready to be used, treating the villagers like an enemy. Enslaved by fear, the villagers could only watch and submit.

In shack after shack, swords skewered rickety beds, fragile furniture and mounted personal memorabilia. Armoured men pitched clothing through windows, rummaged through meagre sleeping quarters. Swords slashed through curtains and clattered through pottery, water jugs and overturned cooking pots.

'There's nothing here, my Lord!' called a samurai over his shoulder to Shigemasa.

Shigemasa nodded in satisfaction and turned his attention towards the village's small Buddhist temple. 'Go in there.'

Samurai thundered through the temple entrance. Their eyes fell on burned offerings of candles, then flowers, and finally Buddhist beads. They scrutinized the incense tables.

'Nothing!' called the head samurai as he exited the temple. 'There is no evidence of Christian observance here.' He bowed towards Daimyo Shigemasa.

The nearest peasant looked up and ventured to speak again. 'As I mentioned, Lord Shigemasa, there are no Christians in this valley.' He cast his eyes down, quickly realising his fault in staring at Shigemasa.

'Grab him and put him in a straw coat! Let him do the *mino odori* – the raincoat dance!' shouted Daimyo Shigemasa. Samurai elbowed the peasant to the dust and spun his face away from the warlord. A samurai sword speared his leg. The man screamed in pain as the blade was pulled free. Soldiers tied his hands behind him as blood pulsed from the wound. They wrapped dry straw around his upper body while other samurai poured hot lamp oil over his head.

'Mercy, Lord!' cried the peasant's wife, falling to her knees. Shigemasa stared at her with a cruel resolve. She wailed hysterically, then stood to shield her daughters from what was about to happen.

Daimyo Shigemasa held a match above his head and glared at the villagers gathered around him. Master Yamaguchi hurried up, interrupting the Daimyo's silent gaze.

'Lord Shigemasa, thank you for visiting. Welcome,' Yamaguchi said.

'I doubt I'm welcome,' Shigemasa said. 'I am here for your taxes.'

'But Lord Shigemasa, we paid our taxes two weeks ago ... *and* on time.' Master Yamaguchi raised his chin. 'I believe our small community is the most reliable in all your lands.'

'Perhaps *too* reliable,' the Daimyo replied. 'If you can pay your taxes with no difficulty, I must not be charging you enough.' He turned to look at the rice paddies, now empty of workers. 'If you can all be in your huts when I come down the mountain and are not working in the fields, then I have been too lenient with you. Beginning today, I am doubling your taxes.'

'But, Lord Shigemasa, our community already pays more taxes than most! We cannot do it!' a man cried out in anguish.

'The next person – man, woman, or child – who questions me will lose their tongue.' Shigemasa looked around, assuring himself they had heard and understood his edict. 'I will return in one month to collect your outstanding amount.' He gazed at the surrounding rice fields with a grin, then continued. 'Rice or a cash payment of 500 silver coins. You may choose how to pay.'

'May I speak, Lord?' Master Yamaguchi beseeched Shigemasa.

'What is it?'

'What if we need more time?'

Shigemasa's gaze flicked to the women and children in front of him before replying with sufficient volume to reach everyone. 'If you fail to make the payment within one month, we will take your women and children as hostages.'

Master Yamaguchi heard a low gasp. The Daimyo raised a hand, motioning for his samurai to head off. 'Before I take leave,' the Daimyo added, 'there is one other way for you to pay your taxes.'

'What, Lord?' a villager cried out. 'What other way?'

'Find Christians who are hiding and inform me of their whereabouts.'

'But we are Buddhists, Lord. We know nothing of Christians.'

'Then let me motivate you,' the Daimyo replied. 'The rewards for information leading to their capture are 300 silver coins for priests, 200 coins for brothers, and 100 coins for any other vile Christian!'

Shigemasa turned his horse to face the mountains as his band of samurai attended to their mounts. He spurred his horse into a walk, saying as he rode away, 'You would be wise to help us root out any hidden Christians in Arima – and not *just* for the money.'

'What do you mean, Lord?' Master Yamaguchi asked, running alongside the horse.

'There are developments in the regime. The Shogun has appointed Mizuno Kawachi as the new governor of Nagasaki. His first task will be to exterminate all Christian dogs from these lands. He arrives in June.'

'We will cooperate in any way we can, Lord.'

'You would be wise to do so,' the Daimyo answered. 'I can assure you the new governor and I will hunt down every hidden Christian and annihilate them – all of them!'

He signalled his flag bearers towards the mountain. As he left the village he called back, 'One month. Or I will take your women and children, and the man wearing the straw coat will dance and burn on my return.'

CHAPTER TWO

For confidential delivery to Father Andre Palmeiro
Visitor of Jesuit Province of Japan and
Vice-Province of China
Mission of the Society of Jesus, Macao, China
22 May, Year of our Lord 1626

Dear Father Andre,

I pray my letter finds you well.

Please accept my first letter to you in your new role as Visitor. I am delighted to learn of your appointment, and am further encouraged that our Paternity in Rome remains responsive to our fast-changing circumstances in the Japans and the Far East.

I perhaps write more than is necessary now in order to give you a present and necessary history of our circumstances, as communication is all but impossible between Macao and Japan and you may not have been given intelligence of our circumstances that is up to date.

As I am sure you are aware, the mission in Japan has become increasingly hazardous over recent years, with hundreds of fathers, brothers, and catechists brutally executed.

Since Tokugawa Iemitsu became the Shogun of Japan three years ago, the number and severity of Christian persecutions and torture has multiplied. Without question, it is now the most hostile environment I have ever witnessed for our Society since my arrival in Japan almost twenty-five years ago.

Shogun Iemitsu feels his authority threatened by our teachings and the Word of God, and he has become the most oppressive leader our Society has ever had to contend with. We are constantly hiding from a militarized regime determined to exterminate us and all things foreign.

The aristocracy in Japan pays him homage, but many in the lower classes find ways to disobey him – a development the Shogun finds inconceivable. His answer is to believe that the peasant classes have been seduced and supported by a foreign power intent on displacing him. Alas, he believes the Society is the channel for that foreign-inspired revolution – a suspicion that has led to our persecution and torture. As a result, I believe circumstances will only get worse for us before they get better.

Our mission on the southern island of Kyushu has become even more perilous. Earlier this year, we heard news that Shogun Iemitsu has appointed Mizuno Kawachi as the new governor of Nagasaki to replace Hasegawa Gonroku, who largely resisted our persecution. Under the express orders of the Shogun, Kawachi has resolved to stamp out Christianity by any means necessary.

This adverse development will spell extreme persecution for all Christians on the island of Kyushu, which includes the city of Nagasaki, our largest Christian foothold, and our nearby community in Arima.

Following months of careful consideration, I will coordinate an exodus of Christians from Arima to Yezo in the north, where I understand Christians can live in less danger of death and persecution.

However, I assure you I will stand steadfast, acting as the anchor for our Mission and our Society in both Nagasaki and Arima. Rest assured, I shall not abandon any Christian while I am alive. As always, I believe we will weather this storm just as we have the many great storms that have battered our faith in the past.

I know that God is with us, and His Word will take foundation in Japan. I believe the great light of our Lord and Father Almighty will shine through the clouds, dispelling the darkness that currently hovers over Japan.

Now more than ever, I place my trust and faith in our Lord and Father.

I remain your most devoted servant,

Father Joaquim Martinez, Society of Jesus

Father Joaquim reread his epistle to the head of the Jesuit Order in Macao, and after a decisive nod, folded up the letter, placed it into an envelope, and used his signet ring to secure it with a wax seal. He paused then drew a Buddhist insignia on the back of the envelope. *A necessity,* he thought. *Our activities must remain covert – at least for now.*

He pondered the information he had conveyed. The situation had been unpredictable for some time, but was even more fragile if reports of Kawachi's brutality were true.

He snapped out of his musings at three short knocks at the door. He glanced around, then shoved the letter under his bed, calling out, 'Enter.'

Furniture scraped back along bare floorboards, followed by

a low creaking sound, and the soft swish of fabric as a young Portuguese man in his mid-twenties appeared, revealing a secret doorway behind him. Father Joaquim appraised the new arrival. Although clean, the man's traditional Japanese clothes were old and ragged, in contrast to his youthful face.

'Catechist Miguel, good morning.'

'And to you, Father.' After a moment's hesitation, Miguel said: 'You wanted to see me?'

'Yes, Miguel. I wanted to let you know I am taking a short trip to Nagasaki tomorrow. I'll leave at sunset.'

'Tomorrow evening? That is sudden. I'm not sure I can make all the necessary preparations by then. Can it not wait?'

'No, it cannot,' Father Joaquim replied. 'I need to visit our good friend Mateus da Costa as soon as possible.' Father Joaquim saw an unspoken question on Miguel's face, sighed, then added, 'Daimyo Shigemasa has increased our taxes beyond our ability to cope. The village can neither produce enough rice nor gain enough silver to pay his demands on time. I must seek Mateus's help. Our situation is becoming more precarious.'

Miguel nodded in agreement but did not look happy. Father Joaquim saw the anxiety on Miguel's face. 'Don't worry, Miguel. I will speak with Master Yamaguchi.'

'Yes, Father. I will wait to hear from you. Yamaguchi-san informs me he is teaching this morning.'

'That's good news,' Father Joaquim exclaimed. 'I always enjoy Master Yamaguchi's lessons. Shall we walk over together?'

Father Joaquim took a moment to gather his *budo* training gear. In exchange for his Christian ministry, he had been under Master Yamaguchi's tutelage in the Way of the Sword since his arrival in

Japan when he was just 22. He had proved himself a gifted martial artist with great potential, according to Yamaguchi-san. Now, at 47, many in the valley considered the tall, athletic priest to be a master himself.

As Master Yamaguchi had advised, Father Joaquim and the others who trained in the village kept their *budo* lessons a secret. Social classes were clear: peasants were peasants, and samurai were samurai. Given that peasants' only purpose was to produce rice and perform other manual labour for the upper classes, the regime prohibited them from owning weapons. According to the Government, there was no need for them to learn *budo* or receive any kind of martial training. To be caught doing so was to invite severe punishment.

With his training gear in hand, Father Joaquim left the hidden room with Catechist Miguel. They slid the concealed door back into place, rehung the Buddhist linen hanging on the wall, and moved the furniture back to conceal any trace of a secret room before exiting on their way to practice.

Outside the hut, a large, fierce-looking young man greeted them. Legs spread wide, he wore a tattered, grey-coloured *gi*, the traditional Japanese martial arts training uniform.

'Good morning, Father.' The young man bowed in formal respect.

'Good morning, Yamamoto-san.' Father Joaquim bowed in return.

He smiled at the young man before taking a deep breath of fresh air. Mist drifted across the surrounding rice fields. Forested hills and verdant mountains rose at the edge of the paddy fields, on which a light rain fell.

Yamamoto strode off down a path and the two men followed.

CHAPTER THREE

22 May 1626
Arima, Shimabara Peninsula, Kyushu

The winding path led to a plain, almost dilapidated building made of grey wooden planks, with a simple thatched straw roof, much like other dwellings in the village. At the end of the pathway they arrived at the entrance to the dojo, the martial arts training hall. They removed their sandals, bowed low, and entered, ready to begin a practice that might one day save their lives.

Father Joaquim wore his black *gi*. He glanced around the dojo at twenty or so other students, most wearing ragged, off-white *gis*. Several were stretching in preparation for Master Yamaguchi's lesson.

A senior student clapped his hands three times, announcing

the Sensei's arrival. Master Yamaguchi entered through a private doorway at the rear of the dojo, carrying a sword.

The students assembled in rows in a kneeling position – a *seiza* – with the most senior in front and the newest at the back. Master Yamaguchi laid his katana in its *saya* or sheath at the front of the room then walked to the centre of the dojo and bowed his head to the assembled students. The students returned the respectful greeting.

Yamaguchi turned to Father Joaquim, bowed again, and invited him to the front of the dojo. '*Hajime*,' he said. *We shall begin.*

'This morning we will learn about the power of hard and soft.' He handed a wooden practice knife to Father Joaquim. Yamaguchi made a gesture specifying the attack he wished the priest to make. Joaquim made no allowance for the frail-looking old man as he attacked. He slashed at Yamaguchi's throat. The sensei stepped back, allowing the knife to sweep past, then in a blur of motion grabbed Joaquim's wrist, twisted and flipped him onto his side. The priest found himself peering up into the crinkled eyes of his teacher. He laughed – no matter how skilled he became, the old man still bested him effortlessly. As the priest gathered himself to rise, he felt a sharp stabbing pain in his wrist, forcing him to drop the knife. He nodded in admiration as he rubbed his arm. 'Impressive.'

The other students nodded to themselves and bowed to their master in appreciation as they absorbed the new technique.

'*Yokemenuchi koetegaeshi tanto-dori*,' said Master Yamaguchi, naming the technique. He bowed again to the dojo, and invited his students to practise it among themselves.

The students paired off. A short while later, Yamaguchi watched Chiba, one of the younger and more excitable students, struggle to disarm his partner. After multiple failed attempts he clearly grew frustrated and kneed his more powerful training partner in the side in order to force him to give up the knife.

The master clapped his hands and the students lowered themselves into a *seiza* position. 'Chiba-san, you seem to be having difficulty disarming Yamamoto-san. Father Joaquim, perhaps you could provide Chiba-san with a demonstration.'

'Yes, Sensei, if you wish.' Joaquim rose to his feet and faced Yamamoto. The priest looked up at the larger man, who attacked without warning, stabbing and yelling with great force. Unfazed, Joaquim stepped back and executed the new defensive technique, slamming the heavier man into the *tatami* and forcing him to drop the knife. The students nodded in approval.

'Solid execution!' Yamaguchi applauded his long-time student. He turned to address the dojo. 'As you can see, one way to overcome great strength like that of Yamamoto-san is to execute perfect technique at speed. Father Joaquim has been training in *budo* for twenty years so his technique is very good. But what about those of you who have not trained for twenty years? Must you have even greater strength to overcome strength?'

Yamaguchi shot Chiba a quick glance then paused, allowing his students time to reflect on the question. 'Many of us feel the need to fight force with even greater force. But there is another way.'

Chiba looked perplexed as Yamaguchi stared through the window at the rain outside.

Yamaguchi continued, 'Today we are learning how soft can beat hard.' He nodded towards the rain-soaked, clay window ledge. 'Water is one of the softest substances in the world, yet it will wear down the hardest rock in time. The key to overcoming great strength ...' – the teacher hunched up, round-shouldered, looking feeble, – '... is to use *soft*.' He lowered his voice to a whisper. 'Hard cannot always overcome hard because there is always something harder. Soft is the only sure way to defeat hard. Let me show you.'

Yamaguchi retrieved the sword he had brought to the dojo, and unsheathed it, revealing a magnificent blade. The entire dojo gasped involuntarily at the sight.

'This magnificent katana once belonged to my former lord, Daimyo Konishi Yukinaga, before he was executed.' Yamaguchi held the sword up high for the entire dojo to see, then he invited Yamamoto to face him on the mat and handed him the blade. He signalled that the student attack him again – but this time with the sword. Yamamoto hesitated, then with a loud grunt executed a vicious strike from the side. Yamaguchi then did the unexpected and stepped into the attack. He blended his arms with those of Yamamoto and twisted his wrist, swinging Yamamoto high in the air. The younger man hit the *tatami* hard. He groaned in defeat as Yamaguchi applied pressure to his wrist, engendering the spontaneous release of his student's handgrip, and removed the sword.

The students watched Yamaguchi in awe. 'As a warrior, you must learn to recognize hard so you can counter with soft. This applies to any weapon and any situation. This is not just a *budo* principle but a life principle. When you grasp that, you will be well on your way to a mastery not just of the way of harmonious spirit, but of life.

'Our true strength comes from the universe. When you understand that, then you will understand that a drop of water can become as powerful as an ocean.'

He looked at Father Joaquim and gave him a short nod and a small, private smile.

CHAPTER FOUR

22 May 1626

In the warmth of the early afternoon, a dozen children giggled and shouted to each other as they played with small wooden toys near their disguised church building while Catechist Tonia watched over them. The older children, meanwhile, were in the rice paddies, working alongside the adults, trying to produce enough rice to meet Lord Shigemasa's demands.

Tonia was tall and slim, a pretty, dark-haired woman in her early twenties dressed in old, worn farm clothes.

'Who was that scary man on the big horse, Tonia-san?' a child asked her.

'Daimyo Matsukura Shigemasa,' Catechist Tonia answered. 'He is warlord of these lands.'

'I don't like him. He frightens me.'

'You're right to be wary of him. Lord Shigemasa is a cruel man. I don't like him either,' Tonia said softly. 'But you need not fear him, for God is with us.'

Tonia had been born in Lagos, in Portugal's Algarve Peninsula. After her mother died of a respiratory ailment, her father, a Portuguese merchant, had brought her with him to the Far East. Soon after their arrival in Macao, however, her father took ill and died as well. There were those who believed he had been poisoned by jealous Dutch merchants resentful of the Portuguese control over trade. Whatever the reason, the orphaned teenager, alone in the world and unprotected, chose to dedicate her life to missionary work.

Disguised as a Portuguese merchant's wife, she had made her way to Nagasaki where she met Father Joaquim, who had taken her under his wing and sheltered her in this small village, some forty miles outside Nagasaki.

Tonia knew her mere presence in the Japans was unusual and risky, especially as a young, unmarried Christian woman. She did not even have the slim protection of being a businessman's wife. She was fortunate that her long black hair and olive skin colouring helped her, from a distance at least, blend in with the Japanese.

'Remember, Haruko-chan,' Tonia said to the child, 'no matter how frightening the Daimyo may seem, God is much, much stronger.'

'Okay,' the child said as she hugged Tonia.

'Tonia-san?'

Tonia turned to a little boy who was tugging on her cloth shirt. His name was Shiro, maybe six years old. He lived with his uncle in Master Yamaguchi's village because life was too impoverished in his native village. Life had become hard in all the villages, as warlords throughout the country escalated their demands on peasants who had no one to appeal to and no way to defend themselves.

Shiro asked, 'Why is Daimyo Shigemasa raising our taxes? My uncle says it is impossible to make more rice.'

'Daimyo Shigemasa needs the extra rice to feed his new samurai,' Tonia said. She reached out a hand and placed it over one of the boy's. 'The Daimyo also needs extra taxes to build a large castle.'

'Why does the Daimyo need so many warriors? Won't they just hunt Christian families like us?'

Tonia turned away, unsure what to say to the boy. The truth? It was too dangerous to try and hide it from him, and yet too harsh to tell him the real answer to his question. She said, finally, 'The adults have disguised our village well, Shiro-kun, so this is not something you need to worry about.'

'My uncle says I have to hide that I'm a Christian because if the Daimyo finds out, he will kill us!'

'Your uncle should not say such things to you, Shiro-kun,' said Tonia, feeling more and more uncomfortable with the conversation.

'He told me one Christian woman on the Daimyo's lands had her hands cut off for praying.'

'Try not to worry about such things, Shiro-kun. God will protect us.'

'Are you sure, Tonia-san?'

'Yes. We are His children and He will look after us. I promise.' Tonia realized the noise of children playing had died down, and turned to see the other children listening to their conversation. Her heart sank as she considered their fears. Children should not be afraid for their safety. But that was not the world they lived in.

'Do you believe this, Shiro-kun?' she asked.

'Yes. I pray for His protection every night.'

'Good. Believing is the first step to receiving the Lord's help and blessings. And prayer is the best way to speak to Him.'

Shiro nodded in agreement, narrowing his eyes and biting his lower lip. For a young boy, Shiro had a sharp mind, and perhaps a too-attentive ear.

'Come, let us all say a short prayer together,' Catechist Tonia said. She motioned for the children to gather around.

CHAPTER FIVE

22 May 1626
Shimabara Castle, Shimabara Peninsula, Kyushu

Matsukura Shigemasa hastened up the tall and spacious stairwell of his newly built castle, accompanied by seven of his most loyal retainers. He ignored the many samurai standing guard outside myriad rooms in his oversized palace. To Shigemasa they were little more than living chess pieces.

Just as inconsequential to the Daimyo – unless one failed at his duties – were the hundreds of samurai outside, who guarded the manicured grounds, each wearing their lord's official colours of red, white, and black.

Shigemasa passed fine Chinese silk and satin embroideries, exceptional large-scale drawings, and various exotic ornaments and statues. But he ignored it all. The lavish evidence of his wealth emphasized his power, nothing more.

As he entered the castle's grand chamber the large audience of retainers and samurai ceased talking. They all assumed a kneeling position, bowed, and waited. Assuming a *seiza* position in front of them, Shigemasa asked curtly, 'So, do you think our visits to the villages have been effective?'

Who there had the courage to speak his mind to such a powerful man? After a moment a bald-headed senior retainer said, 'Yes, Lord. Although I imagine the new taxes may not have pleased some of the peasants.'

'They are peasants. Who cares?' the Daimyo said.

An adviser, still new to his post, ventured, 'But after these new taxes, the peasants will have nothing.'

A more seasoned retainer gave the younger man a furtive head shake. The Daimyo raised an eyebrow and let out a breath. 'Peasants need just enough to eat and survive. They must pay the rest in taxes!'

'Yes, Lord,' the adviser answered, and bowed his head.

Shigemasa scanned his retinue. 'What about hidden Christians? Do you think our forays to the villages will help to uncover any of the remaining vermin?'

'I do not know, my Lord,' a retainer to his left replied. 'They are a resilient group.'

'Then we must put more pressure on them, *neh?*'

'A wise thought, Lord.'

'Agreed. In time they will break and betray one another.' The Daimyo smiled. 'And what about the reward of silver coins? Do you think this tactic will be effective?' He again looked at his followers.

Speaking cautiously a retainer several rows back said, 'If I may be bold, Lord, I am not sure if silver is the most effective way to get the Christians to betray one another.'

'I agree, Lord,' another spoke up. 'These hidden Christians are an incestuous group and support one another.'

'I also agree, Lord,' said a third. 'For them, Christianity is a way of life, akin to the Way of the Sword.'

Shigemasa jutted his chin forward and let out a growl. 'Then give me alternatives. Do not tell me what will *not* work. Tell me what *will*!'

A longtime retainer, seated closest to him, answered: 'Perhaps it would be more effective if we concentrated our efforts on the so-called *apostates*.'

'What do you mean?'

'Might it not be more effective to focus on those who have recanted Christianity? Apostates know who many of these hidden Christians are, and are more amenable to bribes and enticements.'

The Daimyo shook his head. 'Do you think me stupid? We have tried this already. We have exhausted our leads with the apostates; they have already informed on the Christians they knew, yet more still infest my lands. What else can we do? We *must* eliminate any remaining Christians on my lands before Governor Kawachi arrives.'

'Yes, Lord,' his retinue agreed.

'I will not lose my lands because of this scum.'

'Yes, Lord,' one answered. 'If any Christians remain, we will find them.'

'I will never again suffer an embarrassment such as I did when we discovered that filthy Father Navarro hiding on my lands, *neh*.'

A retainer to his right spoke up for the first time. 'Yes, Lord. It was regrettable.'

'Regrettable? Is that what you think?' Eyebrows raised, nostrils flaring, the Daimyo continued: 'Regrettable is losing a dog in a boar hunt. Having the Governor learn of Christians hiding in my lands is *intolerable*!'

'Yes, Lord,' the retainer quickly corrected himself. 'Of course, you are completely correct. It is indeed *intolerable*. We will see it never happens again.'

'Yes, you will.' The Daimyo turned his head towards his senior retainers. 'Let us not forget that the Shogun gifted these lands to me for distinguishing myself in battle at Osaka.'

'Never, Lord,' several replied together.

'I was chosen as daimyo of Shimabara to exterminate Christianity with an iron fist.'

'Yes, Lord.'

'It is for this duty that the Shogun has exempted me from all taxes and dues.' Shigemasa grabbed his katana and smashed it across a table set with a fine tea service. 'I will die before I lose my lands because of this putrid religion!'

Broken glass flew in all directions as black tea and leaves splattered everywhere. Shigemasa continued to rage.

'*Hai*, Lord. We will exterminate Christianity long before that.'

CHAPTER SIX

22 May 1626
Arima, Shimabara Peninsula, Kyushu

Father Joaquim and Catechists Tonia and Miguel huddled together in a tiny, impoverished hut. A small candle illuminated their surroundings, creating a peaceful atmosphere as they shared a small amount of rice from a communal bowl.

'A lot has happened and there has been much change,' Joaquim said.

'Recent events have been worrying,' responded Miguel. He fidgeted his fingers and rocked his knees back and forth.

'That is why I've called you here tonight,' said Father Joaquim. 'I've made some important decisions about our mission. I've discussed the matter with Master Yamaguchi, and we've decided to move the village to the north.'

'Where in the north?' Tonia asked, as her eyes widened.

'Yezo.'

'But that's on the other side of the country!' Miguel exclaimed.

'Are you sure, Father?' Tonia asked.

'Yes. When I'm in Nagasaki, I will dispatch a letter to the new Visitor in Macao.'

For a moment, Miguel contemplated the news as he bit his lip. 'I think I'm relieved about this decision.'

Joaquim raised an eyebrow. 'Why do you *think* you are relieved?'

'Well, Father, the journey will indeed be difficult, but I don't think we will last long if we stay in Arima. In time, Lord Shigemasa will find us and kill us.'

'Don't let the regime frighten you, Miguel,' Joaquim replied.

'Yes, Father,' Miguel answered, though his voice betrayed a lack of conviction.

'And how do you feel, Tonia?' Joaquim asked.

'I have concerns, Father. Every day, I pray to God for His support.'

'That's good, Tonia. Only He can deliver us to the salvation of greener pastures.'

'Father, this morning you mentioned borrowing silver bullion from Mateus,' Miguel said.

'Yes, to help us meet our new taxes.'

'Do you think he will?' Tonia asked.

'I hope so. The trip to Nagasaki could be dangerous. I would like you both to stay here and keep an eye on the village.'

'Yes, Father.' Miguel placed a hand on his chest.

Father Joaquim noticed Miguel's face turn ashen. It was clear the catechist feared to leave the village. His arms clasped his body tightly across his chest; his self-protective stance denoting his insecurities.

'How will you repay the loan?' Tonia asked.

'As you are no doubt aware from your late father, the best Chinese silks imported into Japan arrive on Portuguese galliots. So, I will offer to help Mateus sell this silk at prices above those of the *pancado* system.'

'What's that?' asked Miguel.

'The Japanese have fixed prices for silk,' Tonia explained. 'The Shogun wants to limit the profits of foreign traders.'

'But I thought the Shogun made avoiding his new system illegal.' Miguel appeared pale in the candle's flickering light. 'Won't that draw unnecessary attention to us?'

'It has always been a corrupt business, Miguel. Portuguese merchants are always looking for higher profits,' said Father Joaquim.

'But if the authorities fix the prices, how can we sell at prices above the system?' Tonia said.

'Opportunities present themselves. Wealthy families and warlords will pay higher prices for access to the best.'

'But why does Mateus not do it himself?' Miguel asked. He rubbed the back of his neck. 'Mateus is a merchant, not a Christian Father banned from Japan on pain of death. It's much riskier for you than for him.'

Joaquim said, 'Mateus may know the wealthy families, even the Daimyo, but his Japanese is weak, plus he does not understand Japanese etiquette and customs as well as I do.'

'But he can speak a small amount of Japanese. This is too dangerous. You're a Catholic priest in hiding.'

'The village needs the money,' Father Joaquim replied. He rested his hand on Miguel's shoulder and looked into the young man's blinking eyes. Miguel clutched his hands as the priest continued,

'I believe Daimyo Shigemasa will do terrible things, particularly to the women and children. We cannot let this happen.'

They sat in silence for a few moments. Miguel's distress was obvious.

'Everything will be all right,' Joaquim assured him. 'Like Saint Francis Xavier, the founder of our mission in Japan, I place my faith and hope in the Lord. He will protect us. You must do the same. How can we ask the villagers to have a faith we lack?' Father Joaquim added.

'Yes, Father,' Tonia replied.

Miguel nodded.

'What time will you leave tomorrow?' Tonia asked.

'As soon as the sun goes down. I have a baptism planned for tomorrow morning. It's important to welcome our village newborn into the house of God.'

Joaquim stood up, lowered his head to Tonia and Miguel. As he left the hut, he pondered on his two catechists. Tonia, he thought, showed great courage and aptitude for the mission. Miguel did not appear cut out for the difficulties they were facing. He thought of the trials of Abraham and Job, and wondered why God tested them so. *Is this my test now?* he wondered.

CHAPTER SEVEN

23 May 1626

Father Joaquim scanned the horizon as morning sun, against a clear blue sky, warmed away the chill of morning air. He stationed himself close to a large wooden basin, on a small mound in front of the entire village, ready to perform a baptism. In front of him stood a young Japanese couple, holding their newborn baby before an excited crowd. For a split second, the Jesuit closed his eyes and reconsidered the risks. Under most circumstances, he would never venture outside in daylight – the perils were too great. If caught, torture and a gruesome death awaited him. But this was his favourite holy sacrament.

After requesting Shiro and several other reliable boys keep watch on the mountain for any sign of approaching authorities,

Joaquim's elation inspired him to continue.

'Holy baptism is the basis of all Christian life,' Father Joaquim declared. 'It is the gateway to life in the Spirit. It is also the door that provides access to other sacraments. Through baptism, we are freed from sin and reborn as sons of God.'

The congregation broke into a hymn. When the singing stopped Joaquim said, 'I would like to welcome everyone here today, in particular the parents of this child.' He stretched out his arms, motioned to the young couple, and offered them a warm welcome. 'This moment is joyous, for this child is a gift of God, the Source of life, who now wishes to confer His own life on this little one.'

Joaquim asked the parents: 'What name do you give your child?'

'We name our child Peter,' the father replied, casting a loving glance at his baby son.

'And what do you ask of God's Church?'

'We ask for baptism,' the parents replied in unison. 'We request eternal life for our child.'

As they answered, the parents glanced repeatedly at the top of the neighbouring mountain to reassure themselves no one was coming. They returned their gaze towards their child as they fidgeted with their hands and shuffled their feet.

'By your request, you accept the responsibility of raising him in the faith. Do you understand what you are asking?'

'We do,' the young parents replied. They smiled nervously.

Joaquim's eyes sparkled as he looked down at the child. He made the Sign of the Cross on the child's forehead and said, 'Peter, the Christian community welcomes you with great joy. In its name, I claim you for Christ our Saviour, by the sign of His Cross. I now trace the cross on your forehead and invite your parents to do the same. I will now read from our Holy Book.'

After reading aloud from his Bible, it occurred again to Father Joaquim that this was truly the essence of his life's work. He was in Japan to teach a new nation and baptize its citizens into God's grace.

The moment passed, and he could see that among the attendees he was the one who enjoyed the celebration the most. Their faces reflected happiness for the newborn baby, but their stiff bodies and darting eyes told a different story. They were terrified of any sign of the Daimyo or any of his wandering samurai tasked with checking the villages. They threw repeated glances towards the top of the mountain, praying that the boys assigned to keep watch were doing their jobs to keep the village safe. One mistake would be fatal.

CHAPTER EIGHT

23 May 1626

Father Joaquim heard them again. The villagers had become so accustomed to the incessant, monotonous *wah-wah-wah* sounds – more bird-like than the typical frog croak – that they no longer heard the chorus of hundreds of hungry common brown toads calling out in the nearby rice fields. Like the toads in pursuit of dragonflies, the villagers were all there with a singular focus, Joaquim thought: to pray for him.

The journey to Nagasaki would not be easy. Warlords' eyes watched each path. Samurai stationed at strategic locations would be on the lookout. He fought back a tingling in his fingers and toes. All he could do now was pray and hope he would make it back alive.

He had traded his priest's robes for the more colourful high-quality silk attire of a Portuguese merchant. With large baggy pants, a loose-fitting shirt, a long overcoat and an oversized hat, he was barely recognizable, even to the villagers who knew him well. He'd made this risky trip before, and each time he'd donned the same disguise.

Father Joaquim took the time to study each of his parishioners with heartfelt warmth and affection. He knew full well that this could be the last time he would ever see them. Beloved friends and past residents of the village had disappeared forever, or ended up in Nagasaki, or even the capital, Edo, to endure torture and execution for the most trivial of reasons.

As the horizon eclipsed the last flicker of sunlight, Father Joaquim bowed to the villagers in appreciation, humbled that they cared so much for his welfare and safety. Then he lowered his head in a deep bow to the head of the village, Master Yamaguchi, not only because he was the most senior male in the community, but also because he was a close friend and mentor.

All Christian missionaries were now banned from the country. For many years, dating back to Japan's second Shogun Hidetada, all European merchants had been confined to the port cities of Nagasaki and Hirado. Any foreigner discovered in the hills faced intense interrogation. One wrong answer – or even an interrogator's suspicion – could lead to banishment, imprisonment, or worse.

In the gloom of a fading twilight, Joaquim picked up his European satchel, and left for the mountain. Travelling a precipitous path in the dark of night carried its own set of risks, but it was safer than the threat of being caught by the Daimyo's samurai if he travelled in daylight. He knew his disguise would not keep him particularly safe, as the authorities already suspected Christian Fathers disguised themselves to travel throughout Japan in secret. But it was better than nothing.

Joaquim remembered the days when Christians walked freely through any part of the country, at liberty to share their faith with anyone who would listen. When he'd arrived at Nagasaki twenty-five years earlier, as a teenager, the authorities had accepted Christianity. Missionaries preached without fear.

Father Joaquim gripped a large rock. He grunted as he hauled himself up a steep part of the mountain, his thoughts drawn again to the past. Life then was bright and full of opportunity to spread God's Word. Now, only persecution, torture, and death awaited them. A tear rolled down his cheek as he recalled lost kinsmen, persecuted and killed for their faith.

More than half a century before his own arrival, when the first Jesuit, St Francis Xavier, took his first step in Kagoshima, near the southern tip of the country, not only peasants, but also feudal landowners and warlords had embraced the Society's teachings. Even several influential daimyo had converted to the faith. Religious freedom had continued until 1614, when, fearful of the West's creeping influence on Japan, the first Shogun, Tokugawa Ieyasu, had banished Christianity and all foreign missionaries from the country.

Father Joaquim not only knew this recent Japanese history, he had been a part of it. He knew the Church's mission had made extraordinary progress in converting Japanese to the faith before politics and corruption took its course. By the year of its banishment, the Church had converted some 300,000 Japanese souls. The priest took pride that the Church's mission had made such extraordinary progress in converting Japanese to the faith so quickly.

He also recalled that during the early years of the banishment, the Society had made a bold stand. About ten years ago, however, when the arrests and martyrdoms of Christians took a dramatic upturn, it had become clear that if Christianity were to survive in Japan, it would need to go underground.

Thus it was that in a period of five short years, Father Joaquim's missionary life had gone from public acceptance to severe persecution and martyrdom. The Shogun and his Bakufu regime had ordered that any Christians remaining in the country were subjected to torture and execution. European Fathers were viewed as the most subversive, defiant, and threatening to Japan's long-standing authoritarian culture, and were considered special targets.

With little support from the papacy on account of a dwindling budget, the Jesuit missionaries had only their faith, their wits, and one another to rely on.

Father Joaquim pressed forward up the slopes, armed only with his faith, determined to save his village from death and destruction, and prepared to risk everything for the village – including his life.

CHAPTER NINE

24 May 1626
Shogun's Castle, Toshima District, Edo,
Musashi Province

At the far end of the Fujimi-tamon defence house on the grounds of Edo Castle, Shogun Iemitsu and his retainers were taking pleasure, readying their torture apparatus as several Buddhist monks and the Roju elders who comprised the Bakufu cabinet watched.

In a dark corner of the room stood a senior Buddhist monk in a saffron robe. For years, he had been called to attend these gory torture sessions, and over time he had come to know the Shogun and his father, Hidetada, well. In his view, Iemitsu was a megalomaniac obsessed with power, despising Christians because he abhorred the thought of the Japanese adoring anyone other than himself. It worried him that what was happening to the Christians could easily start happening to fellow Buddhists should the Shogun begin to doubt them. He could not let that happen.

The monk considered Shogun Iemitsu a malicious man, much like his father, though more obsessed with supremacy and control than even his father and grandfather. He had ascended to the title of Shogun in 1623, at 19 becoming Japan's third Shogun. From his early days, Shogun Iemitsu had made it his mission to exterminate Christianity from Japan, and was ruthless in his quest to fulfil that duty.

'You will tell me where your flock is hiding,' Iemitsu growled. The priest was covered in spreading purple welts along his nakedness and was stretched and shackled on a bamboo rack. He gently shook his head. Shogun Iemitsu signalled angrily to the torturers to dispense with their wooden clubs in favour of metal branding pincers. The three men removed the white-hot pincers from a nearby oven and moved towards the wide-eyed prisoner.

The Shogun grinned as he saw fear in the man's eyes and his clenched fists. 'Do you wish to say anything before they begin?'

The priest remained silent, refusing to give the Shogun the satisfaction of any kind of response. Shogun Iemitsu indicated the first torturer should brand the Father on his bare chest. The pincers sizzled, blistering the skin with a sweet, cloying smell. The tortured priest howled and lost consciousness.

Another torturer splashed water on the victim's face. The Shogun waited for him to come to. 'Do you not see the futility of your situation, Father?' the Shogun said. 'Look at where Christianity has brought you … to the edge of an agonizing death. Tell me where the others are hiding.'

The Japanese Father grimaced in pain, blinking to try and remain conscious. The Shogun stared into the priest's eyes, enraged by the lack of response. Surely, the man was mocking him with what he could only describe as pity?

'Christianity is a danger to the Empire and a corruption brought by foreign barbarians!' he bellowed. 'Christians are spies for the Pope and the kings of Portugal and Spain, and all those who wish to invade my country.' His eyes narrowed in contempt as he snarled, 'You are the enemy! A traitor! And you will all die for embracing this faith!'

He instructed another of his men to brand the disfigured priest, this time on his cheek. The Father's face scrunched in agony as the implement made its mark. A piteous scream sprang from his throat as the brand ate into his skin. His shackles clanked as he thrashed and gargled, spitting bloody froth and phlegm, weeping from the continuing agony of his wounds.

Stunned into terrified silence, the Shogun's retinue dared not move a muscle or show any sign of dissent before the Shogun. Cabinet members grimaced and covered their faces with their clothing as the stench of burned flesh filled their noses. They avoided eye contact with each other as the Father's torment continued.

'Where is your God now, priest? See how he has abandoned you and your friends.'

The Father whispered in a cracked voice, 'Jesus watches over me. I am never alone.'

'What did you say?' The Shogun moved closer, his eyes riveted on the man's bruised and reddened eyes.

The priest mustered what little strength remained and said, 'Where I am weak, the Lord is strong.'

'Where is your Jesus now, you pathetic rat?' the Shogun shrieked. He looked around the room at his retinue, each of whom nodded in agreement while trying to avoid the sight of the dying priest.

'To find life, one must be willing to lose it,' the tortured man whispered.

The Shogun gave a disdainful snort. This should have been more satisfying. That it wasn't enraged him. He charged across the room and fetched his own personal short sword. He unsheathed it, whipped the sharp blade through the air, and with one swift stroke severed the priest's head. It fell to the ground and rolled at the feet of one of the Buddhist monks, who involuntarily scooted backwards.

'Burn his body,' the Shogun ordered. He wiped the blood from his blade with a black cloth. 'All of it. We don't want to risk making a martyr of this traitor with his body parts.'

'Do not worry, Lord,' answered Sakai Tadakatsu, one of his cabinet members. 'He never existed.'

CHAPTER TEN

28 May 1626
District of Nagasaki, Kyushu

Too late, Father Joaquim spotted the six samurai blocking the path.

'Halt where you are!' one of them shouted and hurried towards the foreigner. Three of the other five tripped over one another as they chased behind.

'Don't try to escape!' another shouted, his hand on the hilt of his katana as they approached.

Father Joaquim's fingers twitched as he gave the men a darting gaze. Unable to do anything else, he assumed the role of a Portuguese merchant and approached the samurai.

'*Konichiwa*,' he said. He kept his posture strong as he bowed and proceeded towards the field's edge to greet his pursuers.

'We have you!' a zealous samurai bellowed as he grabbed Joaquim and thrust him to his knees with great force. Another samurai shoved his boot in his middle, sending him to the ground.

'I'm on official trading business,' Joaquim said as he caught his breath. He struggled to keep his voice calm as he addressed his samurai captors.

'What official business?' the leader demanded. He thrust his foot into Father Joaquim's side. 'The Shogun prohibits all foreign merchants from leaving Nagasaki and Hirado!'

Another samurai unsheathed his *wakizashi* and pointed the short sword at Joaquim's head.

'I'm on official business on behalf of Governor Hasegawa Gonroku,' Joaquim replied with a stern voice.

'Liar!'

'What business do you have assaulting a trader on official government business?' Father Joaquim did his best to appear offended that an official mission be questioned.

'All foreign traders are forbidden from leaving Nagasaki and Hirado,' the leader repeated.

'Yes, that's true – unless they're authorized by the Governor,' Joaquim answered, still held on the ground by samurai, who were pinning back his arms.

'We are not aware of any exceptions,' the leader countered. Nevertheless, his eyes narrowed and he appeared to be wrestling with his eagerness to harm the foreigner sprawled before him, and a sudden creeping fear he could anger an important official if he acted impetuously. He said, 'What evidence do you have?'

'Documentation, in my satchel.' The Father indicated the bag with his head.

'Grab the bag,' the leader said.

A younger samurai snatched Father Joaquim's satchel and thrust him back down.

'I'm on official government business. What right do you have to hold me like this?' Joaquim asked, channelling his growing fear into a feigned indignation.

'Shut your mouth, *gaijin*, or I'll cut out your tongue!'

Two of the samurai rustled through the Jesuit's bag. The men dug eager hands deep in the bag's interior. They produced a European compass, a map of Kyushu, some food, and a journal.

'Where is this documentation?' one samurai shouted as he breathed heavily while continuing to rummage through the satchel.

'There.' Father Joaquim pointed at an envelope with an official seal.

Irritated, the samurai grabbed the envelope and tore it open, breaking the seal. The others were silent as the samurai read the letter aloud.

'*I write this letter to attest that the Magistrate of Nagasaki provides official permission for Portuguese merchant Joaquim Martinez to travel on foot without restriction between Nagasaki and Hirado ...*'

'As I said – '

'Shut up, dog!' The samurai resumed reading. '*... to fulfil merchant duties as prescribed by the Governor of Nagasaki, Hasegawa Gonroku.*'

'Is it signed and stamped?' asked the leader.

'Yes, by the Governor, and it bears the official seal of the magistrate.'

'Why would the Governor have you travel by foot and not sea?' the leader demanded.

'It is private business,' Father Joaquim said.

'Answer the question!'

'I am a Portuguese representative of the Governor. He has asked me to gauge interest in new silks from some of his closest supporters in the region.'

'For what purpose?'

'To determine their needs and convey them to the Governor. Then I am to monitor these requested items as they arrive on Portuguese ships into Nagasaki from Macao.'

'What else?'

'In Nagasaki, I am to negotiate lower prices for these goods from my fellow Portuguese traders, as Governor Hasegawa Gonroku would like to secure them for his closest allies.'

The samurai tilted their chins down and frowned, appearing deflated by the explanation.

'Grab your things and move on.' The leader had decided. His shoulders slumped and Father Joaquim was allowed to rise to his feet.

A samurai thrust the satchel into his chest and pushed him towards Nagasaki.

As Father Joaquim walked away, it occurred to him that the authorities would have rewarded them a small fortune in silver for apprehending a banned priest in disguise. *Thank you, Lord, for not letting them spot that my documentation was a forgery.*

He picked up his pace towards Nagasaki.

CHAPTER ELEVEN

29 May 1626
Arima, Shimabara Peninsula, Kyushu

In the cool morning sunshine Master Yamaguchi was engaged in his favourite pastime, clipping the leaves of the many bonsai trees in his garden. Shaping the miniature trees relaxed him.

Bonsai was a tradition his family had adopted that dated back more than a millennium in Japan. And, as was his custom, Master Yamaguchi had become a master at the craft, excelling in all bonsai cultivation techniques, including pruning, root reduction, potting, defoliation, and grafting, to produce small trees that mimicked the shape and style of full-size trees. Master Yamaguchi's private garden was spectacular in design, and admired throughout the village.

A knock on his outside gate refocused the old man's attention. Catechist Miguel stood outside the yard.

'Master Yamaguchi, I'm sorry to interrupt. Do you have a moment?'

'Ah, Miguel. Thank you for the visit.' Master Yamaguchi walked over to the gate and opened it.

Once again, Miguel was struck by the magnificence of the garden. Along with abundant bonsai trees and other exotic vegetation, the garden was a magnificent display of colourful flowers, mostly pink, peach, and light blue.

On the right side of the garden was a small waterfall where a stream of water flowed from an adjacent mountain; on the left, blue-throated *ogawa-komadori* birds perched on several handmade miniature wooden houses.

'Master Yamaguchi,' Catechist Miguel said, stopping to gaze about the garden, 'your garden looks even more impressive than the last time I was here.'

'You are too kind, Miguel, but I'm sure that is not why you visit me today. What's on your mind?'

'I'm worried about many things, but I'm most worried about Father Joaquim. He might not make it back from Nagasaki.'

'It is worrying, Miguel, but I have faith he will return safely.'

'But if they discover his identity, they will kill him.'

'Focus your mind on positive outcomes, Miguel.'

'I am trying, Master Yamaguchi, but the world has turned upside down on us in Japan, particularly since the Daimyo's latest ultimatum.'

'I admit, life has changed for Christians, but we must remain optimistic about our future. We must maintain hope.' Master Yamaguchi placed his hand on Miguel's shoulder.

'I see a future filled with death, Master Yamaguchi.' Miguel shook his head. 'It is much worse than I imagined.'

'Why did you come to Japan?' Yamaguchi asked. 'What drew you here?'

'To spread the Word of God.' Miguel took a deep breath, adding, 'That and the excitement of the mission.'

'An exciting mission? What do you mean?'

'In Europe, the mission in Japan is reputed to be the most exhilarating. It is one of the furthest outposts from Rome and holds great prospects in terms of converts. We heard great stories about the missions here, despite the danger.'

'I see.' Master Yamaguchi nodded.

'Now I am finding it to be more than I can bear.' Miguel lowered his eyes, his chest caving. 'From the moment I arrived, the mission seemed almost impossible.' He looked at Master Yamaguchi again. 'And the death toll has only risen.'

Yamaguchi nodded again. 'I agree that recent times have been difficult.'

'I worry the mission will not survive here, Master Yamaguchi. And I fear *I* will not survive.' Miguel dropped his gaze again.

'Time will improve things, Miguel. God will see to it.'

'I wish that were true, but I don't believe it.'

'What do you want, Miguel?'

'I want to go home. I'm scared to death here and cannot sleep. I want to go home where I can live without fear of persecution and torture ... and death. I want to be free again.'

Master Yamaguchi saw the conflict and fear in Miguel's eyes. 'Then it is time for you to return home, Miguel.'

'I wish it were that easy.'

'What do you mean?'

'Father Joaquim … I cannot bear to tell him.'

'He will understand.'

'Father Joaquim is dedicated to the village and the mission, Master Yamaguchi. He is a brave and committed leader. I cannot bear the thought of letting him down.' Tears formed in Miguel's eyes as he continued. 'There is also the question of getting out of here alive. The Shogun exiled the Society of Jesus a long time ago. We are not supposed to be here. If I'm caught trying to leave, they will kill me.'

'Perhaps you should discuss this with Father Joaquim when he returns,' Yamaguchi suggested.

'*If* he returns,' Miguel whispered, giving voice to his worry. 'And who will look after the village if he does not?'

'Miguel, we are not your responsibility. The village *will* survive.'

'I don't know what to think any more,' Miguel confessed as he held his head in his hands.

'Again, I think it best if you discuss matters with Father Joaquim on his return.'

'Even if Father Joaquim can borrow enough silver from Mateus da Costa and is able to make it back here alive, we still have to move to Yezo.' Miguel shook his head again. 'Yezo is too far, and the journey between here and there is much too dangerous. The regime will discover us.'

'Miguel, you should not—'

Miguel cut off Master Yamaguchi mid-sentence. 'Our move will expose us. Do you know what they will do when they capture us? They will torture us. They will cut off our feet and burn us alive! Maybe I should attempt a trip to Nagasaki, pose as a trader, and flee to Macao on my own!'

'Miguel, please, you should discuss matters with Father Joaquim before attempting anything rash.'

'But I cannot stand the thought of torture! Do you have any idea how painful it is for your flesh to burn?'

Yamaguchi raised his baggy trousers.

Miguel's eyes widened at the sight of severe burn marks on his foot and lower leg from his childhood.

'Miguel!'

The young man drew in a sharp sniff and caught his breath before answering. 'Yes, Master Yamaguchi.'

'Would you like tea?'

Miguel nodded. 'Yes, I would like that.' Miguel wiped his tears with his sleeve and calmed himself.

'Come, follow me,' Master Yamaguchi said. He led Miguel through the back door into his small, but tidy, home.

'Enough of worry. Let us talk about something else. Tell me more of your home in Portugal.'

Soon, a sparkle emerged in Miguel's eyes as he reflected on home. 'Ah, Portugal. How I long for home! Portugal is the most beautiful of all European countries. And Lisbon ... far more beautiful than Rome. Maybe it's time!'

CHAPTER TWELVE

30 May 1626
Nagasaki City, District of Nagasaki, Kyushu

From the mountain's summit, Father Joaquim had a panoramic view of Nagasaki's residential quarters and the bustling trading port below. Columns of smoke rose from chimneys in the populated urban areas, while by the seashore, dozens of ships of all sizes, mainly cargo vessels, docked, unloaded wares and passengers, reloaded, and sailed away. In every direction, he saw figures meeting then scurrying through the marketplace. Nothing much had changed – Nagasaki was still the largest international trading hub in Japan.

Weary from the climb, his brow beaded with sweat, Joaquim began a slow descent, hobbling over stones and gravel while taking in the breathtaking vista of green mountains surrounding a huge, deep blue bay. The vibrancy of the city, nicknamed the 'Rome of the Far East', captivated all who visited, residents, foreign traders, and missionaries alike.

Before Father Joaquim's predecessors had arrived in Japan, Nagasaki had been a small fishing village. It had taken only six decades for the city to become the largest trading port in Japan, mainly because of the Portuguese and their strong trading ties with Macao in China and their other colonies.

Joaquim's feet hurt and he stopped to rest by a large boulder lining the pathway. An underfed youth approached him, balancing a small bag of food on his head. On seeing Joaquim, he set it down by his feet. Joaquim's stomach gurgled at the aroma of fresh rice and fish. He had not eaten since the day before.

The boy's curious gaze met Joaquim's. 'Will you buy food?'

'No, my son. But thank you.'

'You're not Japanese, are you?'

'What makes you say that?'

'Well, you look different.'

Joaquim smiled. He'd had little to smile about in recent days and the youth's innocence warmed his soul. 'That's right. I come from Portugal.'

The boy raised an eyebrow. 'Where's that?'

A sigh of nostalgia left Joaquim's lips as he recalled his homeland. 'It's a long way from here. Portugal is a powerful seafaring nation, and the Portuguese were the first to arrive in Asia from Europe.'

The boy raised a quizzical brow, but said nothing.

'There are many Portuguese traders in Nagasaki.'

'Why?'

'They trade – buy and sell things.'

'So they live here? Like you?'

'Yes. Other nationalities have done the same – the Dutch, the French, and the English – but the Portuguese have been the most enduring.'

'Won't you buy my food? You're a rich merchant, aren't you?'

Joaquim chuckled, patting his bag. 'Regretfully, I have no money today, and I have food of my own.' He set his hand on the boy's shoulder, rose to his feet, and bade him farewell.

Two hours later, as Father Joaquim emerged from a trail at the base of the mountain, two city officials dressed in samurai attire met him on the path.

'Where are you coming from?' one official asked.

Joaquim found a leash in his bag. 'Have you seen my dog?' he said.

'What?'

'My dog. He ran up the trail ahead of me. Did you see him?'

The official squinted and shook his head. 'No, we haven't seen a dog.'

Father Joaquim dug into this bag and fetched silver coins. 'Here,' he said as he handed two silver coins to each of the officials. 'It's a large black Portuguese dog. If you see it, please let me know. I live in the foreign quarters – house number thirteen.'

As he passed the officials, he added, 'His name is Cão, and he's been with me a long time. I must get him back.'

The city officials gripped their silver coins, nodded agreement, and continued on their way. Joaquim grinned to himself, thinking, *works every time.* He strutted as though he belonged, towards the foreign residential quarters.

As he walked through the streets of Nagasaki he couldn't help comparing the architecture to that in his village of Arima. Rather than the simple board buildings of his impoverished village, here each street had rows of houses with traditional, gently curved, Japanese-style roofs. The air was scented with cooked food, fresh spices, the tang of burning wood from cooking grills, and lingering tobacco smoke. What struck Father Joaquim as unusual, however, were dozens upon dozens of boarded-up homes.

Minutes later, he arrived at house number thirteen and recognized in surprise the symbol on the door – the Chinese character for Buddhism. Someone had used great care and diligence to engrave the symbol in the wood. He knocked.

Almost right away, the door swung open and a smiling face greeted him. 'Father Joaquim,' a Portuguese man whispered, with eyes that sparkled. 'It's wonderful to see you. Come in, old friend, please.'

'Mateus, it's good to see you, too.' Once inside, the men embraced.

Mateus was short and middle-aged, and, Joaquim noted, a little stouter than he remembered him to be. Mateus had dark hair, olive skin, kind brown eyes, a thick dark beard with subtle streaks of grey in it on one cheek, and an almost ever-present pipe from which sweet-smelling tobacco smoke wafted. Joaquim couldn't think of anyone who didn't like the jovial businessman.

'So, what do you think of the new engraving?' Mateus cocked his head to one side.

'Surprising.' Joaquim smiled.

'A necessary decoy, alas. These days, foreigners must profess their following of Buddha to live in Nagasaki. The symbol keeps the authorities at bay.'

'A sign of the times.' Father Joaquim sighed.

'Indeed.' Mateus nodded and asked, 'What brings you to Nagasaki, Father? Nothing good, I'm sure.'

Smiling at the remark, Joaquim removed his shoes at the door and sat down at Mateus's small kitchen table, atop which sat bottles of traditional Portuguese liqueurs, reams of pungent tobacco, a second smoking pipe, and a trading ledger.

'I'm an optimist, Mateus, you know that. But my burdens have grown heavier, and I need to address problems.'

'What problems?'

'Taxes.'

'Oh.' Mateus took a large puff from his pipe and fetched two wooden mugs. 'Don't get me started about taxes.' He grabbed a bottle of wine and a pitcher of water. 'Wine or water, Father?'

'I think I need wine.' Joaquim rubbed his beard.

Mateus poured red wine into the mugs, and Joaquim took a big sip before continuing. 'Daimyo Matsukura Shigemasa has driven up our taxes again and is putting even greater pressure on all the villages to expose Christians.'

'And your village?' Mateus asked, his brow furrowing.

'We're managing, but I need a favour.'

'Hah! I knew it.' Mateus slapped his thigh and smiled. 'What do you need?'

'Five hundred large silver coins.'

'Holy saints! You must be joking.'

'I wish I were.' Joaquim raised his eyebrows, acknowledging the audacity of his request.

'That's more than I have under my mattress,' Mateus chuckled.

'I thought it might be.'

Mateus thought for a moment, then said, 'I can borrow it.'

'From whom?'

'Other Portuguese traders.'

Joaquim said, 'Will they lend you that much?'

'I'll find out tomorrow night.'

'Are you comfortable asking them this, Mateus?'

Mateus grinned and winked. 'I'll go to the *gaijin* bar where the merchants like to gather and drink. I'll ask when they are drunk and in a good mood.'

'You traders never change,' Father Joaquim replied.

'If there's one thing you can count on, it's the thought of making a quick profit. That, and our love of wine and women.'

'It is different from the missions.'

'And how is that, Father? Things are only getting worse for Christians hiding in Nagasaki. How is life on the outskirts?'

'Difficult, I'm sorry to say, and politics is likely to make it worse.'

'Because of the new Nagasaki governor's arrival?'

'Yes. I've heard reports that Kawachi is vicious. Brothers, sisters, and children, all slaughtered like goats in the streets and in their homes. No one is safe.'

'What will you do?'

Father Joaquim rested his forehead on the outstretched fingers of his right hand. 'You and the others must be vigilant now. For the first time, the Shogun will have one of his own running Nagasaki, and he will not turn a blind eye. As for us, after we pay our taxes, we will slip away to Yezo in the north.'

'That's a long way away. Do you not fear capture?'

'Our Lord will guide us.'

'Father, I'm a believer and a good Christian, but I worry about you.'

'Have no worries, Mateus. "Seek first his kingdom and his

righteousness, and all these things will be given to you as well. Therefore do not worry about tomorrow, for tomorrow will worry about itself.'"

'Bless you, Father.' He paused. 'But I still worry.'

'None of us need worry unduly, Mateus. We need only seek God's help. He will answer our prayers.'

Mateus nodded, taking a moment to think. 'Father, we have been friends a long time.

'Yes, Mateus, a very long time.'

'Is it not time for you to return to Europe?'

'I am not that man any longer, my friend. You know that. There is nothing for me there. That man – the young teacher and faculty member at the College of Jesus, in Coimbra – has been washed away, along with the blood that was on my hands. My home is here. This is where God has sent me to do His work. It is where I must do His bidding. I am His soldier now.'

'You have done all you can here. The padres are no longer welcome and if the authorities catch you, they *will* crucify you.'

'I cannot abandon my converted brethren, Mateus. Never.'

Mateus sat silent for a moment, familiar with Joaquim's resolve. 'I admire you, Father. Your strength and spirit are an inspiration.'

'Praise the Lord, Mateus, not me. My strength comes from Him.'

Mateus let out a long sigh. 'Get some rest, Father. You've had a long journey. Please, take my bed.'

'Are you sure? What will you do?'

'What I always do in the evening – visit the *gaijin* bar in the port. It may be a quiet night, but perhaps I will get lucky with a woman and some cards.' He grinned and shrugged apologetically.

CHAPTER THIRTEEN

31 May 1626
Shogun's Castle

Inside his castle, Shogun Iemitsu prepared for an official assembly. Like the rest of his castle, the Shogun's meeting chambers were enviable. Resplendent Japanese artwork and calligraphy adorned the walls of the chamber's high ceilings, interrupted at precise intervals by strong mahogany beams and light, painted screens. In designing, building, and decorating the magnificent castle, no cost had been spared.

High in the rafters hung the Shogun's flag and family crest. The flag itself was all white, and the Shogun's symbolic family crest, or *mon*, was circular in form, containing three hollyhock leaves. The hollyhock leaf resembled wild ginger, and the triple hollyhock had become a recognized icon throughout Japan, symbolizing the strength of the Tokugawa clan and the Shogun's dominance over the country.

Shogun Iemitsu was proud of his family symbol, which could be traced back to his grandfather, Ieyasu. Young Iemitsu was especially proud that his grandfather had begun his rule of Japan after a famous battle – the Battle of Sekigahara in the year 1600 – when Ieyasu had defeated all opposing forces to become master of the country.

Among attendees at the meeting today were the Shogun's father, Hidetada, the Shogun's Roju advisory cabinet, multiple high-ranking samurai, and the appointee for Governor of Nagasaki, Mizuno Kawachi.

The Shogun lifted his chin and inflated his chest as he glared around the room. Gathered before him were the most powerful men in Japan, and all owed fealty to him. He felt proud that at 19 he was the richest and most powerful samurai in all Japan.

Iemitsu and his Roju cabinet controlled Japan's finances with a tight grip. The daimyo were required to pay tax subsidies to him in the form of predefined quantities of rice, called *kokus*, which acted as the country's main currency. Although other forms of currency existed, such as silver coins, the true measure of a man's wealth was rice production, and Iemitsu controlled the entire system. The key for the daimyos who actually produced the rice was to secure as much productive land from Iemitsu as possible, and warlords manoeuvred and sometimes fought each other for this privilege.

Iemitsu held his head high, his knees anchored on a beautiful golden satin cushion atop an elevated platform. The room became silent. Buddhist monks wearing yellow robes lined the room's periphery.

The Shogun turned to his right. 'Official Mizuno Kawachi-san, we have called this meeting because soon you will leave for Nagasaki.'

'Yes, Lord.' Kawachi bowed low in deference to the Shogun.

'Before you leave, we want to ensure you are clear about your role and our expectations in the south.'

'Yes, Lord. I am here to serve.'

'Your role is to annihilate Christianity in Nagasaki and throughout Kyushu ... ' – the Shogun paused, – '... by whatever means necessary.'

'Yes, Lord.'

'I officially appoint you *bugyo* of Nagasaki. You will replace the existing governor, Hasegawa Gonroku.'

'Thank you, Lord Shogun. Your appointment is a great honour.'

'You will also act as my official representative in Nagasaki, and I empower you to oversee all of Kyushu's warlords in exterminating Christianity. Furthermore, you will keep a close eye on Kyushu's daimyo to monitor their eradication of these vermin. Do you understand your duties?'

'Yes, Lord, I understand.'

'I want you to place spies in all the domains to ensure that none of my subjects give sanctuary to any Christians. I will also place my own spies in the region.'

'Yes, Lord.'

'If you discover hidden Christians, I want to know.'

'I will keep you informed, Lord Shogun.'

'If our daimyo are neglectful in their domains, I want to know.' The Shogun clenched his fists in emphasis. 'I will punish them, and if they are lucky they will lose only their lands. Do you have any questions, Governor?'

'No, Lord. I look forward to being your Iron Hand,' Kawachi

replied with a determined nod.

'When do you leave?' asked Sakai, a member of the Shogun's cabinet.

'In one week,' Kawachi said.

'What will you do upon your arrival in Nagasaki, Kawachi-san?' the Shogun's father, Hidetada, asked.

'I will crucify Christians as a warning to others.'

'Good.' Hidetada nodded an approval.

'I want to send a strong message to Nagasaki and all the domains. I want the whole island to know that Christianity will perish. I have *no* compunction about burning Christians alive, or dismembering them one limb at a time.'

'Your resolve is praiseworthy, Kawachi-san,' the Shogun said. He nodded his head with his shoulders back. 'Make us proud of your appointment.'

Light chatter broke out in the chamber as the attendees appeared pleased with their progress, but was quickly silenced by the Shogun's father, Hidetada, who raised a hand in the air. 'I would also like you to keep an eye on the foreigners in Nagasaki.' He paused and questioned Kawachi. 'You understand *why* we must watch them with sharp eyes, do you not?'

'To ensure they don't smuggle in any more priests or missionaries, Hidetada-san,' the Governor replied.

'Not only that,' Hidetada continued. 'We need you to gather intelligence about a potential raid or invasion of our lands by the foreign barbarians.'

'Yes, Lord, of course.'

'This is vital. The Spanish have already established a base in the Philippines.'

'Yes, Lord. I know about their base in Manila.'

'Do not take this duty lightly, Kawachi-san. The Spanish are a conquering nation.'

'The Council has educated me in their tactics, Lord. First, they send Christians to infiltrate, convert, and gather intelligence. Then, they send their army.'

'Correct,' Hidetada replied. 'Let us not forget that the English and Dutch have already warned us about the King of Spain. The Spanish have conquered so much of the new world to their west, why would they not also seek to go further and conquer Japan?'

The Governor nodded.

'I have studied the world maps of the Spanish, the Portuguese, and the Dutch,' Shogun Iemitsu interjected. 'Our country is small in size and might seem insignificant to the greater world. Foreigners could invade and conquer Japan and plunder our wealth, just as they have done elsewhere.'

'I will deploy spies to learn all we can,' the Governor said.

'You must!' Hidetada's voice rose as he clenched his jaw. 'The Christians are the beginning. They report not just to the Pope, but to the kings of their native lands. All foreigners are in league together, to threaten us and divide the spoils of Japan among themselves. First the Bible, then the sword and the lash.'

Whispers buzzed throughout the chamber.

'Don't trust anyone,' the Shogun interjected. 'Imagine if the Japanese Christians, the foreigner barbarians, and the ronin were to join forces!'

The murmurs grew louder.

'Let us not underestimate the ronin,' stated Abe Masatsugu, the most senior member of the cabinet. 'Those leaderless samurai roam our lands and remain a serious threat to the Empire.'

'The Shogun is correct,' Hidetada exclaimed as his eyes darted around the room. 'Imagine the ronin joining forces with a foreign army. They could overthrow us!'

The murmurs in the meeting chamber grew louder as the Roju cabinet members exchanged worried glances. Meanwhile several samurai on the periphery of the room grumbled at the suggestion.

'I despise those masterless samurai.' The Shogun's face was red, the veins in his forehead visible. 'You have an important role in the south, Governor,' Hidetada added. 'You must keep watch on everything.'

'Yes, Lord Hidetada. I am a loyal servant of the Shogun. I will not let you down.'

'First, kill the Christians.' The Shogun's fury resounded throughout the room. 'Second, watch the Spanish and Portuguese traders; they know things. Third, keep an eye on those unemployed ronin that roam our lands without purpose. They're dangerous, and must not conspire against us.'

'Yes, Lord.'

'Good. This is *my* country.' Iemitsu withdrew a knife from inside his garment and stabbed it into the elegant *tatami* mat before him. 'And I will not give it up to anyone.'

CHAPTER FOURTEEN

31 May 1626
Nagasaki City, District of Nagasaki, Kyushu

Unlike Father Joaquim's own straw bed, Mateus's was large, elevated on an elegant wooden frame, and filled with an abundance of plush feathers. Joaquim rose, stretched, then knelt beside the bed. He searched inside his jacket, located a secret compartment, and withdrew a small, worn-out Bible.

He opened the book of Luke and read: 'The harvest is plentiful, but the workers are few. Ask the Lord of the harvest, therefore, to send out workers into his harvest field. Go! I am sending you out like lambs among wolves.'

Joaquim turned his head at a light knock on the door. Mateus da Costa entered. 'Ah, Father, good morning. How did you sleep?'

'Well, Mateus. How was your night?' Joaquim sat on the edge of the bed.

'Terrific,' Mateus answered with a smile that hinted at satisfaction. 'I always enjoy my nights in the port.'

'Was it prosperous?'

'Always!' Mateus smirked. 'Japanese women love Portuguese traders.'

'Good for you, but you know I fill my cup in other ways.'

'Ah, Father, we traders cannot help ourselves. We enjoy the best that Nagasaki offers.'

'And how is business, Mateus?'

'More bureaucracy and barriers,' Mateus replied, sighing. 'The Shogun appears bent on closing the country to outsiders. Did you know that Japan is now influencing ships that depart from Macao?' Mateus leaned against the doorframe.

'I don't understand.'

'The Shogun's cabinet has stationed a Japanese official in Macao.'

'For what reason?'

'They are inspecting all prospective passengers and preventing anyone who looks suspicious from coming to Japan. They are creating pre-boarding lists, along with descriptions of everyone on board.'

Joaquim shook his head. 'For what purpose?'

'An official gives a copy of the list to the ship's captain, who must deliver it to the authorities in Nagasaki before anchoring. If there is any discrepancy between the list and the persons arriving, they kill the captain.'

'Another measure to prevent missionaries from arriving?'

'Sadly, yes.'

'Unbelievable. The country is closing itself off.' Joaquim banged the table in frustration.

'It's ridiculous.' Mateus's face mirrored the priest's look of despair. 'They expelled the Spanish two years ago. I think the Portuguese may be next.'

'But we have traded with Japan for over seventy years – longer than anyone else.'

'Nothing lasts forever, Father. Trade has become much more challenging, for the Portuguese and even the local merchants. Did you see all those boarded-up houses on the way here?'

Joaquim nodded. 'It looks like they are growing in number.'

'Those are former homes of Japanese Christians. The local authorities have seized them because of their beliefs.'

'But I thought Governor Gonroku turned a blind eye to Christianity?'

'When he can,' Mateus replied. 'The Governor cannot *always* turn a blind eye. When Christian worship is blatant he must act, or face the Shogun's wrath.'

'I was not aware Governor Gonroku had become a persecutor.'

'I do not think he has much choice these days. The Shogun controls religion now. He decides everyone's faith.'

'It's sad that religious freedom has ended,' said Joaquim.

'I fear it will only get worse.'

'Because of the expected arrival of Mizuno Kawachi?'

'Yes. Any remaining, hidden Christians in Nagasaki are worried about his arrival, the traders too.'

'Why the traders?'

'Because Portuguese traders and merchants used to run Nagasaki.'

'And that is changing?'

'It's rumoured that through the new governor, the Shogun will exert greater control over future trade.'

'That's not good.' Father Joaquim's shoulders slumped.

Mateus nodded. 'The Shogun does not like the Portuguese making so much money at the expense of the Japanese. It's as though he thinks we're picking his pockets.'

'Hence the *pancado* system.'

'Yes. More and more, the Governor and the authorities are meddling in trade issues, squeezing our profits.'

With a hint of mischief in his voice Joaquim said, 'All the more reason to sell on the black market then.'

Mateus could not stop an explosive laugh at the priest's grasp of moral ambiguity. 'Exactly so, Father. Some merchandise we sell under the *pancado* system, and some – our best – we sell on the black market.'

'The Japanese do love their Chinese silk,' said the priest.

'Without question, and right now everyone wants their silk in red and black.'

'And this is where I would like to help – with the silk trade.'

'Oh?' Mateus raised an eyebrow.

'My silver loan is not a gift; I want to repay you, and I have the language skills and knowledge of local customs to help you.'

'What do you mean?'

'Let me negotiate for you on the black market.'

Mateus paused for a moment, considering Joaquim's proposal. 'It's a tempting offer, Father, but I'm not so sure. There are more complications now. The Dutch are growing more jealous of our strongholds in Nagasaki and Macao.'

'Some things never change.'

'They do a little.' Mateus shifted his footing. 'The Dutch are becoming more aggressive in their tactics.'

'That is nothing new. Are they still sacking our ships at sea?'

'They try.'

'And still moaning about their lousy port in Hirado?'

'Yes. I suspect they'll never be happy with that small fishing village. They want to control Nagasaki and they're jealous and unpredictable in their troublemaking.'

'I still would like to help, Mateus. I would like the ability to pay back the loan.'

'It could be very dangerous for you, Father. If the authorities discover your identity, they will kill you, painfully.'

'We cannot live our lives in fear, Mateus.'

The merchant was quiet. 'Let me think about it. I need to secure the loan first.'

'As you wish. You will make enquiries tonight?'

'All the influential Portuguese traders with the deep pockets will be at the *gaijin* bar tonight. Let's see how the night goes.'

'Thank you, Mateus.' Father Joaquim placed a hand on his chest and bowed. 'Your help will save lives.'

CHAPTER FIFTEEN

31 May 1626
Fukae, Shimabara Peninsula, Kyushu

Daimyo Shigemasa, a dozen of his most senior samurai on horseback and a hundred on foot entered a village in Fukae, one of the largest farming communities in his domain. A number of villagers scurried out of sight making for their homes, while others bravely stayed with their families to greet their daimyo.

'Welcome, Lord Shigemasa!' a farmer cried out.

'Welcome, Lord,' a crowd echoed, and bowed several times.

'I remember this village,' Shigemasa said sourly. He scrutinized it from atop his tall black horse. 'Always behind on rice production.'

Shigemasa crossed his arms and gazed around at the tired-looking villagers. He saw a plethora of women and elderly people, but few strong-looking men able to perform the heavy manual farming work he required. He observed their bones outlined through their skinny frames and the dark circles under their eyes due to a lack of sleep.

'We try our best, Lord Shigemasa!' a peasant exclaimed. He ran up to the Daimyo, carrying a wooden pot filled with cold water. 'Please, have cool water after your long journey.' A samurai pushed the man away roughly.

Shigemasa ignored the peasant and continued, 'This village is the most unproductive in my entire domain. You have the greatest number of farmers but produce the least amount of rice.'

'We work hard for you, Lord, every day! Our fields are not as fertile as others, but we work day and night,' a man dared to say.

'Do not offer me excuses for your laziness!'

A senior farmer approached Shigemasa and his large horse with another pot of water. 'Please, Lord, take cold water. You and your horse must be very thirsty.'

'I'm here for rice, not water!' Shigemasa roared. He kicked the pot out of the farmer's hands, sending it to the ground, where it shattered.

The terrified farmer took a few steps back.

'This soil looks perfectly fertile,' the Daimyo announced.

Another farmer stepped forward. 'Lord, we would not lie to you nor make excuses, but the soil on these lands is not deep and there are many rocks.'

'Silence!'

'Please, Lord, let us move to another parcel of land,' a young peasant cried out. 'We can improve our production on better soil.'

'You will not move to other lands. *These* are your lands!' The

Daimyo observed the stacks of filled rice bags. 'Bring me your rice production – at once.'

'Yes, Lord,' the peasants answered and ran in all directions to collect every bag of rice in the village.

'How many sacks of rice do I see before me?' the warlord asked.

A peasant counted the bags. 'Almost forty large sacks of rice, Lord,' he answered as he looked down and bit his lips.

'I require *one hundred* sacks of rice from this village. This is less than *half* of your production quota.'

'Please, Lord, it is not possible,' a distressed woman near the rear of the crowd cried out.

'Silence!' The Daimyo glared at the peasants. 'All across my domain I hear excuses for failing to meet quotas, but your village is the worst.'

'Please, Lord, you own our entire lives,' another farmer lamented. 'It is not possible to work any harder.'

'Nonsense. You are slacking in the fields and there must be a reason. Are there Christians among you?'

'No, Lord,' the village leader replied. 'We are Buddhists. You know this.'

'Then why are you slacking in the fields?'

No one dared reply.

'The other daimyo are getting richer and producing more rice, but not me!' Shigemasa shouted in frustration. 'If you are not slackening because of Christianity, then it means you are slackening because you are too old to work in the fields.' He glared at the elderly in the village.

'Who is the oldest among you?' The Daimyo scanned the villagers.

No one spoke.

'Find me the oldest farmer in this village.'

Shigemasa's samurai rustled through the villagers. After a few minutes of manhandling the farmers, the samurai pushed two old men to the front of the crowd.

'Bind their hands behind their backs,' Shigemasa commanded. He turned to the terrified villagers. 'If you are slow in the rice fields, it means you do not have the proper motivation.'

The Daimyo faced the samurai detaining the two elders. 'Put them in straw coats.'

The samurai bound layers of straw over the older men as peasants pleaded for mercy for them.

'Set them alight.'

The bound men cried out in terror and tried to run, but they were old and hampered, and easily caught. The Daimyo's samurai held them and poured oil over them. Then a samurai struck a wooden match and lit their straw coats.

The flames roared up in a flash as the oil-soaked straw caught fire. The bound men screamed as their flesh burned, and scampered back and forth, twisting and turning in agony in a grotesque imitation of dancing. As the flames burned brightly the men shrieked in high-pitched tones few had ever heard before.

'Look! They're dancing.' A samurai laughed at the burning men.

'The *mino odori* – raincoat dance!' another warrior mocked, to the entertainment of his companions.

As the stench of burning flesh caused the villagers to cover their noses and some to gag, Shigemasa leaned back in his saddle and said, 'I have no tolerance for poor productivity.' He pointed his riding crop at the burning bodies. 'If you do not meet your next quota, I will find two more victims on my return. I trust this will be sufficient motivation to work harder.'

The Daimyo and his retainers left, leaving the charred bodies and wailing villagers in his wake. His work had just begun.

CHAPTER SIXTEEN

31 May 1626
Gaijin Bar, Port of Nagasaki

Mateus da Costa sat with his liqueurs and tobacco pipe in the company of four other Portuguese traders, in the back corner of a dark, smoky *gaijin* bar along Nagasaki's harbour front. A Portuguese merchant ran the establishment, which held a dozen tightly packed tables. Most of the patrons were European and wore colourful, oversized European clothes, with large boots, baggy pants, and majestic shirts sporting multiple buttons, with excess cloth hanging from the shoulders. Apart from a hint of Japanese ambience, they could have been in a bar on the Lisbon waterfront.

As the evening wore on and Mateus judged that his friends had consumed enough spirits, he decided it was time. 'Gentlemen,

I need you to look deep into your hearts and then dig deep into your pockets. Father Joaquim Martinez and his village of Catholic converts need five hundred pieces of silver, fast. If he does not get it, the authorities will probably kill him.' Mateus set down his mug of ale with a thump, as if for emphasis. Liquid spilled out of it. 'The Daimyo might also kill the villagers too – even the children and a newborn.'

'Why should *we* help, Mateus?' a trader asked, swigging half his beer in one large gulp.

Mateus puffed on his pipe and exhaled. 'Because it's the right thing to do.'

'Mateus …' The man leaned forward and grinned. 'I'm a businessman. The right thing for *me* to do is make as much money as I can.' He leaned back and took another large swig from his mug.

'He's right,' a second trader agreed. 'It's almost June, and the July trading season is on our doorstep. We all need as much working capital as possible.'

'Gentlemen, we need to think beyond trade and working capital. As Catholics, we've an obligation to help the Church.'

Mateus tried to make eye contact with his fellow traders. It wasn't easy. Their eyes were squinty, reddened, and glossy from drink and tobacco smoke. But the shrewdness was still there, though hidden among scruffy beards, bad teeth, and long greasy hair.

'Five hundred silver coins is a hell of a lot of money, *meu amigo*,' a third trader said.

'Why can't Rome support the Fathers?' another asked.

'Because Rome is halfway around the world, busy fighting Protestant heretics, and near-broke, and we all know it. Father Joaquim needs our help now.'

'Why this priest? Between you and me, I find most of them tedious when they're not trying to lecture me, or make me feel guilty about drinking and women.'

'Father Joaquim and I travelled to Japan on the same ship. He and I have known each other for a long time, and he would do anything to help me – or any one of you. Defying the Shogun's laws for as long as he has, he is one of the bravest men I know. Please, gentlemen, divided five ways it is just one hundred silver coins each.'

'*Just* one hundred!' the third trader scoffed. 'Do you know how many nights with Japanese *yūjo* one hundred silver coins could buy?'

'Oh, he knows,' the first trader quipped. He turned to face Mateus. 'How do we know the Father will pay us back? If what you say is true, he'll likely be dead in a week.'

'Agreed,' the second trader added. 'All the priests are becoming extinct out here.'

'Then lend *me* the money, and *I* will pay you back. I will help the Father.'

'So we lend *you* the money, Mateus, not the priest?' the first trader asked.

'Yes. *I* will take responsibility for repayment.'

'When will we get our money back?' the second trader asked, slurring his words.

'Before the new year,' Mateus said.

He poured shots of sake for all at the table.

The traders shot back their drinks and then puffed on their pipes as they considered the matter. Mateus poured more shots.

'Ten per cent interest,' the third trader said.

'No interest,' Mateus said. 'This isn't a commercial transaction, it's for the Church.'

The traders puffed on their pipes and cigars again.

'Fine,' said the first trader. 'I will lend *you* the money on *your* creditworthiness.'

'Agreed,' the other traders echoed.

'So, we are agreed.' Mateus smiled and held up his sake cup. 'Tomorrow afternoon, I will visit each of your quarters to collect.' He tossed back the rice wine in one shot. '*Saúde!*' he said, and stepped away from the table, holding his hat in an exaggerated bow to the group, and exiting the smoky bar.

Outside, Mateus took a deep breath. That had been easier than he had imagined it would be. He pinched tobacco into his pipe, lit it, and meandered down the street. He ambled towards his home, feeling tipsy. Before he realized what had happened, he felt himself falling to the ground, his head throbbing and feeling wet. He touched his fingers to his scalp and then, as he examined the blood, heard the distinct sounds of Dutch voices. Dazed and trembling, he glanced up and saw his two attackers. One was medium height with brown hair, blue eyes, with a scar on his face. The other was tall, heavy-set, and powerful-looking.

'Look what we have here,' the big Dutchman said, glaring down.

'A bleeding Roman Portuguese pig,' the smaller one added.

Mateus moaned as he lay in the street, blood streaming from the gash the bottle had made when the big man had slammed it against his head. He felt nauseous and his vision was becoming blurry as he tried to focus on his dimly lit surroundings.

'Look, the pig's squirming in the dirt,' the smaller Dutchman said, breaking into a hearty laugh. 'We see too much of you, little pig. Every time we trade, we see you.'

'We have grown tired of your smell.' The larger man kicked Mateus in his chest to reinforce his point.

'Time to start eliminating the competition,' the smaller man added. He walked over to Mateus, knelt and punched him in the face.

Blood spurted from his nose in a large gush and his head snapped back onto the street. Dizziness threatened to overcome him. Was this his end? He glanced around him looking for help. But there was none, not even if he could gather his wits enough to cry out for help.

Spitting blood, Mateus gasped for breath, feeling the pain in his side sharpen with each breath. 'Nagasaki is Portuguese and always will be, especially to heretics like you.'

'Think again, Roman,' the larger man said. He kicked Mateus in his side, and felt the cracking of several ribs. Mateus's breathing became laboured and shallow. The world fluttered and images in the dark became less distinct. Only a stabbing pain in his side provided any clarity.

Mateus cried out, 'Go back to Holland, you Protestant scum!' Holding his ribs, he lay curled up in the street, feeling the blood streaming across his face.

'Sit him up,' the small Dutchman directed his companion.

The large Dutchman gripped Mateus by his collar and pulled him forward while Mateus gripped his arms ineffectually in a futile effort to stop him.

'Kiss the Pope for me, Portugee!' the smaller whispered into his ear from behind. He pulled a knife from his jacket. Mateus struggled as he saw the metal glint of the blade in the moonlight. He thought to scream for help but only a dull gurgle emerged as the knife sliced open his throat from left to right. They let him go and he sank like a collapsing bag of air into the gutter.

'Quick, find his bag. Get the money!' the smaller Dutchman said.

His companion opened Mateus's bag, replacing the few coins he had left with several articles, including a Bible and a large crucifix.

CHAPTER SEVENTEEN

1 June 1626
Gaijin Residential Quarters, Nagasaki City

Father Joaquim knelt against Mateus's bed murmuring a prayer in the early morning light, his knees sore on the cold ground. He was reaching for his Bible when the front door of the house crashed open.

Joaquim rose to his feet and stashed his Bible under the bed-covers. He went to the front room with a terror gripping his chest that the authorities had come for him. The Jesuit immediately saw four stern-looking officers, who had smashed in Mateus's door. They wore official navy-blue uniforms, along with matching hats.

'Halt where you are!' the first official shouted as Joaquim entered the room. The officers spread out, doing their best to encircle the priest.

'What are you doing here?' another demanded. 'Are you Christian? Are you praying?'

'Who are you?' the first official asked. 'Stand still!'

Joaquim faced the officials, unaware that he had adopted a sideways defensive posture and was balancing on the balls of his feet. He noted that each had his hand on the hilt of his sword.

'You're under arrest,' an official said forcefully.

'Please, calm down,' Father Joaquim replied. 'I'm a trader, a colleague of Mateus da Costa, the man who lives here. He will straighten out all of this upon his return.'

'Mateus da Costa is dead!' the lead official declared. 'You are a Christian priest!'

'What?' Joaquim exclaimed, wondering how they could possibly know. It dawned on him that it didn't matter whether they thought it true or not. He was a foreigner – that was enough these days.

His shoulders tightened and his hands began to sweat. He found his breath becoming rapid and shallow. Blinking, he forced himself to ignore the news of his friend's death and deal with the immediate situation. With an instinct born of years of practice facing martial arts opponents, Joaquim forced himself to deepen and slow his breathing and relax his body.

'Someone murdered him in the port area last night. And now you are under arrest.'

'We will crucify you, Padre,' another official declared with an intense stare. 'Come with us!'

'I don't want to hurt anyone, but I cannot go with you today,' Joaquim answered.

'Don't be stupid, Padre. We will kill you if you resist.' In a show of force, the officials unsheathed their swords and advanced. The leading official raised his katana for a swiping downward blow, so Joaquim stepped towards him and inside his raised arms. Taking advantage of a momentary surprise on the official's face he grabbed one sword arm and delivered an open-handed blow to his chest, forcing him backwards into the other three officials. They became a jumbled mass of arms and legs in the confined space. In the confusion, Joaquim stabbed his thumb into the back of the wrist nearest him, causing a sharp, involuntary spasm of pain through the man's hand. His fingers flew open, releasing his sword, leaving him disarmed. One of the officers at the back of the group who was still standing took a threatening step towards the priest, and with the skill of a seasoned master Joaquim delivered precise, savage throat slashes to the leading men. Two of his attackers collapsed, as fountains of arterial blood sprayed from their wounds.

'Put down your sword,' one of the two remaining officials shouted nervously.

'You first.'

'Kill him!' The lead official charged at Joaquim, swiping his sword from left to right. The second official hesitated. With a deft strike, Joaquim knocked the sword from the first attacker's hand and kicked him in the chest, sending him flying into his colleague. Each lost his balance and stumbled sideways. As they tried to stand, Joaquim cut them down with precise slashes to their necks.

Surveying the carnage, sword still in hand, Joaquim prayed, 'Lord, forgive me, for I have sinned.' He stared at his gore-drenched hands and dropped the sword. Then he grabbed his bag and recovered the hidden Bible.

For years, he had studied the craft of war from Master Yamaguchi, but it had always been an exercise to develop a mastery of self-control. Now he finally understood what he had been studying, what 'self-defence' really meant.

The priest dropped his head and said a prayer for the men he had just murdered, knowing that they had left him no choice but to kill them before they killed him. It still felt like it was not a good enough reason. He struggled to reconcile his actions with his faith. He forced himself to change quickly out of his bloody clothes into simple clean ones, then stepping through the blood-soaked door, fled Mateus da Costa's home as though the archangel Michael was hot on his heels.

CHAPTER EIGHTEEN

1 June 1626
Arima

Master Yamaguchi carried a large old pot and paced among the villagers, pouring water into wooden cups for the exhausted villagers working the rice paddies.

He finished pouring and stood up straight. 'Listen,' he said, 'let's play a game.'

The children cheered as they leaped from the ground and rushed towards him.

'What game shall we play, Master Yamaguchi?' a girl asked, tugging at the old man's worn-out garments.

'I propose a competition: adults versus children. The winners get to take the rest of the day off.' Master Yamaguchi smiled down at the children.

'What's the game? What's the game?' the children squealed as they bounced from foot to foot.

'The game is simple,' Master Yamaguchi replied. 'It's called *rocks in the pot*.'

'What's that?'

'Let me explain.' Master Yamaguchi held out his hands, beckoning the children to settle down and listen.

'Here is the pot, and there are the rocks.' Master Yamaguchi pointed at a small pile of rocks near the edge of the rice field.

'From a distance of ten feet, you will throw rocks into the pot. The group with the most rocks in the pot takes the rest of the day off.'

'Competition accepted!' a parent shouted as he leaped from his feet and ran towards the rocks. 'We will not let these measly children beat us.'

'You're right,' a mother laughed. 'I think the adults deserve a day off, not these cheeky children.'

For a moment at least, the mood changed, and the villagers were living, not just working to avoid death.

'There are twelve children, so we need twelve adults!' Master Yamaguchi shouted as he set the rules. 'Two rocks per player.'

The children cheered as they ran to the front of the group, pushing to be the first to throw.

Master Yamaguchi intervened, settling the matter. At the front, young Shiro fended off the other children.

'Well, it looks like Shiro-kun will be the first to throw,' Master Yamaguchi declared.

Master Yamaguchi knew the village recognized Shiro as a talented boy. Not only was he strong in the flesh, but the villagers regarded him as intelligent and spiritual. By the age of four, when he wasn't working in the fields, Shiro could already read and write. Regarded as a child prodigy, he spent much of his time with Catechist Tonia, becoming proficient in Latin and Portuguese, and memorizing hundreds of verses from the Bible. By the age of six, he had already developed a strong faith in God and become a leader and role model for the other village children. It was thus no surprise that Shiro would be the first child to throw.

'Let us start,' Master Yamaguchi instructed.

Shiro focused on the task and closed his eyes for a few seconds, taking a moment to pray. When he opened them, the other children cheered as they wished him well in his throw. With no hesitation, young Shiro threw his stone ten feet into the air, landing it dead centre in Master Yamaguchi's pot.

The children cheered again, this time in delight. Master Yamaguchi and the parents in the village applauded.

'I will be the next to throw,' Shiro's uncle stated as he paraded to the front, edging his nephew out of the way with a smile. 'I think you will find the adults just as capable.'

With his shoulders back and chin high, Shiro's uncle threw his stone high in the air, and it also landed in Master Yamaguchi's pot. Most of the adults gave him a clap of congratulation while the children looked on in anticipation.

The throwing continued until almost all the stones were tossed, the adults keeping the score equal until the final lobs of the game. The score was seven to seven, with one child and one adult left to throw.

The last child walked up to the line: a young girl of nine, with long dark hair and a cheery smile. The crowd chanted with enthusiasm, aware this would be the children's last throw.

'You can do it! You can do it!' the children cheered.

'Set your mind on things above, not on earthly things, Miwa-chan!' Shiro shouted. 'Visualize your rock in the pot and it will be so.'

Young Miwa clasped her hands in prayer, then grabbed her stone and threw it high into the air, right into the centre of the pot. The children shrieked in delight, jumping and dancing around little Miwa.

'It's not over yet!' an adult yelled. 'We still have one more throw.'

The children settled down as the final adult walked up to the line.

Without delay, the adult tossed the stone … and missed.

For several minutes the children screamed in joy and danced before the adults.

'Catechists Tonia and Miguel have been hiding inside all day,' Master Yamaguchi said. 'I am sure they are very lonely. Who would like to join them for some playtime and stories?'

'Yay!' the children cheered again. 'No more work in the field today!'

'Come with me then,' Master Yamaguchi said as he led the children towards one of the small dwellings, where Tonia and Miguel kept cover.

Meanwhile, the adults knew what was in store for them. Like every other day, it would be non-stop work until the dark hours. The village could not afford to miss their new production quota.

CHAPTER NINETEEN

1 June 1626
Magistrate's Office, Nagasaki City

Governor Hasegawa Gonroku sat in his office and stared at a map of Nagasaki on his wall. So, he thought, the Shogun has finally decided to have *his* man in this important post. Gonroku knew *he* was not that man: he lacked the stomach for the brutal governing the Shogun demanded – often including torture and crucifixion. Gonroku himself had suggested that he wasn't the right man for the job, so it was no surprise that the Shogun had appointed Mizuno Kawachi in his place. Until Kawachi's arrival, however, Gonroku had a job to do and despite his distaste for the violent parts of the responsibility, he was resolved to leave office without losing face.

And then, in the middle of what had been a quiet day, two officials had rushed into the Governor's office barely able to catch their breath. '*Bugyo*, we have serious news!'

'Speak,' the Governor said.

'Criminals have murdered four officials in the residential quarters!' said the first official.

'What?' At that moment Gonroku knew he would not be able to end his term untroubled.

'They murdered our officials inside the home of a *gaijin* trader,' the second official added.

Stunned, the Governor leaped from his relaxed kneeling position. 'A *gaijin* killed my officials? Have you arrested him?'

'No, your honour. Someone murdered the *gaijin* trader in the streets near the port last night.'

He closed his eyes for a moment, and rested his forehead on his right hand, then asked, 'What else?'

'The trader was an avid Christian and was carrying a cross, a Bible, and other items of Christian worship,' the first official said.

'When our officials confirmed his identity, they went straight to his quarters to investigate,' the second official added.

'Who was he?'

'A well-known, long-standing trader,' the first official answered.

'His name?'

'Mateus da Costa, a Portuguese trader,' came the response.

'I know that man!' exclaimed Gonroku clasping a hand over his mouth. He had met with Mateus not long ago. 'He's traded in Nagasaki for decades.'

'Was he a devout Christian, Governor?' the second official asked.

Deep in thought, the Governor replied, 'I don't think so.' He shook his head. 'What did his home reveal?'

'That someone had murdered all four officials when they arrived,' the second official said.

'But what did you find in his home?'

'A lot of blood and business papers,' the first official answered.

The second official then offered his assessment. 'I think the murderers were professional killers, Governor.'

'Why do you think that?'

'They were all killed by single slashes to their throats. There were no other cuts or wounds, so the murderers were very likely expert swordsmen.'

'How many criminals were involved?'

'We don't know, Governor, but there must have been several. It would take several men at least to kill our officials like this. We train our officials very well.'

The Governor knelt down next to a small table and stared at the wall. He recalled that Mateus had given him some gifts, including an expensive terrestrial globe and dozens of pieces of exotic art work imported from Macao. He also recalled receiving these in exchange for granting Mateus additional trading privileges.

'This is horrible news. I do *not* need a Christian scandal during my last days as Governor. It will be a humiliation for me before the Shogun.'

'What should we do?' the first official asked.

'Lock down the city and put every official in Nagasaki and the entire district on high alert. I want anything out of the ordinary investigated.'

'What else, Governor?'

'Get the tracking dogs. Find these criminals at once. I *cannot* suffer such embarrassment before the Shogun.'

* * *

Dressed in flamboyant Portuguese trading attire once again, Father Joaquim approached the Government checkpoint with deliberate false confidence and a broad smile of fake bonhomie. As the priest strolled up to the outpost he could not stop his legs from shaking, and the tremor in his hands, as the violence from earlier that morning continued to haunt him.

'What is the purpose of your travel?' asked a guard.

'I'm travelling to Hirado to negotiate commercial dealings on behalf of the Governor.' He was shocked at the tremor in his usually calm voice.

A second guard wandered over and looked Joaquim up and down. '*Gaijin* are not permitted land-travel outside of the city. You should know this, and travel by boat if necessary.'

'I understand, sir, but I have documents from the Governor granting special permission,' Joaquim insisted.

'I never heard of this,' said the new official. He was clearly the more senior of the two men. 'Let me see this documentation!'

Father Joaquim reached into his bag and withdrew the letter he had used earlier.

'This seal is broken,' rebuked the lead official. 'And it looks crumpled. Governor Gonroku would never issue official documentation in such decrepit condition.'

'I can assure you the documentation is legitimate,' responded Joaquim, feeling his anxiety rise. He kicked himself for forgetting to reseal the letter at Mateus's home. Distracted by the sudden conflict earlier, he had forgotten to reorganize his papers. He felt an itchy bead of sweat slowly work its way along the inside of his shirt collar.

The lead official scrutinized Joaquim intently. 'This documentation and situation is most unusual. We cannot permit you to travel until we receive explicit confirmation from the Governor.'

'But I assure you these papers are legitimate,' Joaquim pleaded. 'Please, the Governor is relying on me and I don't want any problems.'

'Why is there blood on your bag?!' asked the first official. He swiped a finger on a spot on the bag and showed the smear to his superior. 'Look!'

Joaquim spotted the superior nod to his junior. Before he could react, the senior official shouted, 'You are under arrest!' and the younger official put Joaquim in a headlock from behind, knocking off Joaquim's broad-brimmed hat.

'Please, I don't want any trouble,' Joaquim said. He was taller than the Japanese official holding him and struggled to maintain his full height as the official persisted in his headlock but failed to put a knee into his back. In a half-strangled voice, Joaquim said, 'Let me go and everything will end in peace.'

'You are not going anywhere, *gaijin*, until the Governor interrogates you!'

'I'm afraid I cannot let that happen.' Joaquim dropped almost to his knees while gripping one of the official's wrists, then stood and torqued until he heard the snap of the wrist. The young official screamed with pain and fell to the ground, nursing his injured arm. The senior official immediately drew his katana, assumed a *tachi-ai* standing posture, and pointed the sword at Joaquim's face.

The priest felt strangely calm as he stared not at the weapon, but into the official's eyes. His heart pounded, and he felt a gentle breeze caress his face briefly as the leaves on nearby trees rustled then fell silent. Somewhere a bird chirped, and the man on the ground continued to moan with pain. Joaquim realized that although the official before him was clearly angry, he was also wary of getting too close to this unarmed *gaijin*. 'Kneel and raise your hands or I will kill you!' the official commanded.

'I cannot, sir. An entire village depends on me. Please, lower your weapon and let me pass ... and I will let you live.'

The swordsman bellowed a roar that seemed to start from the pit of his stomach and charged at Joaquim. He took a massive swipe that would have split Joaquim from shoulder to waist had it landed. Joaquim felt the wind of the blade on his face as he deftly sidestepped and moved inside the blow as Master Yamaguchi had taught him. He delivered a blow with his elbow to the senior official's face, feeling the nose break, while at the same time grabbing for the man's sword hand. A precisely chosen pressure point proved too painful and the man's weapon clattered to the ground.

With blood flowing freely down his face and his long dark hair flying wildly in the air, the senior official drew his short sword, or *wakizashi*, and stabbed at Joaquim's face with another yell. The Jesuit felt the shock of steel on steel in combat for the first time as he swung the katana to block the strike, throwing the *wakizashi* backwards and exposing the official's now unprotected head. With an instinct born of years of training Joaquim followed his defence with a yell of his own and a counterstrike that severed the official's head from his shoulders.

The injured man cried with rage and leaped to his feet, drawing his sword with his good hand. He charged at Father Joaquim with equal fervour. Joaquim easily blocked the weak blow and countered by stabbing his sword through the man's throat and killing him.

* * *

He could not be sure how long he had been sitting in the dust in the middle of the road, listening to the rushing of the air and the rustling of the leaves in nearby trees, but when Father Joaquim finally regained some sort of composure he found himself staring at two corpses lying in pools of their own blood. Looking down he saw he had spatters of it on his face, hands, and clothing. It occurred to him that he could not remain there and he had better move. He'd be able to make better time in the dark on his way down the other side of the mountain, away from Nagasaki and towards Arima.

He sighed and scanned the nearby terrain. He realized it would be safest to leave the main trail and head through the thick brush of the forest. He rubbed dirt on his colourful jacket to dull its brightness and disguise the bloodstains, then used it to try and clean and dry his hands.

Oh, Lord Father, please help me understand Your ways. Mateus da Costa was our only hope and now he is gone and, in your name, I have become a murderer. What penance must I do for these acts and to save my people?

Joaquim looked skyward as he prayed aloud for his friend and for himself. He set off, pushing his way through the forest undergrowth, deliberately abandoning the weapons at the guard station.

The trail, such as it was, took him uphill, until hours later he reached the mountain peak from where he could see all of Nagasaki and the neighbouring mountain peaks, where government guards monitored all travellers entering and exiting the region. He sat and took in the view, catching his breath, head in his hands, thinking, and was finally moved to prayer.

Oh Lord, forgive my wickedness. How are we going to pay the Daimyo his 500 silver coins? Should we just escape to Yezo without paying our taxes? Shigemasa will surely hunt us down. Show me the way, Lord. Show me the way.

It was early evening when Joaquim descended the mountain in moonless starlight. It was imperative he return to his village as soon as possible. But how would they resolve their worsening situation?

CHAPTER TWENTY

6 June 1626
Arima, Shimabara Peninsula, Kyushu

An orange dawn slowly cracked the horizon as Father Joaquim worked his way through the foothills and the new day became warmer. After sleeping under thick brush during the day and travelling through the thick Kyushu mountainous forests at night for several days, the priest was exhausted. He approached the village and its people at a plodding walk.

Joaquim sought to console himself. *Things will be okay. It's good to be back! This village is my home. Lord, thank you!*

He made his way to Master Yamaguchi's small, dilapidated home and glanced inside to see if his dear friend was awake. Candlelight flickered inside.

'Is that you, Father?' Yamaguchi said.

'Yes, Sensei, I hope I didn't wake you.'

Yamaguchi said, 'Nonsense. You know I am an early riser.'

'How did you know it was me? You didn't even look out of the window.'

'I dreamed you would arrive today, and here you are. You look tired. Come in and rest.'

'Thank you, Yamaguchi-san.'

The priest was a picture of horror covered in mud, dirt and blood from head to toe. Joaquim let out a breath that rattled his lips as he bowed, then stepped inside, and took off his shoes.

'Would you like some tea?' Yamaguchi asked.

Joaquim nodded before dropping to his knees, across from Master Yamaguchi.

'How was your visit to Nagasaki?'

'I have bad news.'

'Oh?'

'Mateus da Costa is dead – murdered in the street, in the middle of the night.'

'That is awful. Do you know who killed him?'

Joaquim shook his head. 'Perhaps it was the Dutch, or another competitor. Or a Japanese thief. I don't know.' The priest paused and took a deep breath. 'When the authorities arrived to investigate, they discovered me in Mateus's home.'

'And yet you are here.'

'They tried to arrest me.'

'And?'

'A fight broke out. I killed them. I suspect every government official in Nagasaki is looking for me now.'

'I had reservations about this trip, Father.'

'Yes, I know, Yamaguchi-san, but I had to see if Mateus could provide us with a loan.'

'You did your best. You cannot fault yourself for this.'

'But I killed men, Sensei. My conscience weighs on me.' The Jesuit made the sign of the cross over himself and buried his face in his hands.

'I understand, but, Father, I am sure they would have killed you if they had had the chance, *neh*? These are dangerous times.'

Father Joaquim shook his head. This was no consolation for his actions.

'You are alive because it is the will of God.'

Raising his head, the priest said, 'Thank you, Yamaguchi-san. My purpose was so clear to me before, but I must admit I do not always understand His ways.'

'Perhaps the Lord has another plan for us.' Yamaguchi took a sip of tea.

Father Joaquim sipped his tea as well.

'And how is the village, Yamaguchi-san?'

'Everyone is fine, Father. We continue to work non-stop.'

'How is that going?'

'The mood is low, and we are falling behind. It will be impossible to meet Daimyo Shigemasa's quota.'

'We knew that would be the case. That is why we must pray.'

Yamaguchi nodded. 'And in the meantime?'

'We can only try to produce as much rice as possible. The closer we are to Daimyo Shigemasa's quota, the better.'

'I agree.'

'And I will help.'

'Help?'

'Yes, I will also work in the fields.'

'That is not wise, Father.' Father Joaquim could see the concern in Yamaguchi's expression.

'I will wear a good disguise.'

'There are spies everywhere. You risk your life if you are exposed.'

'My life is already at risk, and so is the life of everyone in this village if we do not make our quota.'

'Agreed. But working in broad daylight is taking it too far.'

'We must remember the Lord is with us. We *cannot* live in fear.'

'It is too risky.'

'Please do not worry, Yamaguchi-san. God has a higher purpose for us. After we pay our taxes, we will move the village somewhere better. We will *not* be persecuted forever.'

* * *

After changing his clothes, and checking on his young catechists, Father Joaquim made his way to the rice fields and beckoned the villagers to come and hear his news.

As a few drops of rain fell from grey skies, Joaquim made the sign of the cross to the people crowding around him.

'As you all know, for several years now a storm of trials and persecutions has assailed us. Alas, it appears conditions will only get worse before they get better.' He looked out at the anxious faces in the crowd. Joaquim wished he could make the approaching dangers disappear.

'We must maintain our faith. Circumstances change, but our

God does not. The God we serve today is the same God who parted the sea for Moses and the Israelites. Have faith in Him.'

'What is the news from Nagasaki?' a farmer asked. 'I thought you had a friend there who could help us.'

'I will not lie to you,' Joaquim answered. 'Someone killed my friend. There will be no help from Nagasaki.'

The crowd murmured as bodies began to fidget.

'What happened to him?' a woman asked.

'He was murdered. I do not know by whom, or why. I only know that door has been closed to us.'

As the priest looked at their faces, he saw tears in the eyes of grown men as well as women.

'We cannot produce Lord Shigemasa's new quota, no matter how hard we work,' one of the older farmers declared. 'What will we do?'

The murmurs intensified.

'We must do our best,' Joaquim answered.

'But what about Lord Shigemasa? He has no mercy,' the farmer continued. 'Our best will not be enough. If we cannot meet his quota, he will destroy our families.'

'We must try hard,' Joaquim replied. He took a moment to make eye contact with several of the village's elders before adding, 'And pray to the Lord.'

'But what if the Lord does not hear us?' Tamiko, a young mother asked. 'I cannot let the Daimyo take my children.'

'The Lord *always* hears your prayers,' Father Joaquim said. 'Even before you ask, the Lord has answered you.'

'How do you know that?'

The priest saw the desperation in the woman's face. 'From the

Scriptures,' he answered. 'The prophet Isaiah tells us: "And it shall come to pass, that before they call, I will answer." This means that even before you pray, the Lord has heard you.'

'What should we pray for?'

'For the Lord to look after us – to protect us and ensure our survival. We must have faith. He will answer.'

'That seems very wishful. What more can we do?' a villager named Noboru asked.

Father Joaquim closed his eyes. He lifted his head skyward before replying. 'You can *see* God helping you and thank Him for it.' Looking back at Noboru, he continued. 'The greater your thankfulness, the stronger His response. The Lord *always* responds to those who believe and have faith – *always*! This is His promise.'

A teenage girl stepped forward. 'Father, I prayed for the Lord's help, but He didn't answer me.'

'What do you mean?'

'I prayed for help from Nagasaki, from your friend Mateus, but we did not receive it. Why did the Lord not answer?'

'The Lord *always* answers your prayers, Hanako-chan, but sometimes it may not be the way you like or expect.'

'But why not in Nagasaki?'

'I don't know, but the Lord has infinite wisdom. Perhaps He means for us to follow a different path.'

Father Joaquim put his hand on Hanako's shoulder and continued. 'The key is to trust the Lord and have faith that He *will* answer. Don't worry about *how* God will answer; just have faith He *will*.'

Hanako nodded her head, as did several other villagers. She smiled thinly.

Father Joaquim looked out over the crowd. 'A storm is coming, but if you have faith in God, He *will* protect us.'

CHAPTER TWENTY-ONE

17 June 1626
Magistrate's Office, Nagasaki City

Mizuno Kawachi was a sinister-looking man with rough features and small, dark eyes. As he rode into the city at the head of a retinue of mounted samurai and foot soldiers he scrutinized Nagasaki. Relative to other major cities in Japan, Nagasaki had a more commercial feel to it, owing to it being the country's largest international trading port.

He continued to make his way towards the city centre. Buildings in the city's core were several storeys high. Dozens of active merchants lined street-level stalls and shops with a variety of things for sale from around the country, as well as the world, including food, spices, art, clothing, and above all, silk from

China. Everywhere he looked there was a flurry of commercial activity: buying, selling, negotiating, and bartering by Japanese and Europeans.

Kawachi noted all of it, including the beauty of the city centre, where long vertical flags hung from tall poles along the streets. Elegant lanterns hung from wires that ran the length of the roads, alongside ubiquitous, eye-catching displays and signs.

Surrounded by his samurai entourage, Kawachi bumped his way through the bustling streets, gazing at its odd European influences and items for sale as he passed its residents, who gazed at him in reverence. He could see many had been expecting his arrival and this pleased him. As residents stared at him atop his tall horse, he lifted his chin and pushed out his chest. This was all his now.

Not far away, Governor Hasegawa Gonroku was reading a document in his room at the Nagasaki magistrate's office. The afternoon was warm, even for mid-June.

In two weeks, Portuguese ships would arrive in Nagasaki from Macao laden with silk, for the busy trading season. Outside the Governor's door, two officials reviewed documents that required official approval, affixing the magistrate's official stamp to various papers.

They were interrupted by a band of samurai and officials who barged through the front door. The officials gasped at the rudeness of the unexpected arrival and straightaway put down their paperwork and bowed to the high-ranking officials. '*Bugyo*, Gonroku-san,' one called out, drawing the Governor's attention.

'What?' Governor Gonroku looked up from his work through an open door.

'We have an official visit. Please, come right away.'

The Governor rushed into the front room. He scanned the delegation and recognized the new Nagasaki governor straightaway.

'Mizuno Kawachi-san.' Gonroku bowed. 'Welcome.'

Kawachi and the members of his entourage bowed perfunctorily in return.

Gonroku said, 'I was not expecting you for another week or two.'

'I wanted to make an impact,' Kawachi responded. He squinted with distaste as he looked around the office. 'Under the Shogun's orders, I am here to relieve you of your duties – right now. Go home.'

Speechless, Governor Gonroku's mouth fell open before he continued. 'This is very unexpected. I have work to complete, murders to investigate, documents to process.' The Governor's frustration and growing humiliation were evident in his tone and reddened face.

'That will not be necessary. You may leave now.' Kawachi spoke dismissively, and narrowed his eyes in contempt as he stared at his predecessor.

'Do you dishonour me?' Gonroku returned his replacement's contemptuous glare.

'You have dishonoured yourself.' Kawachi scanned the office, planning how best to use it.

'Of what do you speak? Elaborate!'

'Your main task was to exterminate Christianity in the District of Nagasaki, but you closed your eyes to this disease infecting our land. Your dishonour is your own.'

'That is nonsense. I have Christian prisoners, including priests, locked up now!'

'Why are they not dead?'

Kawachi locked eyes with Gonroku. The latter shifted his gaze to the table. 'It is not the right time.'

'Nonsense! You delay crucifying them because you have a soft heart.'

'I do not.'

'For years, you have abstained from your duties!'

'What?' Gonroku's face turned red as his body quivered.

'You have pronounced a lack of evidence to convict; you have forewarned Christians to run; you have even let Christians go free! You have *failed* the Shogun!'

'I have not!'

'It matters not. You wished to be relieved of your duties, and now you have been.' Kawachi waved his hand towards the door. 'Go.'

'But I have work to conclude, trading approvals to complete.'

'Another area of concern to the Shogun. Even this you cannot do well.'

'What do you mean?'

'The Dutch complain that you favour the Portuguese. Even local Japanese complain that you favour them.'

'That is trade. Someone always complains about their share.'

'Are you taking bribes?'

Kawachi watched the blood drain from Gonroku's face.

'That is preposterous! What accusations are you making?' Gonroku's agitation became more pronounced.

'If the shame is too great, Gonroku, you may commit *seppuku*.'

'I will not commit *seppuku*. I have taken no bribes!'

'It is clear you are not fit for your post. Why would we permit you to continue your work? Now go. Leave my presence.'

Governor Gonroku stormed into the next room and snatched his bag as Kawachi and his retinue looked on, their satisfaction apparent. Disgraced and humiliated, the former governor exited the front door with his head down.

The District of Nagasaki had a new ruler.

CHAPTER TWENTY-TWO

18 June 1626
Arima

Yori was supposed to be on guard duty, but the morning sun had quickly warmed the fields, and the shade of leafy branches, the buzzing of insects, and chirping of birds had lulled the boy into dozing off against a thick tree trunk. By the time the seven-year-old heard and then spotted Daimyo Shigemasa and his detachment of samurai, they were almost on top of him.

One of the Daimyo's samurai charged his horse to within inches of Yori.

'Aaaaagghh!' Yori screamed.

'Shut up, boy!' Shigemasa snarled as he rode up. He stared him into silence, gazing at him with cruel, narrowed eyes.

'Master Yamaguchi, working the end of the field closest to the mountain, heard the scream and, looking up, spotted the approaching samurai. He sprinted as fast as his old legs could carry him and ran towards Father Joaquim, who was working at the other end of the field.

'You must hide! Now! Shigemasa is coming!'

'Alert the village. Get as many of the women and children inside as possible,' Joaquim said.

'You must also hide, Father.'

'I will hide behind my wall, as usual, but I will need someone to seal it behind me.'

'I will send someone. Now, move!'

The peasants had only minutes to spare, and all the arrangements had to be perfect or the consequences would be dire. But with so little time, coordination was poor. Some women tried to place too many children into confined spaces, under floorboards, or in secret rooms behind hidden walls, but there was not enough space and they would not all fit. Eyes wide with jerking arm movements, the women cried as they tried to shove their children inside. Elsewhere villagers sought to hide as many of their Christian relics as possible, replacing them with Buddhist items of worship. To maintain their ruse, it was imperative to keep their Buddhist story consistent.

Shigemasa and his men would be in the village within minutes, but still preparations were not complete.

Yamaguchi hiked to the edge of the village to greet the Daimyo. Behind him several peasant farmers followed to pay homage to the man who could dictate their fate. Shigemasa stopped his procession at the entrance to the village as Yamaguchi approached.

'Daimyo Shigemasa, it is a pleasure. We were not expecting

you.' He bowed a welcome. Behind him, the villagers also bowed low.

'I know you were not expecting me. We are early.'

'Yes, Lord,' Yamaguchi replied. 'How can we serve you, Lord?'

'I am here to collect the taxes you owe me.'

'We are working very hard on your new quota, Lord. I am sure you will be proud of us.'

'Then where is it?' Shigemasa said.

'It is not yet time, Lord. You gave us a month.' Yamaguchi wrinkled his brow and rubbed his face.

'I changed my mind. Show me what you have.'

'But this is very unusual, Lord. I must insist you permit us the full month given to us.'

'Nonsense! Show me what you have ... *now!*'

'Fetch Daimyo Shigemasa's production,' Master Yamaguchi said as he turned to face his fellow villagers. Peasants ran off to various storage areas to retrieve sacks of rice.

As he waited, Shigemasa scanned the village and counted the peasants. 'Where are the rest of your villagers?'

'What do you mean, Lord?' Yamaguchi said.

'Where are the rest of the women and children? I recall seeing more last time.'

Men returned, placing their bags of rice before the warlord and bowing, diverting the Daimyo's attention from his question about missing villagers.

'Is that it?' Shigemasa snarled.

'We have more bags in the fields,' Yamaguchi answered.

'Bring them.'

'They are coming, Lord.'

Moments later, a few more men arrived from the fields, gasping for air as they hauled several more half-filled sacks behind them.

'Is that it?'

'Yes, Lord. I think this is a record production for us, given the time we have had to work.' Yamaguchi prayed that Shigemasa's concern over the rice production would cause him to forget his question about the missing villagers.

'Silence!' Shigemasa examined the bags before him.

'I see only a few dozen sacks here. This production is embarrassing for this village.'

'It is a good production,' a twitchy peasant shouted from the back of the crowd.

'Do you disrespect me?'

'No, Lord,' Yamaguchi interjected. 'We would never disrespect you. We serve you to the best of our abilities.'

'This production is insulting! How dare you present this? You are all lazy mutts!'

'But, Lord—' Yamaguchi started to protest.

'Silence, or my samurai will silence you for me.' Shigemasa looked around. 'I know why your production is so low.' He turned in his saddle to observe the village in the distance. 'Some of your people are hiding from me when they should be out here working. Now, where are the rest of the villagers?'

'We always honour your presence with as many as we can,' Yamaguchi answered.

'Do not patronize me, old man.'

Shigemasa addressed his samurai: 'Find the rest of the women and children!'

Dozens of samurai dismounted from their horses and advanced

on the villagers' homes. They kicked down doors and punched holes through walls. Once inside, the samurai extended even less respect as they ransacked entire homes, breaking possessions, scattering belongings, even lifting floorboards in search of concealed villagers.

'Daimyo Shigemasa, I do not think this is necessary,' Yamaguchi protested.

'Shut up, old man. I will deal with you in a moment.'

Amid the crashing and destruction, Yamaguchi heard women and children screaming. Soon, several samurai appeared, dragging the women by their hair, with their terrified children following and sobbing.

'You deceived me, old man,' Shigemasa roared as he dismounted. 'Keep looking,' he ordered. 'I am sure there are more!'

Several young samurai smashed through more homes, ripping doors off their hinges and demolishing the houses' meagre contents. In one home they ripped up the shack's flooring and discovered the foreign catechists Tonia and Miguel.

'Lord Shigemasa, we found *gaijin*!' Several samurai shoved Tonia and Miguel ahead of them.

To discover a Japanese Christian was a triumph, but to uncover two foreign Christians was an astonishing find for the Daimyo. Although the Shogun would be angry over their continued presence, he would be pleased at their capture.

As villagers watched in horror, samurai beat the catechists with a flurry of savage kicks and punches.

'Let me see these Christian dogs!' Shigemasa yelled. He jumped down from his horse and pushed his way through the samurai.

'This is unbelievable,' Shigemasa declared. He approached the two beaten catechists lying on the ground. Yamaguchi looked on with a pained stare.

Turning to his second-in-command, Shigemasa said, 'Tear down this village. I want every inch of it searched. No one escapes!'

The villagers wailed. The soldiers set about systematically demolishing the buildings and yanking outside anyone in hiding. The villagers cried as the samurai destroyed their few possessions. The soldiers tore buildings from their foundations, broke narrow wooden beams, and ripped apart roof thatching.

It did not take long for a group of samurai to descend on the dishevelled hut where Father Joaquim's tiny room lay hidden. The samurai tore at the outer walls of the structure with their knives and hands. Inside, they found the priest, defenceless and hiding under the flooring beneath his bed, doing his best to avoid detection. They beat and kicked him until he lay still, curled in a ball on the ground. Then they yanked him to his feet.

A samurai pushed his way through the crowd, dragging the priest until they reached the Daimyo. 'Lord Shigemasa, I have discovered another *gaijin*. This one looks like a priest!'

'Bring the entire village to me,' Shigemasa roared.

Minutes later, with everyone assembled, the Daimyo announced, 'This village is no more. You have all deceived me.'

Shigemasa pivoted and walked over to Master Yamaguchi, who stood before him. 'And you, old man, you have deceived me for the last time. Your disrespect is the greatest of all!'

Shigemasa drew his katana and swung it through Yamaguchi's neck, severing it. A trail of gore spilled from the wound, baptizing the wretched soil. Red. Relentless. Until the pulsing of his heart stopped. The old man's head rolled into the field.

Joaquim was not able to see much through the blood and bruising on his face and his swelling black eyes, but he heard the wailing and sobbing of the villagers. Unable to control himself, Joaquim struggled to his feet. 'What have you done?!'

Several samurai pounded him to the ground. As he lay in the dirt, a half-dozen more samurai stood over him and recommenced punching and kicking him while shouting obscenities. Despite the thrashing, the priest managed to cry out, 'He was a peaceful man.'

'Silence!' The Daimyo turned his head, making eye contact with several villagers who immediately looked away in shame. 'You are all under arrest for breaking the Shogun's anti-Christian laws.' He turned again to his second-in-command. 'Burn the village.'

Dark smoke and flames soon filled the sky as the villagers were rounded up. They wailed and cried and were beaten for their misery, tied to long bamboo poles, and dragged up the mountainside. Amid the flames of the burning village behind them, the villagers looked back to see Master Yamaguchi's decapitated body burn with their village.

CHAPTER TWENTY-THREE

18 June 1626
Shogun's Castle

When Masayoshi took part in his first torture as a member of a class, he vomited. His superiors immediately forced him to clean it up. The first lesson of his new profession had been, control your stomach. It took many more months for his soul to became calloused enough to endure the smells, the pleading, the screams, and the crying. After two years as one of the Shogun's torturers, he'd learned to separate himself from his work. When he was here he was detached, someone else.

With him in the torture chamber at the moment were members of the Shogun's Bakufu cabinet and several Buddhist warrior monks. The cabinet members and monks, who witnessed the almost daily torture sessions, were also becoming inured to the pain inflicted on prisoners – most of them Christians.

Today, torturers had shackled a young Japanese man by his wrists and ankles to metal plates fixed to the wall. After months of imprisonment he was filthy and starving, but, given the circumstances, still relatively healthy. And, as yet, the torture had not bent his spirit. The Shogun was determined to change that.

Masayoshi stood to one side, awaiting orders as the young Shogun approached the man, almost the same age as himself. 'You are Akihiko, *neh*?' the Shogun said.

'Yes,' the shackled young man answered in a soft voice.

'Do you know who I am?'

'*Hai*.'

'They say you are strong.' The Shogun eyed the young man. 'I'm told you have survived six months in my jail. That is impressive.'

Akihiko did not reply.

'They also tell me you give your food to save other prisoners.'

Akihiko continued to remain silent. Masayoshi watched him, knowing they would soon call upon him to burn or cut parts of this young man's body – it was his job. But today, for some reason, detaching himself was more difficult.

The prison was narrow and dark, and stank of sweat, human evacuations, mould, gore, and terror. There was a small opening through which guards passed tiny amounts of food to the gaunt, hungry inmates. The prison's ceiling was so low most prisoners could not stand upright. Outside, prison guards yelled and screamed at all hours to deprive the prisoners of sleep. Inside, the jail master crammed 150 prisoners into a space built to hold half that number. Each prisoner had a space less than the width of his shoulders. Quarrels and fights were common.

The heat in the summer was blistering, and if a prisoner wanted to wear clothing, the others would loudly object. Clothing took up space and made their neighbours hot. There was no water to wash with, nor were they allowed to cut their hair, shave their beards, or trim their nails. Food was sparse, and for some, nonexistent. Masayoshi's closest comrades often allowed the prisoners to starve to death, leaving their corpses to lie where they died, emitting hideous smells for days.

Over time, Masayoshi had noticed that Akihiko was not only one of the strongest inmates in the prison, he was also the most generous. On several occasions, he had watched Akihiko give away his food to others and pray with men on their deathbed. It left Masayoshi confused.

Most prisoners in the Edo jail were murderers, rapists, thieves, and other characters who had offended the Shogun. Like Christians and ronin they all somehow posed a threat to his dominance. The truth, Masayoshi admitted to himself, was that Akihiko was probably the least deserving of the torture he was about to endure – much of it at Masayoshi's hands.

The Shogun stood close to Akihiko, staring at him with cold, narrowed eyes. 'It seems my jail is not weakening you, so let us see how you respond to mutilation.'

The Shogun looked towards the Buddhist monks and torturers. 'What do you think?'

'I think he chose the wrong religion,' one of the monks answered with a sneer.

'I think you're right,' said the Shogun. 'But we will show him the path to enlightenment, *neh*?'

'I do not fear death,' Akihiko said. He stared at the Shogun, raising his chin.

'Your courage is admirable,' the Shogun commented. 'It's too bad you don't serve *me*. I am always in need of courageous retainers.'

'I serve only my Lord Jesus Christ.'

'And that is the problem, isn't it?' the Shogun said. 'The peasants of this country exist to serve *me*, not some dead man named Jesus.'

'He is the true Lord,' Akihiko whispered.

The Shogun's eyes narrowed. '*I* am your true Lord. *I* am the only one people should worship. Your Christianity imperils the fabric of our entire society. And I *will* stamp it out.'

'Man was born free to make choices. I choose to follow my Lord Jesus Christ, Son of God.'

'Let's see if we can make you choose otherwise,' the Shogun said. He walked over to a large table displaying instruments of torture. Taking a moment to study them, he selected a large pair of sharp metal scissors and handed them to Yasu, the torturer standing next to Masayoshi.

Yasu grabbed the scissors and bowed to the Shogun.

Together, the Shogun and the two torturers approached Akihiko.

The Shogun stared at Akihiko. 'You are a beautiful young man. Let's see if we can change that.' He gestured to Akihiko's face. 'Start by removing his ears.' The Shogun took several steps back.

Masayoshi grabbed Akihiko's head from behind so Yasu could perform his grisly task. Despite their sharpness, the torturer had to chop several times as blood gushed and Akihiko screamed in pain. Masayoshi's stomach began to turn – something he hadn't experienced in years.

At last, Yasu's lips curled into a smile. He held up a severed ear up for all to see.

'Throw it on the floor in front of him,' the Shogun commanded.

The bloody ear landed with a slap.

Akihiko sagged with exhaustion and pain, looking ashen.

'*This* is what your Lord Jesus brings you.' the Shogun said. 'I am the mightiest Lord in Japan, *neh*?'

Akihiko shook his head from side to side.

The Shogun bellowed. 'Cut off the other ear!'

Masayoshi felt a moment's remorse, but he could not defy the Shogun. Again, he grabbed Akihiko's head and held it still as Yasu took the scissors to the other ear.

Akihiko screamed in pain as blood again poured from his head.

Yasu dropped the second ear next to the first in front of Akihiko.

Akihiko's eyes fluttered as he continued to roll his head from side to side.

'You do not seem so strong any more,' the Shogun stated. 'Are you ready yet to pronounce *me* your true Lord?'

Akihiko tried to shake his head, but instead collapsed. Only the chains binding him to the wall held him up. Blood and tears of pain coursed down his face and dripped onto the floor.

'Imbecile!' the Shogun yelled in frustration. 'How dare he deny me!'

The Shogun scurried over to the table. 'What shall we choose next?'

One of the Buddhist monks approached the table and chose a bamboo saw. 'I think we should saw off his feet.'

'Do it. Hold his feet,' the Shogun ordered the torturers. 'Take him down and saw them off.'

Akihiko was freed from his chains, and held down on the ground. The monks held him down and readied his body for the removal of his feet. Akihiko came to and resisted, straining to free himself. For a moment his struggling worked, then Yasu grabbed a metal pipe and pounded Akihiko's head and body until he was unsciousness again.

The Shogun gave Yasu an approving look and nodded.

With a determination borne of fear for his own life and limbs, Masayoshi took the saw and sliced off Akihiko's left foot, just below the ankle, while Yasu sawed off the right foot. The young Christian's blood splattered over everyone standing nearby, but after a few minutes of gruelling work, Akihiko's feet were removed.

'Place his ears and feet in that basket,' the Shogun instructed, 'and leave them in front of him where he can see them. Hang him back up. And bring in the physician. I do not want this man to die yet.'

'But why?' a Buddhist monk asked.

'These Christians die too fast,' the Shogun answered. 'I want to heal him so we can torture him again.'

'As you wish, Lord Shogun,' the monk replied. Several of his comrades ran off to find a physician.

The Shogun stared at the unconscious Christian hanging from the wall. 'As Nami Amida Buddha himself is my witness, this Christian man will profess me, the Shogun of Japan, his Lord before his last day.'

CHAPTER TWENTY-FOUR

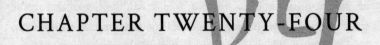

18 June 1626
Nagasaki City, District of Nagasaki, Kyushu

As the early evening air cooled, Governor Mizuno Kawachi and a small entourage of senior officials walked up a long road towards the home of Deputy-Lieutenant Governor Heizo Suetsugu Masanao.

Elegant trees and shrubs lined the immaculate road leading to the Deputy-Lieutenant's home, where workers had placed large boulders and rocks to enhance the appeal of the pathway. Perched on a small slope on the mountainside, the Deputy-Lieutenant's home had a spectacular view of the city below, affording a serene panorama of the sea and the surrounding leafy green mountains.

Governor Kawachi and his entourage made their way towards the majestic gates, where dozens of staff and samurai greeted them.

Servants escorted the new Governor and his retainers through an immaculate garden with a stream, waterfalls, and magnificent bonsai trees to the front entrance of Daikan Suetsugu's home, which boasted an immense curved thatched roof, at least half the size of the overall structure. Residents of Nagasaki could see the impressive roof from a great distance. Shaped in a temple style, the curved eaves, exquisite in their simplicity, extended beyond the walls, covering the verandas.

It was commonly known that Suetsugu was deeply involved in international trade. He often seized illegitimate vessels, taking for his own any slaves on board, as evidenced by some of his house staff.

Kawachi's group bowed in cordial fashion and entered the Deputy-Lieutenant's house, where all removed their street sandals. Suetsugu appeared hurriedly from behind a crowd of servants and approached the new arrivals.

'Welcome to Nagasaki, Governor.' Suetsugu stuck out his chest. 'I thought it more hospitable to host you at my home, rather than meeting at the magistrate's office.'

'Thank you.'

Within the Bakufu hierarchy, while Kawachi was the more senior figure than Suetsugu, the *Daikan* or Deputy-Lieutenant was by far the richer of the two men. Capitalizing on his family connections, Suetsugu had built one of the most powerful trading franchises in Nagasaki.

Nevertheless, despite the deputy's affluence and power, Suetsugu was all too aware that the Shogun could confiscate his wealth at a moment's notice if he so chose. The fact caused him endless sleepless nights.

Suetsugu was always scheming ways to manipulate the Bakufu hierarchy in his favour.

At the top was the Shogun, the country's chief warlord and military leader. Supporting him was the Roju cabinet, then the administrative officials and feudal daimyo.

Most daimyo were wealthy warlords who had inherited their lands, generating additional wealth by taxing the peasant class over whom they ruled, and resorting to bribery and corruption in their quest for more money, land, and power.

Governors and deputy-lieutenant governors helped administer and enforce the laws of the Bakufu regime and were appointed by the Shogun. These officials also served as his spies in the five major shogunate cities: Osaka, Kyoto, Edo, Sakai, and Nagasaki.

For each town, the Shogun appointed a governor to keep watch, rule, and administer. And to assist the governor, the Shogun also appointed a *daikan*.

As the newly appointed governor, Kawachi studied Deputy Suetsugu's magnificent home, trying to gain the measure of the man. It was easy to see the extent of Suetsugu's incredible wealth. His walls displayed exceptional Chinese art and multiple Buddhist statues, exotic art, and exceptional calligraphy.

Rumours had it that Suetsugu had multiple warehouses throughout Nagasaki to store his more significant assets. His wealth comprised dozens of boxes of gold and silver, vast piles of precious lumber, boxes of coral and exotic foreign tea sets, hundreds of pictures by Chinese artists, thousands of boxes of Chinese articles, dozens of folding screens, and hundreds of swords and other high-quality weapons.

'Please, make yourself comfortable. May we offer you tea?' The Deputy lowered himself into a *seiza* or kneeling position.

The governor nodded and gave a short grunt as he also lowered himself on the opposite side of the table.

'And how do you find your time in Nagasaki thus far, Governor?'

'I do not bother with pleasantries. I am here to execute the Shogun's orders.'

'Ah. You mean the Christians?'

'Yes.'

'Governor Gonroku disappointed the Shogun,' the deputy said.

'I know. It was me who told him about Gonroku's failings.'

'*You* told him?'

'Yes, but I was not the only one. The Shogun has many spies in Nagasaki.'

'It appears little goes unnoticed here.'

'The Shogun knows everything.' The Deputy signalled his servants to pour tea, starting with the Governor. 'So, Governor, how will you conduct your administration in a different way from your unfortunate predecessor?'

'Tomorrow, I will roast several Christians to death.'

'Ah.'

'I want my presence felt immediately. I want any remaining Christians to know that their slaughter is coming.'

'I'm impressed.' The Deputy nodded his head and gave a small smile. 'I'm sure this will please the Shogun.'

'The Shogun has honoured me with this appointment and I will not disappoint him. I want him to know that under *my* name, we will completely exterminate Christians from Nagasaki and surrounding areas.'

'And how will you accomplish this, Governor?'

'Death and torture.'

'That's it?'

'Far from it.'

'Alas, not all Christians fear death. Some even relish it.'

'I will use every means available, Deputy-Lieutenant. I will use death and torture first to show that, unlike my predecessor, I am not averse to bloodshed. Killing is easy but not the complete solution.'

'What do you mean?'

'It's easy to create large piles of bodies to put on display as warnings. I want *apostates*!'

'You prefer them to renounce their faith rather than suffer death?'

'Yes. I want to force these Christians to publicly abandon their useless faith.'

'I'm intrigued. And how will you do this?'

'I will make beggars of them. I shall conduct raids and routine searches of every home in Nagasaki.'

'For what purpose?'

'To discover the occupants' true identity.'

'That will take a great deal of men,' the deputy said.

'I will offer incentives. If one family betrays another, they will inherit the other family's home and all their belongings.'

'A wise plan,' the Deputy nodded. 'You will give them a strong incentive to inform on their neighbours.'

'Greed and fear are powerful tools, used correctly.'

'Indeed. And if a family is adept at hiding their faith?'

'I will put pressure on their communities to give them up and place the onus on them. If we discover a Christian hiding in a community, we will kill their neighbours as punishment.'

The Governor sipped his tea with a blank stare and leaned back before continuing. 'I will also take their homes and deprive them of work, food, and sustenance. I will take everything they have to force them to inform on their neighbours.'

'Very thorough, Governor. And if all these measures are insufficient?'

'Death, Deputy. If they do not recant, they will face torture and death. Can I count on your help?'

'Of course, Governor. I have no reservations about persecuting Christians.'

'Are you sure?'

'Why would you question my resolve?' The Deputy sat upright, his body rigid.

'Because you used to be a Christian.'

'I apostatized a long time ago.' The Deputy raised his hands. 'My loyalties lie with the Shogun and the Bakufu now.'

'The Shogun hopes that is the case, Deputy.'

Suetsugu placed his tea on the table. 'Governor Kawachi, look around you. Do you think I would give up all this wealth because of a repulsive foreign religion?' Suetsugu stared at the governor. 'I chose money over God a long time ago.'

Kawachi studied him for a few moments. Then he seemed to come to a conclusion, nodded curtly and said, 'Good.'

'Rest assured, Governor. My apostasy is irrevocable and resolute, and I will prove it to you.'

'Oh?'

'With your own eyes you will witness me executing Christians.'

CHAPTER TWENTY-FIVE

19 June 1626
Fields of Arima, Shimabara Peninsula

Even though she was only six years old, Haruko had quickly learned not to cry out as she slid along through the mud like a small anchor. Several backhands to the sides of her face had made a convincing impression, but her tired legs could not keep up, and her whimpering was involuntary as the other nineteen villagers, tied by their wrists to a bamboo pole, dragged her through the pouring rain, yanked from the front by a burly, short-tempered samurai.

The Daimyo's samurai moved the villagers as fast as possible in the soggy conditions. There were three poles and at the front of each were the tallest, mostly men, followed by the women, with the shortest and children at the rear. At the back, the youngest children, like Haruko, were dragged like debris if they couldn't keep up.

Haruko's mother near the front could only pray, as she twisted her head to steal glimpses of her quietly weeping child. With no food, little sleep, and the falling rain as their only water source, samurai had tugged, pushed, and whipped the villagers non-stop since their village had burned twenty-four hours earlier. Along with their physical exhaustion, despair at the death of Master Yamaguchi had overtaken many of the villagers, evidenced by their sagging posture, resignation to their fate, and red eyes. He had been more than the village leader; he'd been an intimate friend and confidant to young and old, imparting wisdom to any willing to hear it.

When a samurai abandoned his section of a pole to urinate at the side of the path, some of the prisoners saw an opportunity to whisper.

'Where are they taking us?' Miguel was tied to a pole behind Father Joaquim.

'I don't know, Miguel,' Joaquim said. 'Maybe to the court in Nagasaki.'

'What will they do to us?'

'I don't know.' Joaquim's body felt like one massive bruise. He thought perhaps he had at least one cracked rib as his side hurt constantly and his breathing was painful. His swollen, blackened eyes made it hard to see where he was going, while his split lips made it painful trying to drink the rainwater pounding on him. His ears were still ringing from the many blows to the head he'd received, and it was hard to hear anything over the roar of the splattering rain and the sounds of feet pulling against the sucking mud.

'They will torture and kill us, won't they?'

'Try to rid your mind of such thoughts, Miguel. They will not help you.'

'But what's the point? There is nothing we can do now.'

'Miguel, this is a test of our faith. Through this, God is proving to us that our faith is real, that we are truly His children. Your faith will give you strength.'

Miguel stumbled and fell, but quickly righted himself lest a samurai beat him for slowing the procession.

'What shall we do, Father?' a farmer asked.

'We do the only thing we can, my son. Pray. We are in His hands now.'

Father Joaquim heard a sharp snap and felt a burning pain across his back.

'I told you to shut up,' a samurai snarled, leather whip in hand.

The samurai put his whip around the farmer's neck and began strangling him. His face turned purple as the leather crushed his throat. Turning blue, he slumped, clamouring for air.

'Let this be a warning, priest. Open *your* mouth, *he* will suffer.' Seconds before it was too late, the samurai released his grip on the farmer's throat, allowing him to breathe. Jiro made a loud gasping sound as he sucked air into his lungs.

As the group stumbled on, many of the children, including Haruko, continued to slip and fall in the mud, causing delays and frequent stops.

'Damn this weather and these stupid children,' a frustrated samurai cursed. He approached Haruko, who had just fallen again. 'Get up, stupid girl.' The samurai hit her hard on the side of the head with his fist. She crumpled to the ground, face down in the mud, where she struggled to stay conscious and breathe. The samurai grabbed her by her hair, and hauled her to her feet.

With rasping breaths, Haruko held one hand to her swollen head and cried as her mother looked on, helpless.

'If you fall one more time,' the samurai growled, 'I *will* beat you to death!'

Father Joaquim could no longer contain himself. 'What kind of samurai are you to strike a child like that?' he shouted. 'Hit *me*, not her. Let's see if you're brave enough to hit a man!'

With a guttural roar, the samurai charged at Joaquim, knocking him to the ground, and forcing the entire pole of victims to fall over into the mud. The samurai then kicked Joaquim repeatedly. Still fuming, he drew his sword and delivered a series of powerful blows with the butt end of his weapon.

'Enough!' Shigemasa shouted. He walked over to get a better look at Joaquim, who was on his knees, held up by his bound hands on the pole, bleeding afresh and coughing. 'We can beat these mongrels only so many times.'

'But this dog barked at me, Lord,' the furious samurai protested. 'We should kill him for dishonouring me.'

'I do not want to deliver dead Christians to the new governor. Do you? His death awaits him in Nagasaki.'

The samurai took a step back, clearly still frustrated.

Joaquim picked himself up off the muddy ground, and the others also rose.

'Everyone, listen,' Shigemasa ordered. 'This journey is taking far too long.'

Pinching their lips together, the warlord's samurai grumbled in agreement.

'This cursed weather will force our journey to take three days instead of the usual two, but I see no reason it should take any longer.'

'*Hai*!' the samurai echoed in agreement.

'From this moment forward, all samurai and retainers will keep their thrashings to a minimum to hasten our travel.'

Responding to the grumblings from the ranks, Shigemasa added, 'Have no concern, men. I can assure you all these Christian dogs will meet their end soon enough.'

* * *

In Nagasaki, Governor Kawachi, Deputy-Lieutenant Suetsugu and a large number of officials and samurai stood on the edge of the village in the rain, watching workmen erect stakes for a mass execution.

'How many stakes do you wish to raise, Governor?' the deputy-lieutenant asked.

'At least fifty.'

'You want to kill that many?' the Deputy-Lieutenant asked, wide-eyed.

'We should erect more than we need. I want to remind everyone in Nagasaki that the remaining empty stakes are waiting for them.'

'A wise plan, Governor.'

'Christians should always fear for their lives. These extra stakes will remind them to live in fear.'

'How many shall we execute tomorrow?'

'I'm not sure yet.'

'How about thirteen?' Suetsugu suggested.

'Why thirteen?'

'Because thirteen is an unlucky number for Christians.'

'Why unlucky?'

'Because their Lord, Jesus Christ, was betrayed by his thirteenth disciple, Judas,' Suetsugu answered.

'Your knowledge of Christianity is useful, Deputy-Lieutenant.'

'"Know your enemy, and you shall win a hundred battles without loss."'

'So, are you my Judas or my Sun Tzu?' the governor asked with a grin.

'Oh no,' the deputy answered with the hint of a chuckle, 'I am *far* richer than Judas.'

With upturned faces, both laughed at the joke.

'Fine, thirteen crucifixions,' the governor declared. 'But make sure we have more stakes available.'

'We will raise at least fifty.'

'Good. Tomorrow will be a momentous day. Under *my* watch, let all of Nagasaki see Christianity die.'

CHAPTER TWENTY-SIX

21 June 1626
District of Nagasaki, Kyushu

The rain subsided as Daimyo Shigemasa led his captives to the first official guard station at the edge of Nagasaki. Given his prominence as a powerful warlord, almost everyone recognized him around the south of Kyushu. Exhausted, famished, and dehydrated, the villagers looked around at the expansive mountains that surrounded their entry into the city and deep blue sea port beyond, seeing a hopeless natural cage.

Two senior guards scurried forward and extended a warm greeting to the Daimyo. Behind the officials a large number of samurai watched the arriving party of prisoners, fascinated especially by Father Joaquim and the foreign catechists tied to bamboo poles. The capture of a foreign priest and his catechists was a rare occurrence these days.

'Daimyo Shigemasa, it's an honour,' the ranking guard stated. 'How may we assist?'

'I have uncovered an entire village of Christians. They have sheltered this foreign priest and his aides.'

'An impressive capture, Lord,' said the guard with admiration.

'I am taking them to the Nagasaki Court of Justice for sentencing by the governor.'

'Please proceed, Lord Shigemasa.' The senior guard motioned them forward. 'Several officials will escort you.'

Shigemasa's procession made its way down the mountain towards the city. Soon, the villagers would arrive at the Court of Justice, where they would face judgement.

'What will happen to us, Father?' Catechist Miguel asked, clearly terrified.

'Judgement and sentencing.'

'So the end is near?'

'These men have no power over us, Miguel. We are in *God's* hands now, remember that.'

* * *

Magistrate's Office, Nagasaki

'I never said the Shogun does not want you to make money,' Governor Kawachi told Deputy Suetsugu. 'I only said he does not wish for your activities to disadvantage the regime.'

'What does that mean?' the Daikan said, sounding frustrated.

'It means your decisions need to be better aligned with the Bakufu.'

'Give me an example.'

'The Portuguese.'

'What about them?'

'You favour them in trade and give them special privileges.'

'My family has long-standing ties to government officials in Macao.'

'So?' The Governor glared, unblinking.

'The Portuguese are long established as intermediaries between Japan and Macao.' Suetsugu felt his temper rising.

'And what about the Dutch?'

'They are Christians too. I don't trust them.'

'Why?'

'Well, to begin with, they ransack our ships at sea. And they're violent troublemakers.'

'Maybe they cause trouble because they cannot get a legitimate foothold in Macao or Nagasaki. The Shogun may not want to trade *only* through the Portuguese. He may wish to have more balance.'

'That does not make sense.' Suetsugu shook his head. 'It was the Shogun who expelled the Spanish three years ago.'

'That was different,' the governor replied. 'The Shogun had good reason to suspect Spain may try to invade Japan.'

'But who planted that idea in the Shogun's mind?'

Sounding irritated, Kawachi said, 'What do you mean?'

'It was the Dutch. I tell you, they're troublemakers. You'll be swapping one group of troublesome Christians for another.' Suetsugu took a deep breath, trying to master his frustration. 'The Dutch and the English planted that thought in his mind to suit their own interests!'

'It doesn't matter. He is Shogun, and he decides policy.'

'So what would the Shogun have me do?'

'Provide the Dutch with more opportunity in Nagasaki.'

Feeling his temper boil once more, Suetsugu shook his head. 'It doesn't make sense. I can control the Portuguese, predict what they are going to do far more effectively than I can the Dutch.'

'The Shogun is interested to learn the *real* reason the Portuguese monopolize trade in Nagasaki.'

'The Shogun, or you Governor?'

'It's the same thing.'

'I already told you. The Portuguese have control of Macao, our largest trading partner.'

'The Shogun has concerns you are taking bribes from the Portuguese to give them a monopoly on trade in Nagasaki.'

'Bribes?' Suetsugu turned away, having a hard time looking at Kawachi.

'Are you taking bribes and not sharing the proceeds?'

'Absolutely not!' Suetsugu's nostrils flared. 'I am dishonoured by the insinuation!'

'The Shogun has a right to ask questions. His regime controls trade in Japan, *not* the merchants.'

'I do not dispute the Shogun's control.'

'Perhaps there is another reason you favour the Portuguese.'

'Of what do you speak?!'

'You have too many outstanding loans with them,' answered Kawachi. 'The only way the Portuguese can pay you back is if you continue to allow them a monopoly in Nagasaki.'

Suetsugu's face reddened as he clenched his fists. 'That is absurd!' The Deputy-Lieutenant's agitation was becoming more pronounced as his gaze bounced around the room.

'It is not absurd. You are making too much money from these loans, Deputy. You extended loans to the Portuguese at interest rates much higher than the Shogun considers proper.'

'Give me an example.'

Shoulders loose, Kawachi paused for a moment before answering, as if trying to get a rise out of Suetsugu. 'Some of your interest rates are almost thirty per cent.'

'It's my money; I can lend it out at whatever rate I wish.'

'The Shogun worries you are profiting too much from your position.'

'I do not see why I should lower my interest rates!'

'It is not only your rates,' the Governor replied as he leaned back. 'The Shogun thinks you may be in too deep now with your loans, so your personal interests are not aligned with the regime.'

Suetsugu gripped his tea cup so hard it broke.

'That is preposterous!' The Deputy-Lieutenant shouted in frustration as he grabbed a cloth and wiped some of the spilled tea. 'I bring our country the best silk from China!'

The Governor turned at the sound of runners approaching.

'Governor, we have an urgent message from a guard on the edge of the city,' an official blurted out. 'Daimyo Matsukura Shigemasa has captured an entire Christian village in Arima. He is bringing them to the Court of Justice now.'

'He has also captured a Portuguese Christian Father and his foreign aides,' a second messenger announced.

'Take them to the court!' Kawachi commanded.

'Yes, Governor.'

'The Deputy-Lieutenant and I will be there directly.'

'Another foreign priest?' asked Suetsugu, stupefied.

'It appears so,' responded the Governor. 'Come, let us go. We can resume our discussion later. It is time to destroy more Christians.'

* * *

Court of Justice, Nagasaki City

To maintain order in the overcrowded court, officials crammed the villagers into a corner of the room and forced them to kneel. Filthy and bloodied, with dark circles under their eyes, the villagers appeared overwhelmed, exhausted, and anxious as they awaited Kawachi and the Deputy-Lieutenant.

Moments later, Kawachi arrived and gazed at Father Joaquim, his catechists, and the villagers who stared up at him in dazed shock.

'You will bow,' the Governor commanded. 'How dare you not acknowledge my presence!'

The villagers prostrated themselves before the new governor.

'You are very lucky,' Kawachi announced. 'Had you arrived yesterday, you would have all perished in our great fire, when I celebrated my arrival by burning thirteen Christians to death.' The Governor smiled grimly. 'Deputy, please remind me of some of their names.'

On hearing the victims' names, Father Joaquim experienced a deep sense of sorrow at more friends lost to the holocaust. They had given so much to the faith, but now they were dead, like hundreds of other Christians before them.

'This Court of Justice will not convene long today,' the

Governor declared. 'You are all criminals according to the law of the Shogun. Take these mutts to the prison. Tomorrow, we will pronounce judgement on them.'

CHAPTER TWENTY-SEVEN

22 June 1626
Nagasaki Prison, Nagasaki City

It was the smell that hit him first. Father Joaquim lifted his eyes from his downward gaze and studied the dim surroundings and his fellow prisoners as best he could in the dark. The prisoners had to make do, crammed next to each other, naked, cold, and in their own filth. He pinched his nose at the putrid stench. It was past midnight, of that he felt certain, and many of the exhausted inmates were struggling to fall asleep. There were no beds or blankets, just an overcrowded, cold concrete prison filled with the sounds of snoring, weeping, and moaning.

The priest was still mourning the loss of his friend and *sensei*. Added to his grief now was the discovered loss of friends in the

Society. *Lord, I do not understand Your ways*, he prayed, staring into the darkness. *Please, grant me vision.* Father Joaquim covered his eyes and face with his hands, using his fingers to massage his temples. The rancid smell, along with the pervasive moans of his fellow prisoners, continued to make him gag, and gave him a headache.

'I don't understand.' Catechist Miguel turned towards Tonia. 'Why did Master Yamaguchi not defend himself against the Daimyo?'

'I don't know,' Tonia replied. 'Master Yamaguchi defended himself against such an attack a thousand times.'

'He even taught us that technique several weeks ago,' Miguel continued.

'Perhaps he was afraid the Daimyo and his samurai would have killed us all,' Tonia responded.

Father Joaquim said, 'Yamaguchi-san always placed others first.'

'I guess it doesn't matter any more.' Miguel shrugged.

'Miguel, please, try to have faith,' Joaquim said.

'Faith in what?'

'That we *will* survive.'

'Do you truly believe that, Father?'

'Yes, Miguel.'

'Look around you – this is the end for us.'

'If you feel that, then you do not have faith, Miguel. You must believe.'

'Believe in what?'

'Our survival, Miguel. Do you believe the Lord will protect us?'

Miguel sighed as his brows drew together and his face tightened. 'I want to believe, Father, but look at where we are, in prison, facing a death sentence, with no way of escape.'

'Our reality is what we *believe*, Miguel. I have asked the Lord for help, and I believe we *will* survive.'

'I believe, Father,' Tonia interjected. 'I believe we will be free again one day.'

Miguel shook his head in frustration. 'I'm sorry, Father. I have the greatest respect for your faith, but I have seen nothing but bad luck since I arrived in this God-forsaken country.'

'Then pray, Miguel, for our survival, and for Japan.'

Miguel sighed again and closed his eyes to retreat from the conversation. 'I am tired. I will try, Father – I will.'

* * *

Kawachi, Shigemasa, and Suetsugu gathered in the Nagasaki magistrate's office.

'So what do we do with them all?' the Governor asked. He sat behind the magistrate's desk.

'Execute them at once,' said Suetsugu.

'I don't care,' Shigemasa stated. 'It doesn't matter, just as long as I get credit for their arrest.'

'You already have credit for that,' the Governor answered.

'But I want the Shogun to know I captured and arrested them.'

'Yes, yes, you will get your credit,' the Governor grunted.

Daimyo Shigemasa continued to press Kawachi for recognition of the Christians' discovery and arrest. 'This is important, Governor. I want the Shogun to know that I am doing everything possible to capture these despicable Christians on my lands.' Shigemasa looked at the Governor with narrowed eyes. 'And I want him to know I am producing results.'

With a pinched expression, the Governor huffed. 'Yes, Lord

Shigemasa, I will make him aware.'

'So are we all agreed?' Suetsugu interjected. 'We will execute the entire village tomorrow?'

'Slow down, Deputy. We should think about this in a careful manner,' the Governor answered.

'What is there to think about? The answer is simple: we exterminate them.'

'I know you want to them dead, but I want what is in our best interests.'

'What do you mean?'

'I mean, how can *we* gain the most favour with the Shogun?'

'The Shogun wants us to execute hidden Christians.' Suetsugu did not conceal his impatience. 'There is nothing more to discuss.'

'The Shogun also likes to torture Christians himself,' the Governor replied.

'What are you saying?'

'Why not send them all to the Shogun and let *him* torture and execute them?'

'That is a good idea,' Shigemasa agreed. 'But there are too many. The women and children tire easily, and it would take far too long to get them to Edo.'

'Then maybe we should split them up?' the Governor suggested. 'Split the men from the women and children.'

Yes,' Shigemasa nodded. 'We can take the men to Edo with ease.'

'Then it is decided.' The Governor leaned back, satisfied.

'What about the foreign priest and his aides?' Shigemasa asked. 'One of them is a young woman.'

'Is she strong?' the governor asked.

'Yes, she is the strongest among all the women of the village.'

'Then take all the men and the three foreigners to the Shogun. The Shogun has never tortured a foreign woman before.'

The men in the room smiled. The Governor was not the only one amused at the thought of the Shogun torturing a young Portuguese woman.

'The real prize will be the torture and death of the foreign priest.' Feeling proud that he was already producing results so early in his post, the Governor smiled at the others. 'The Shogun views the priests as the primary agents poisoning Japan.'

'Who will take the men to Edo?' the Deputy-Lieutenant asked.

'I will!' Daimyo Shigemasa blurted.

'Edo is almost a two-week journey, Daimyo.'

'It matters not. I want to hand these dogs over to the Shogun in person.'

'Fine, you have earned it. Take them to Edo.' The Governor's decision resounded with authority.

'And what about the women and children?' the Deputy-Lieutenant asked.

'What about them?'

'Shall we execute them?'

'I prefer apostates over martyrs.'

'For sure, if we send half the Christians to Edo, we can execute the women and children.'

'Our execution yesterday did not please me, Deputy.'

'Why not? The Christians are dead. Even their ashes do not remain. It was a great victory.'

'They were fearless; this bothers me. They chose death rather than recant their faith.'

'It is still a victory,' the Deputy replied as he shrugged his shoulders.

'A complete victory would be for them to do something against their will. I want apostates, not martyrs.'

'And how will you achieve that?'

'We will achieve it through unbearable torture.'

'Splendid, Governor. I would like to be in charge of this.'

'Are you sure you have the stomach to torture women and children?'

'If I can torture my own mother and sister, who were previously Christian, then without question, I can torture unknown women and children.'

'Did you really torture your own family?'

'Yes, Governor. Their Christian beliefs compromised my business.'

Kawachi raised his eyebrows at Suetsugu, and then shrugged it off, giving Suetsugu's behaviour no further thought.

'Then it looks like we have the right man for the job.' The Governor smiled and nodded his approval. 'Wake the Christian dogs and remove them from the kennel.'

CHAPTER TWENTY-EIGHT

22 June 1626
Nagasaki Court of Justice

Father Joaquim watched Governor Kawachi march into the Nagasaki Court of Justice followed by a phalanx of senior officials. The villagers stood next to the priest. All looked pale with dark circles under the eyes and smelled horrible. Many were sick and exhausted, with slouched shoulders.

The Jesuit watched the Governor and his senior officials prepare to address the courtroom. In their demeanour, he could see intense hatred and vindictiveness. The priest felt helpless. *Maybe this wasn't the right moment*, he thought. *Perhaps a better opportunity to stand up to the authorities and get them out of this horrible situation would reveal itself later.* He tapped his fingers to release energy, struggling to control his emotions. The priest did not hate the new governor and the other officials, but at the same time, he did not like them. For now, he thought it wise to take stock of Kawachi's verdict, and plan thereafter.

'Line up these mutts so they may face their judgement,' the Governor ordered. He made his way to the front of the courtroom and took his seat as prosecutor and judge.

Officials forced the villagers into rows near the front of the courtroom, shoving the children forward, followed by the women, keeping the men at the rear.

'This hearing will be short,' the Governor exclaimed. 'By law of the Shogun and the Bakufu regime, you are all criminals and will suffer great torments for your crimes. There is only one way to reduce your suffering – renounce your useless faith.'

The room was silent.

'Who among you will recant?' The Governor scanned the room, looking for those most likely to break.

Kawachi studied the women, especially those with young children, who hugged their mothers desperately. With his head tilted back, he expected them to crack – at least for the sake of their children.

More silence.

'The Governor asked you a question, you stupid dogs,' the Deputy-Lieutenant bellowed. 'Who will recant?'

With bulging eyes and full body tremors, some of the smaller children wailed. The adults remained silent.

From the back of the room, Father Joaquim locked eyes with the Governor, the man's rage apparent. 'Bring the foreign priest here,' the Governor commanded.

Two samurai guards grabbed Joaquim and dragged him to the front.

'State your name,' the governor said.

'Father Joaquim Martinez.'

'You admit to being a priest?'

'I am a Father in the order of the Jesuits.'

'Why are you in Japan? Your time here has expired.'

'My mission is to spread the Word of God and to shepherd the converted.' Joaquim heard mumblings from the guards.

'Will you recant?'

'No, sir, I cannot.'

Kawachi stared at the Jesuit from the magistrate's bench and crossed his arms. 'And what of your flock? Will they recant this false religion?'

'They are free to make their own choices. I do not command them.'

'Which of you will recant and live? Step forward at once!'

No response.

As the village remained silent, Father Joaquim's eyes gleamed. He felt a sense of pride to be Christian. *For sure*, he thought, *recanting would at least benefit the children in the short term.* But he knew that recanting the children's faith on their behalf would damn them. Mortal life was short, and who was he to forsake their eternal life.

'Read your sentences,' Joaquim said.

'Do you not wish to save their lives, Priest?' the Governor sneered. 'You should *make* them recant.'

'Only God can save us.'

'Your faith will not help you here,' the Deputy-Lieutenant interjected.

'Our Lord Jesus cautioned his disciples that they would meet with opposition when they spread His word. I am not afraid.'

'You should be, Priest. Your death will be the most painful and gruesome of all,' the Deputy-Lieutenant sneered.

'You should never have voyaged to Japan,' Kawachi said. 'The Shogun is Lord here and there is no place for your Jesus. Your teachings corrupt the minds of our people.'

'The people of Japan have a right to choose whom they serve.'

'Wrong. The people of Japan exist to serve the Shogun and the daimyo who own the lands they work.'

Daimyo Shigemasa grinned.

'Well, then …' The Governor shook his head as he gazed over the assembled villagers. 'We will divide the village into two. Daimyo Shigemasa will march the men and foreigners to Edo, where the Shogun will have the pleasure of choosing the manner of their demise. The women and children will remain incarcerated in Nagasaki, where they will recant through torture or face death.'

Without waiting, samurai and officials divided the villagers, pushing the men and foreigners to one side of the court and the women and children to the other.

The crying and wailing grew louder as officials tore families apart. Samurai assaulted several villagers as husbands and wives tried to embrace for the last time. One wife tried to give her husband a last kiss but an official punched her hard in the face, spattering blood around the courtroom. As her children wailed, samurai kicked them in the face, telling them to shut up or die. The husband tried to rescue his family, but a samurai slammed him in the head with the butt end of a sword. He collapsed onto the floor and lay unconscious, covered in blood that oozed from a large gash.

'This court is dismissed!' the Governor shouted. 'May you all lament the day you adopted this useless faith!'

CHAPTER TWENTY-NINE

23 June 1626
Streets of Nagasaki City

Samurai forced the women and children down the street towards an empty warehouse near the harbour. Their orders were to treat them like animals and mock them. Every moan or whimper led to a blow. As they moved through the streets, the guards yanked on the ropes binding the prisoners, causing them to trip and fall to the ground.

Deputy-Lieutenant Suetsugu strutted down the street, leading the march.

'This is what happens to Christians!' the Deputy-Lieutenant shouted. He paraded the captives past a group of locals who gathered near the centre of the city.

Suetsugu noticed the shock on the faces of several local women. As the deputy observed their reaction, he smiled. 'Remove the women's clothing!' he commanded.

'Here?' an official asked.

'What better place to humiliate them?'

Scores of Nagasaki residents looked on in horror and disgust. Suetsugu saw their revulsion and fed on it. The samurai did as ordered. The women barely resisted. They could only cry.

'Leave my aunt alone!' young Shiro shouted. He ran over to the samurai who had torn off her clothing, and tried to kick him.

'Discipline that brat!' the deputy yelled.

With the butt end of their swords, several samurai hammered away at Shiro, leaving him senseless.

'Don't touch him!' his aunt screamed. Despite her nakedness, she tried to run over and protect him. A samurai knocked her to the ground.

Suetsugu stood over the naked woman, and said, 'No Christian will be spared from my wrath. Not even the children. Nits make lice.'

The woman tried to get up.

'Stay down,' the Deputy-Lieutenant commanded, and put a foot in her back. He stood above the woman with a large whip in his hand. 'Crawl like the dog you are!'

The woman turned and stared up at the Deputy.

'You mutts are far too disobedient. You need to listen to your masters!' Suetsugu shouted again. 'Now crawl!'

The woman remained motionless.

'Crawl, I said!' Suetsugu's whip cracked through the air, drawing blood. She cried out and began crawling down the road. Horrified at her treatment, women in the streets gasped.

Motivated by the laughter of the samurai, Suetsugu ordered all the women to crawl down the road. With heads down, the women crawled on all fours, their faces flushed red, their bodies shivering. After several minutes of amusement, Suetsugu signalled for the samurai to pick them up from the ground.

'We can't let these mutts crawl all day,' he said. 'We'll never get to the warehouse.'

Walking again, the group finally arrived at Suetsugu's empty warehouse on the waterfront.

'Shove them in.'

The officials untied the ropes binding the women and children together, then pushed them into the dark warehouse, tossing their clothes in after them.

'You can recant or suffer more humiliation and an excruciating death,' Suetsugu announced. He slammed the door closed and abandoned them to the darkness.

CHAPTER THIRTY

24 June 1626
Omura Prison, District of Nagasaki

Under different circumstances, the brilliant orange-and-red sunset outlining the mountain would have been a marvel. But Daimyo Shigemasa, his son Katsuie, and the warlord's samurai were too focused on driving the band of exhausted prisoners up the mountain slope to notice, and the prisoners too fatigued and miserable to care.

Omura Prison was located twenty miles north of Nagasaki, and Shigemasa had marched them non-stop from the court in Nagasaki.

As the group continued uphill, several prison guards walked down to greet them. At the top, somewhat concealed by tall trees, stood Omura Prison, guarded by twelve more guards.

'Daimyo Shigemasa, welcome to Omura Prison,' Yuzuru Matsumoto, the prison master said. He bowed low. 'I see you have prisoners.'

'Yes, and they are all Christians.'

Shigemasa led Matsumoto away from the group to speak in private. 'We found them on my lands – in a village in Arima,' the Daimyo confided.

'I'm sorry, Lord. But it is a good capture for you, is it not? How many do you have?' Matsumoto looked over the prisoners.

'Twenty-one, including three foreign dogs. Each will be a delightful gift for the Shogun.'

'So how can we help, Lord Shigemasa?'

'I need to visit my castle tomorrow before I lead our long march to Edo. I have more gifts for the Shogun I need to collect. It is also necessary to gather supplies for the journey, so I would like to leave these prisoners here for two nights while I make preparations. Do you have the space to imprison them?'

Half-turning his head and scowling, Matsumoto answered: 'Hmm … I don't know. The prison is already well over capacity. I don't know where I could put twenty-one new prisoners. Perhaps we could execute some?'

Shigemasa shook his head. 'No, I do not want to kill anyone. They are valuable gifts for the Shogun. I want him to see all the fruit of my labours.'

'We cannot execute any of our existing prisoners,' Matsumoto replied. 'I have instructions to make them suffer more.'

'Well then, let us force them all together for a few days. They will all suffer more, and I can get what I need.'

'It will mean piling them on top of one another.'

For a moment, Shigemasa visualized all the prisoners piled on top of one another in a horrid tangle of human bodies with no escape. The thought made him laugh as he smirked and lifted his chin.

'Why do I care?'

'They won't sleep. Some go insane and kill for more space.'

'But my prisoners are gifts for the Shogun.'

'Perhaps we could use a new underground prison cell I have built. It is almost complete.'

Matsumoto's enthusiasm pleased Shigemasa almost as much as the offer itself. 'A new prison cell?'

The man nodded, proud of his accomplishment. 'I built it for the most vile criminals. It is a deep concrete hole in the ground. It can fit one or two, maybe three if they stand and lean against each other.'

'Why is it for the most vile?'

'Because there is almost no air in the hole, and it is unbearably hot. Sometimes we fill it with human waste, so it is foul.'

'Good. We will put my most despicable criminals in it – the Christian priest and his aides. I cannot risk them being killed.'

'That is fine, Lord. But they will get sick.'

'Sick dogs are less likely to run away.' Shigemasa grinned at his good fortune.

'And the rest of the Christians?'

'Shove them into the main prison. I don't care if we have to pile them on top of one another. It is not me in there.'

'As you command, Lord. It will be like hell for them.'

CHAPTER THIRTY-ONE

24 June 1626

Father Joaquim and the two young catechists stood in a hole nine feet deep and less than three and a half feet in diameter, soaked in the urine Matsumoto and several of his guards had deposited on them earlier.

Their exhausted bodies slouched but lacked the room required to sit. Not wanting to recline in the vile waste that surrounded them – even if they had had the room – the three stood amid the foul smell, staring downwards as they discussed their situation.

'When will this end, Father?' Tonia moaned as she pressed against the side of the hole.

'When we are dead,' Miguel said despondently.

'I know I have said this before, but have faith, my friends. We *will* survive this,' Father Joaquim said.

Miguel mumbled: 'I'm sorry, Father, but God has abandoned us.'

'That is the time to renew your faith, Miguel. Perhaps you need to pray. We could do so together if you like ...'

'I have prayed *every* night since our capture. Yet still they persecute us. And it is only getting worse!'

'Give the Lord a chance to respond, Miguel.'

'He has had plenty of time.'

'The Lord will respond in *His* time, Miguel, not yours. Never lose faith. God will answer us.' He embraced the young catechist. 'God's Spirit lives inside you. When you have genuine faith, when you feel it, He will know.'

'It no longer matters. We are dead men.'

'That's not true. Miguel. It does matter, because one day it could save you.'

* * *

25 June 1626

Rats scurried near the top of the prison hole while the two young catechists appeared to doze on their feet. Father Joaquim heard voices above, not far away. The priest listened carefully, focusing his attention.

'Keep these mutts locked in their cages while I'm away,' Shigemasa ordered. 'I'll be back before sunset tomorrow.'

'Yes, Daimyo,' Joaquim heard Matsumoto answer. 'I will not open the door even to feed them.'

'And keep the lid on the pit. I don't want the padre or his aides to see daylight.'

'The lid will remain locked until you return, Lord. The only contact with the priest and his aides will be my men urinating on them,' Matsumoto boasted.

Father Joaquim heard the hoof beats of Shigemasa's horses moving away.

'Come,' the priest then heard the prison master say, 'let's give the mutts an early morning shower.'

Joaquim prayed as he anticipated Miguel's reaction to the abuse they were about to suffer.

The laughter from Matsumoto and his guards aroused the dozing catechists just in time to look up into the streams of urine raining down on them from their tormentors.

'Damn you, you heartless bastards!' Miguel yelled. He cursed under his breath, grimaced, and pinched his lips together.

But his words only encouraged the chortling guards.

'Have no worries, Miguel. Our torments will end.'

'When, Father? When will they end?'

'Soon, Miguel. The Lord will wash us clean.'

'How can men treat other humans like this?' Tonia shook the waste from her hair.

'Try to feel pity for them, Tonia,' Joaquim said, as he wiped her face.

'I want to kill them,' Miguel yelled in a sudden outburst. He wrinkled his nose and flinched as he tried to shake his body to clean himself.

Tonia reached out and placed her hand on Miguel's shoulders to console him.

'Mind your emotions, Miguel,' Father Joaquim said. 'Anger is self-destructive. Focus on love. Love your enemy as the Lord loves us.'

'These men should pay for their inhumanity!' Miguel shouted.

'It is not your job to carry out vengeance, Miguel. Focus on our freedom, and we will have it.'

* * *

As the sun set, a gathering wind signalled the approach of rain. One of the prison guards spotted a grey-haired man in his sixties with the bearing and gait of a samurai approaching the prison from a nearby field. As he reached the bottom of the hill, several other guards intercepted him. The old man was carrying a small box.

Despite his age, the old man appeared strong, and his weathered face suggested he spent most of his time outdoors. As he neared the guards, he smiled.

Noticing the crest of Daimyo Shigemasa on the man's shoulder, the guards bowed to him. 'Welcome,' the senior guard said, acknowledging the samurai's allegiance. 'What brings you to Omura Prison?'

'I am here to present a gift to the prison master and all the guards on behalf of Lord Shigemasa.'

'We are honoured,' the senior guard answered. 'What do you have for us?'

'It is Lord Shigemasa's finest imported tea. He hopes you will all partake of it tonight. He recommended it as it will keep you awake to look after his Christian dogs.'

'Looking after the Lord's dogs is a pleasure and it is an honour to receive this gift. Please, profess our deepest gratitude to Lord Shigemasa.'

'I will. And thank *you* for looking after these mutts.'

* * *

In their cramped hole in the ground, the steady rain seeped through the cracks in the lid to the hole that covered Father Joaquim and the catechists. It wasn't enough to wash away the waste the guards had covered them with, but just enough to give them chills.

'It's quiet tonight,' Tonia said. 'Nothing like last night.'

Joaquim concentrated on subtle sounds above ground. 'Shhhh,' he insisted. 'Did you hear that?'

'It must be a guard,' Tonia whispered.

'No, it's not a guard. This is something else.'

'Look!' A bright blue flame glinted through the cracks in the slab.

'What's that?' Miguel asked, appearing fearful.

'I don't know,' Joaquim answered, bewildered by the light.

There was a strange, almost alcoholic tang in the air, mixed with something indefinable, as the mysterious blue flame burned quickly through the wood, despite the heavy rain.

Soon, the lid popped off and the silhouette of a man hovered above the pit. Heavy rain continued to pour down as the filth washed from the three surprised prisoners.

The end of a short, knotted rope dropped into the hole beside them.

'Who are you?' Tonia broke the silence.

'My pupils call me Master Watanabe. Hurry, take the rope.'

'Do it,' Father Joaquim told Tonia. 'You go first.'

Master Watanabe hauled Tonia out of the pit in a matter of seconds, before tossing the end of the rope back in.

'Who's next?' Master Watanabe asked.

'Miguel. Quick, grab the rope.'

Miguel did as he was told. A few minutes later Joaquim stood under a starlit night, breathing the sweetness of fresh air.

'Where are the guards?' Miguel asked. He cast fearful looks around.

'Resting,' the old man said with a hint of a smile.

'Who are you?' Joaquim asked him.

'The man helping you to escape. We don't have much time.'

'I cannot leave the others.' Joaquim looked towards the main prison building, which housed the rest of the village men.

'We are almost out of time, Father. We must go. You will save them later, but not now.'

'Why should we trust you?'

'Do you have a better option?'

'Fine,' Joaquim agreed. He sighed and breathed heavily. 'But this is only temporary. I will *not* abandon the others.'

'Agreed,' Master Watanabe nodded. 'But for now, let's go – quickly!'

CHAPTER THIRTY-TWO

26 June 1626

Matsumoto awoke to the squalling sound of cats fighting outside his window. He shook his groggy head several times. Panic welled up inside as he tried to remember – something, anything … his name, where he was. Shaking his head a few more times, he recalled, *I am Yuzuru Matsumoto. I am the master of Omura Prison.* He took a few steps to his bedroom door and walked outside. The guard stationed outside his door was on the floor, unconscious. Matsumoto kicked the guard, and the man woke up. All of a sudden, Matsumoto remembered the prisoners Daimyo Shigemasa had left under his watch.

He rushed to the main prison building, where he inspected the sealed lock, then entered. The prisoners were all still inside. He breathed a sigh of relief.

Then he remembered the pit and dashed over to it. To his horror, the pit was empty. Panic set in as he cursed and ran to the guardhouse. Opening the door, he burst inside and yelled, 'Wake up! Wake up, you imbeciles! The Christian foreigners have escaped!'

Like the prison master, the guards were groggy and confused.

'Get up.' Matsumoto's body shook as he paced around the guard house. 'The Christian priest and his aides have escaped!'

'What happened?' the most senior guard asked. He stepped forward, shaking his head just as Matsumoto had done when he'd awoken.

'Drugged, poisoned … I don't know, but it all started with that tea!'

'But that was a gift from Daimyo Shigemasa,' the senior guard answered.

'It doesn't matter now. All that matters is that we find the missing prisoners before the Daimyo returns! I want the six strongest and fastest men to gather arms and head for the forest at once.'

'Yes, Master. Why the forest?'

Matsumoto rolled his eyes. 'Use your head. They're foreigners and fugitives. They *must* run to the forest to avoid detection.'

'Yes, Master, you're right, of course. I am sorry.'

'Bring them back alive,' Matsumoto ordered. 'The Daimyo will be furious if we return them dead.'

'Yes, Master, but what if it is not possible to return them alive?'

'Then kill them. It is better to return them dead than not at all. Go, and find them right away! They are tired and ill, so it should not take you too long. Remember, the Daimyo will return before sunset, so make sure you bring the dogs back before then.'

***

Matsumoto surprised Shigemasa as he walked down the path to meet him.

'Welcome back, Lord Shigemasa,' the prison master said, bowing to the Daimyo and his samurai.

'How are my prisoners?'

Matsumoto paused. Then he said, 'We have a problem.'

Shigemasa dismounted. 'What problem?' He glared at Matsumoto.

'Our Japanese prisoners are still incarcerated, but the foreign priest and his aides are missing.'

Shigemasa exploded in fury. Without a word, he punched Matsumoto in the face, driving him to the ground, where he delivered a ferocious kick to his chest.

'We'll get them back,' Matsumoto struggled to say, crawling away.

'Get up!' the Daimyo ordered. 'Take me to the pit. I want to see what happened!'

Matsumoto rose to his feet and scurried up the hill, with Shigemasa and his samurai following.

'Look,' Shigemasa exclaimed when they arrived at the pit. 'The lock is intact!'

'Yes, Lord, I know.'

'Then how did they get out?'

'See. They burned through a plank – making just enough space to slip out.'

'You're telling me three half-naked captives standing in rain and filth managed to set fire to a wet wooden lid nine feet above them? Do you mock me?'

'No, Lord.' Matsumoto looked down in shame.

'It was your tea, Lord,' said the senior guard, standing nearby.

'My tea?'

'Yesterday, your retainer delivered us a gift of English tea.'

'My retainer?'

'Yes, Lord. He wore your crest on his shoulder and knew about the Christian dogs. He offered us an entire box to keep us awake.'

'Do you dare play with me on such important matters?'

'No, Lord, I swear it's the truth,' the senior guard replied.

'So, a mysterious retainer I know nothing about offered you English tea to keep you awake – yet you all fell asleep? And while you were sleeping, three half-naked Christians at the bottom of a cesspit escaped with no one noticing.'

Afraid to look Shigemasa in the eye, Matsumoto nodded but remained silent.

'Stand over there.' Shigemasa pointed to a spot next to the pit.

Trembling, Matsumoto did as he was ordered.

Shigemasa turned to scan the row of prison guards, each of whom stared studiously straight ahead, before he turned back to face Matsumoto.

'Never in my life have I witnessed such incompetence. You are too stupid or too disobedient to go on living!'

With a sudden twist of his body, the Daimyo drew his long sword and plunged it into Matsumoto's stomach.

Matsumoto fell slowly to his knees. Shigemasa stared into the prison master's eyes, withdrew his sword, then severed Matsumoto's head, sending it rolling towards the pit. Shigemasa kicked it, and it splashed into the waste at the bottom. Then, with another powerful kick, he shoved Matsumoto's body down after it.

The Daimyo pointed at the senior prison guard. 'You're next. Come here.'

The terrified senior guard stayed rooted to the spot. Two powerful samurai grabbed his arms and dragged him towards Shigemasa, who still stood at the edge of the pit.

'No! No! It's not my fau—' Shigemasa drove his sword into the man's chest. As the two samurai released his arms Shigemasa decapitated the guard.

'Never mock your lord.' Wiping the blood spatter off his face and hands, Shigemasa kicked the senior guard's head and body into the pit, before spitting after him in contempt. 'These men have jeopardized my lands and do not deserve to live!' Shigemasa shouted. 'Now, we must catch those wild dogs.'

'What about the rest of the guards?' a samurai asked. 'Shall we also throw them into the pit?'

The Daimyo thought for a moment.

'No, throw them into the prison with the inmates. We might have questions for them later, if they survive.'

'And who will run the prison, Lord?' a retainer asked.

'We will.'

As they walked towards the guardhouse, Shigemasa spoke to his samurai. 'The Nagasaki magistrate sent a letter to the Shogun informing him we have a gift of twenty-one Christians for him to slay, including a foreign Christian priest. What will the Shogun say when we arrive with only eighteen and no priest?'

'I don't know, Lord. Perhaps it will upset him,' a retainer replied.

'Upset? He will be furious. He could take my lands. I will be a peasant!'

'What is our plan, Lord? We must decide at once.'

'We will mobilize every samurai at my disposal.'

'All three thousand?'

'Yes. We will scour every piece of land and forest until we capture them. Our soldiers will use horses to outrun them.'

'Don't worry, Lord. Our samurai will find them,' the retainer assured him.

CHAPTER THIRTY-THREE

26 June 1626

'I need to rest,' Tonia said.

'Rest will come,' Master Watanabe replied. 'Do you see that small hill?'

'Yes,' Tonia nodded.

'Underneath, there's a cave where we can rest. So, please, we must continue.'

Pushing themselves, the group continued for another mile, until they arrived at the base of the hill where Watanabe pointed out a small, hidden cave.

As they entered, Tonia fell to the floor, exhausted. Miguel, lay down next to her. They were both asleep in minutes.

Father Joaquim sat against the cave wall. 'Now I must ask,

Master Watanabe: Who are you, and what is going on?'

Watanabe sat across from Joaquim. 'I am an old friend of Master Yamaguchi. And, like Yamaguchi-san, over the years I have learned to listen to the still, small voice inside when it speaks. The voice told me something terrible had happened to my old friend and his village. When I arrived I found his head, the charred remains of his body, the houses burned to the ground, and the village deserted.

'For the entire day, I prayed, and then that little voice told me to make my way to Omura Prison – and to take Master Yamaguchi's sword. I have learned that miraculous things happen when I obey that voice. It has saved my life more than once, so I listen now.'

'Where did you find his sword?' asked the priest.

'In his home, by the front door, uncharred by the fire,' answered Master Watanabe. 'It felt like he left it there for me.'

Captivated by the sword and intrigued by the mysterious man before him, Joaquim felt both confused and in awe. As he pondered a myriad of thoughts at the same time, he wondered about this man who had risked himself for them and rescued Yamaguchi-san's sword. The thought of Yamaguchi brought back fond memories of his friend and *sensei*.

'Perhaps, Father, we too should sleep now,' the old man said, noticing the priest's eyes flutter.

Joaquim shook his head trying to shake himself awake. But he was as exhausted as his catechists. 'What's your plan?'

'To continue our retreat and regroup in a place of safety.'

'Where?'

'The Goto Islands. They are not far, and some of them are sanctuaries for Christians.'

'What will we do there?'

'Plan the rescue of your villagers.'

'Good,' Joaquim replied. 'Do you think a large force is hunting us?'

'Yes, Father. A very large one.'

* * *

28 June 1626
Hizen Province, Kyushu

Lord Shigemasa's plan to recapture the escapees was simple: the city and prefecture were on the south-west part of the island, with water on three sides. The only logical escape route was to head north-east following the direction of the land. Based on Nagasaki's density and the number of officials in and around the city, Shigemasa determined that Father Joaquim would not head south. He and his retainers calculated how far Father Joaquim and the two catechists could have travelled given the time available to them, and thus established a perimeter based on their expected distance from Omura Prison.

He then dispatched horsemen to the edges of the grid to sweep inward until they either captured their prey or forced them into the arms of Shigemasa's foot soldiers coming up from the south.

* * *

At the far northern end of Shigemasa's search grid, peasants in a small village were labouring in the hot afternoon sun when the thunder of hooves and the rattle of armour interrupted their quiet toil. A regiment of a hundred samurai approached the rice fields. Back when the authorities tolerated Christianity and allowed priests to travel at liberty throughout the land, Father Joaquim had ministered to this village on several occasions.

The samurai Chikayoshi, a large, heavy-set man with a battle-scarred face that attested to a long military background, sat atop a massive black stallion, examining the village. He wore the armour and colours of his master Daimyo Shigemasa, a lacquered metal breastplate overlaid with layers of protective metal plates. Motivated by the warlord's promise of generous rewards, and by his orders, Chikayoshi eased himself into the saddle and furrowed his brow. He was determined to be the one to find the escaped Christians. Motioning towards the village, Chikayoshi and his men moved forward.

As the samurai arrived in the village, most of the children hid behind their mothers, while the men scurried into the centre of the village to pay homage.

'Where are they?' Chikayoshi shouted.

'Who?' a frightened farmer asked, his head bowed and eyes downcast.

'Don't play stupid, you worthless peasant. Where are they? If they are here, tell us at once or we will torch your village and everyone in it!'

Chikayoshi made a hand signal, and twenty samurai dismounted and charged into the dishevelled homes, ransacking them as they searched. As they plundered the dwellings, they smashed anything breakable. They destroyed cooking ware, clothing was pitched outside and trampled on, children's toys were broken and furniture crushed.

Inside the dwellings, terrified women and children screamed in distress as samurai whipped them around like rag dolls and pushed them to the floor. The men wailed in protest, and several ran to their homes to help their families, only to be assaulted by the samurai's heavy fists and the butt-ends of weapons. Any man who dared try to restrain a samurai was beaten bloody and left on the ground.

'Set that one on fire.' Chikayoshi pointed to a large old home built of straw and wood in the centre of the village. As smoke curled into the air, a woman and two children ran out, crying.

'Round up all the children!' Chikayoshi yelled. 'Bring them here.'

Samurai shoved mothers to the ground and grabbed their crying children. A child tried to run, but was thrown to the ground and trampled. Her mother tried to save her, but they broke her neck with a shovel. The village men tried to protest but soldiers pummelled any man who tried to intervene. Chikayoshi did not notice the panic among the villagers. His thoughts were too focused on reaping the reward for finding the escaped Christians.

'Tell me where they are or we will shove your children into the burning house.'

'Please! Who are you looking for?' a farmer cried in despair.

'Three escaped foreign Christians. Where are they?'

'We don't know. I promise you, we have not seen foreigners.'

'Look at that fire. Look at it with close attention,' Chikayoshi ordered the villagers. 'If we discover you have lied to us, we will incinerate every child in this village. As commander of this unit, this is my word!' Chikayoshi turned in his saddle, surveying the villagers. 'Now, I will ask one more time. Have you seen three runaway Christians?'

'No,' several peasants replied.

'Harbouring Christians is harbouring *criminals*,' Chikayoshi bellowed. 'Violation of this law will warrant immediate death. Do you understand?'

'We have seen no foreigners. We promise you!' a farmer yelled, his voice cracking with fear.

'Do you pledge your children's lives on this?'

'Yes. It has been years since we have seen *any* foreigner,' the same farmer replied.

Chikayoshi scanned the faces of the villagers to make sure they were petrified and got the message. 'Don't get too comfortable. We *will* return to verify your claims.' Turning his horse around, Chikayoshi faced his samurai.

'How are our supplies?'

'Low,' his second-in-command answered. 'The men are hungry.'

'Help yourselves to whatever you need,' Chikayoshi said. 'These peasants exist to support us.'

Dozens of hungry samurai raided the village supplies, taking all of the food and filling their metal water containers. The villagers could only watch as the army emptied their stock of food and water.

'Don't be disheartened,' Chikayoshi joked as he observed their forlorn faces. 'You still have your fields. Get out there and harvest more.' As Chikayoshi and his fellow samurai left, the commander yelled out, 'I order you to keep your eyes open for the fugitives!'

'But what can we do?' a downcast farmer asked.

'Send men into the forest to look for them.'

'But we have a new, strict quota to meet.'

'That is not my problem. Until we capture them, no one is safe – and we will keep coming back!'

CHAPTER THIRTY-FOUR

29 June 1626

Master Watanabe and the Europeans sat at the edge of the forest and stared at a large, open field in front of them. They had to cross it before the pursuing army caught up with them, but it was so exposed. They had already managed to skirt several villages to avoid detection, but from the edge of the forest they had caught sight of a large company of samurai following on their tail, though the samurai had not yet seen them. *It was only a matter of time though*, Joaquim thought. It was still morning, and the day was growing hotter, but the group knew waiting in the shade of the forest for nightfall would make them more vulnerable, not less.

Half a mile later Tonia's pace slowed. 'I'm exhausted,' she said.

Her breathing was laboured. They were all beginning to tire, and Joaquim was concerned for her. 'I'm sorry, Father, but I really need to rest. My feet hurt and I'm pretty sure I have blisters, but I'm frightened that if I take off my shoes I won't be able to get them back on again. When can we stop?'

'Not now.' Master Watanabe shook his head, his eyes scanning the horizon. 'We can't rest in an open field. It's too dangerous.'

Tonia placed her hands on her thighs, and hunched over.

'Here, drink.' Watanabe offered her a skin filled with water.

'It's all right, Tonia. We'll rest for a while,' Father Joaquim said as he helped her find a place to sit. 'We will take care of you.'

Miguel approached Tonia and put his arm around her shoulders to comfort her, then he raised his head. 'God preserve us!' He pointed to the edge of the forest. 'Look at their numbers! We're doomed for sure!'

They gazed into the distance as several hundred samurai approached from across the plain, with a dozen on horseback. All appeared heavily armed.

'We are far from doomed, Miguel,' Watanabe replied.

'Now what?' Joaquim asked.

'The Chikugo-gawa is close to here. We can escape them in the water.'

'Can we get there before they catch us?'

Watanabe nodded. 'If we hurry.'

Extending their hands to Tonia, Joaquim and Watanabe pulled her to her feet.

'Can you run, Tonia?' Joaquim asked.

'I must,' she said simply.

Watanabe led the group in a jog across the large open space.

They had not gone far when they heard the echo of a cry from the distant samurai.

'There they are! After them!'

The small group of mounted samurai led a charge towards them, leaving the ground forces far behind as they raced at full speed. Behind them, hundreds of samurai followed on foot.

'The horsemen are gaining on us!' Miguel cried, as he looked back.

Tonia bounced on her feet and sprinted as fast as she could, but tripped and crashed to the ground. Joaquim and Watanabe pulled her back up.

The fugitives increased their pace, but the gap between them and the horsemen continued to narrow.

Every time they looked back they saw the samurai gaining ground. They sprinted until their breath came in ragged gasps, their sides ached, and their vision began to blur.

Joaquim called a halt to grab their breath. Hands on his thighs he said to Watanabe, 'We won't make the river at this pace. Give me Yamaguchi-san's sword. I will slow them down.'

'I will help you,' Watanabe offered.

'No, you must help Miguel and Tonia. Quick, pass me the sword.'

Holding the sword, Joaquim turned to face the enemy. 'Lord, grant me skill to defend my people,' he prayed.

The first horseman arrived almost immediately. With shoulders back, Father Joaquim stood in the middle of the field as his friends raced for the protection of the far side. With the sword hidden behind his back, Joaquim stood motionless, encouraging the samurai to rush him. He saw the white foam on the horse's chest, heard its wheezing gallop, and smelled its odour as the rider drew abreast, aiming to use the horse to knock him to the ground.

The rider had not drawn his sword but had left it in its sheath. *They want to take me alive if they can,* Joaquim thought.

He turned his body like a matador avoiding a charging bull, and swung his sword at the attacking samurai. The blade grazed the top of the horse's head and passed through the samurai's shoulder, throwing him from his horse. He hit the ground hard and lay still. The horse stumbled, broke its leg with a hideous scream, and crashed to the ground in a cloud of dust.

Joaquim dashed to the unconscious samurai and grabbed his bow and arrows. Taking cover behind the injured horse, the Jesuit cut its throat to put it out of its misery, notched the bow quickly, and fired a series of arrows at the remaining horsemen as they closed in on him.

Arrow after arrow flew at the attacking samurai. The leading riders were helpless to protect themselves from arrows that hit either them or their horses. The riders who survived injury to their mounts fell to the ground only to be struck in the chest, shoulders and legs as they stood up. A few were crushed by injured horses. Several more at the rear of the group pulled themselves short, but the majority fell some fifty yards or so from Joaquim's position. The ones at the back readied their bows and arrows, and several arrows struck the ground and the horse near Joaquim. But the samurai were exposed and, he knew, would not retreat.

Taking advantage of their vulnerability, Joaquim fired again and again, the arrows whistling on the air, finding their targets, ripping through exposed chinks in the horsemen's armour. One by one they fell, their wounded mounts thrashing on the ground, screaming their distress.

Finally, only the wounded remained, unable to do anything

other than try to stem the blood, as it discoloured the surrounding grass. The injured samurai waited, immobile, anticipating their ignominious demise from their enfeebled, prone positions.

But no one came. No swaggering victor, eager to gaze into their eyes as they gasped their last. An uneasy hiatus confused their warrior expectations. Had there been more than four to decimate their cavalry so quickly? Where were they now?

The samurai footmen were still some distance away. Joaquim looked sadly at the pathetic scene before him, then turned and ran towards the river.

It didn't take long to catch up with Master Watanabe, but the gap between them and the ground troops was still narrowing. Tonia struggled to keep up, clearly in pain as she gasped for air. She was not so much running as lurching now.

'Nearly there!' Master Watanabe shouted. 'Our escape is at hand.'

Joaquim and Miguel ran alongside Tonia, grabbing her hands and pulling her forward. At last they reached the edge of the wide Chikugo-gawa River.

Recent heavy rains had made the river overflow and now its wild and fast-moving waters raced and swirled past them. They would likely drown in these tumbling waters. But the samurai would certainly kill them if they fell into their hands.

'This is where we will escape them,' Watanabe said. He approached the river's edge and put his hand in the water.

'Where's the boat?' Miguel asked, clutching his stomach.

'We don't have a boat,' Watanabe answered.

'How on earth are we going to cross?' asked Miguel. He watched the wild waters rush by in horror.

'With our feet, Miguel.'

'What? Where's the bridge?'

'There is no bridge. We will walk across.'

'Are you mad?' Miguel blurted as his eyes bulged. 'Do you think you're Jesus?'

'Please, I have no time to explain. You must trust me. Have faith. I will help you take the first step.'

Watanabe stepped into the wild waters. With his feet planted wide, he stood firm in the river as the rushing waters flowed around him. Joaquim was astounded.

'Tonia, quick, take my hand.' Watanabe reached for her. 'Miguel, hold onto her other hand. Father, take Miguel's hand. Form a line.'

Tonia and Miguel remained frozen to the spot. Behind them, hundreds of samurai approached across the great field, their weapons glinting in the sun, the sound of their thudding feet carried on the breeze. The distance between them and the fugitives lessened with every step they took.

'Do as he says!' Father Joaquim commanded.

Tonia and Miguel stepped into the water and formed a line. Watanabe closed his eyes, lifted his head towards the sky, and meditated for a moment. Then he walked with deliberation through the rushing water, guiding Tonia, Miguel, and Father Joaquim forward.

'Trust in God,' Watanabe said. He continued to step deeper as the rough waters rushed up to his thighs. In the rear, Joaquim was flabbergasted. He felt the strong current pull at him, but somehow, defying logical reasoning, they remained linked and resolute and firmly anchored in a way the priest could not comprehend.

'Is this a dream?' Tonia asked. They continued to walk into the heart of the raging waters, as though it was bracing them rather than attacking.

'It's as real as you are,' Watanabe said.

'The current is very strong in the middle!' Miguel shouted. He bit his lip as the waters propelled him off-balance and ahead of the group. Only the linked hands kept him upright.

'Fasten your inner eye on the power of God to support us. When you do this, the water becomes as solid as rock.'

Miguel held Tonia's hand tightly, keeping his eyes closed, feeling the cold water pushing and pulling as it swirled around his legs up to his waist, his feet seeming to find purchase, but on what, he couldn't say for certain. Immersed in prayer, Father Joaquim kept his eyes closed and gripped Miguel's hand tightly as he walked through the powerful waters.

They took their final steps onto the far riverbank just as the samurai arrived at the other side. The soldiers let out a ferocious war cry and loosed a hail of arrows that arced across the raging waters, forcing Joaquim and the others to take cover behind nearby rocks.

Dozens more samurai arrived. Many, eager to impress Shigemasa and gain a rich reward, ran into the water and tried to swim to the far bank.

But the river's current was too strong. The turbulent water crashed over the samurai, dragging them down in their heavy armour, driving them towards the rapids further downstream. The relentless undercurrent swallowed them whole, tossing their helpless bodies on to the rocks as they were swept to their death.

CHAPTER THIRTY-FIVE

Father Joaquim and his companions breathed a sigh of relief and clasped their hands in prayer. After offering thanks, the priest laid a hand on his heart and looked to the sky. Despite feeling grateful, Joaquim knew their reprieve was temporary. He wanted to rest – they all did – but he knew they could not. Shigemasa's warriors would be enraged after seeing their comrades swept to their deaths, and Joaquim knew they had to put as much distance as possible between themselves and the samurai.

Mindful of Tonia's need to recoup her strength, Joaquim and Watanabe agreed silently to walk for a while in order to give her a chance to recover a little. If they did not, Joaquim feared they might end up having to carry her, which would really slow them down.

Tonia stopped limping after a while, and eventually broke the silence between them. She caught up to Master Watanabe. 'I must know. How on earth did you perform that miracle?'

'Of what do you speak, Tonia?'

'How did we walk across the river?'

'*I* did nothing, child. It was our communion with the Source that saved us.'

'You mean, God?' Father Joaquim said.

'If you wish. Does the name really matter?'

'But why call Him "the Source"?'

'Is God not the *source* of all creation?'

'Yes.'

'Then we can also call Him the Source. It is through the Source we can accomplish these deeds. I cannot do these things on my own.'

'Then why cannot I do them?' Miguel asked.

'Who says you cannot?'

The young man shook his head. 'No, I can't.'

'You must believe that you *can*.'

'It's impossible.'

'Really? Does your Bible not say, "Greater works than these shall you also do"?'

Joaquim nodded in agreement.

'Help me with the passage, Father,' Watanabe added.

The padre nodded. 'In the book of John, Jesus says, "Very truly I tell you, whoever believes in me will do the works I have been doing, and they will do even greater things than these, because I am going to the Father."'

'Correct,' Master Watanabe replied. 'Jesus was always in communion with the Father.'

'But I cannot do this,' Father Joaquim protested. 'I'm a normal man.'

'Are you suggesting that Jesus was lying or trying to deceive when He said that?'

'No, of course not. But I'm just an ordinary man.'

'So Jesus spoke this passage only to supernatural men?'

The padre shook his head. 'I didn't say that.'

'Then it's time to put away your doubts and start to *truly* believe in your inherent powers.'

'It sounds like fantasy,' Miguel said.

'Did you not just walk through a raging river, Miguel?'

'Yes, but that was only because of *you*.'

'I told you, *I* can do nothing. Everything I achieve is through my faith in the Source. But the belief starts in you. Believe that He lives in you.'

'I believe this,' Father Joaquim avowed.

'I know you do, Father. Your faith is strong, and you are close to doing these great works on your own. Now it is time for you to *know* you can do these things yourself. And *thanking* Him is the strongest form of knowing.'

'I will try,' Joaquim replied.

'There is no trying. You must *do*. When you *know*, the outcome is assured.'

Father Joaquim looked at Watanabe. 'So when I pray, I should also give thanks?'

'Yes.'

'Is it not arrogant to give thanks for what you are yet to receive?'

'Thanking is the greatest form of faith.'

'What about asking?' Miguel enquired. 'Is it not important to ask?'

'Asking is like trying. If you ask too many times, it means you are uncertain about the outcome. When you are uncertain about the outcome, you cannot know, and the circle cannot complete itself. The best way to know is to thank.'

Tonia took a deep breath. 'Can we rest a short while?'

'Not yet. The legion will have found a way to cross the river by now.'

CHAPTER THIRTY-SIX

29 June 1626
Shogun's Castle, Toshima District, Edo,
Musashi Province

'I should kill you! I gave clear orders not to disturb me.' Shogun Iemitsu rose naked from his bed and wrapped himself in a plush silk robe.

'Forgive me, Lord. I would never disturb you unless it was to bring you news of the greatest importance,' the retainer stammered.

'What is so important that you violate my strict orders?'

'One of your spies on Kyushu sent a carrier pigeon. Some of your new prisoners have escaped.'

'Which prisoners?'

'Some of the Christians at Omura Prison.'

The Shogun grabbed an elegant sake flask and smashed it against the wall, sending pottery flying. Turning on the retainer he asked with quiet menace, 'Under whose command did these prisoners escape?'

'Daimyo Matsukura Shigemasa, Lord, but he was at his castle when it occurred. They escaped under the prison master's watch.'

'Fools!' the Shogun shouted. 'They are all fools. There will be consequences for this!'

'The prison master is already dead, Lord. Daimyo Shigemasa executed him.'

'Good.' The Shogun dressed himself as he continued: 'Perhaps we should sanction Daimyo Shigemasa as well.'

'He has organized a massive manhunt, my Lord, and deployed a force of 3,000 samurai to recapture them.'

'Which prisoners escaped?'

'The foreign priest and his aides, Lord.'

In a second burst of anger, the Shogun kicked over an expensive Chinese table, smashing the exotic sculptures resting on it.

'I despise those foreign mongrels. They carry a disease that challenges *my* dominion. They are the ones I most want to mutilate!'

'What shall we do, Lord?'

'Fetch my sword. We will go to the streets of Edo so I can vent my anger.'

'Yes, Lord.'

* * *

An hour later, still raging, Shogun Iemitsu led dozens of his samurai and retainers down the streets of Edo, as residents and passers-by ran away, frantic to avoid him.

At his side swung a long, glinting sword, the Shogun's hand on the hilt. He itched to draw and use it. Taking a turn down a street, he caught sight of a man sleeping beneath a filthy blanket. He dashed towards him.

'Stand up, worthless vagrant!' The Shogun kicked him in the gut.

'What? Who is it?' the man asked as he woke up.

'Get up, I said!'

The man tried to rise, but he moved slowly, which vexed the Shogun, who had found an easy target for his fury. He plunged his weapon into the soft belly of the homeless man, his excitement rising as he withdrew his sword and watched the blood seep thickly on to the road.

'This sword is razor-sharp!' exclaimed the Shogun, his flushed appearance denoting his mania. 'It's perfect.'

The homeless man fell forward, grabbing the Shogun's garment in a vain attempt to steady himself, incomprehension etched on his face.

'Don't touch me, filthy creature!' the Shogun roared in disgust. 'Get away from me!' Pushing the man away, he knocked him to his knees. With a swift downward swing, the blade glinted in the twilight as the Shogun severed the man's head, sending it rolling a short distance away.

'Vagrants are society's waste,' the despot declared as he handed an aide his sword to wipe off the blood. He retrieved his now gleaming weapon. 'Now, what else can we find to test my blade on?'

All of a sudden, a young Buddhist monk walked around the corner of a building and gasped at the bloody sight before him. A pot of rice clattered to the ground from his shaking hands.

'Who are you?' the Shogun demanded, lips pressed together as he narrowed his eyes.

'A follower of Buddha. I was coming to bring this man food.' He indicated the corpse at the Shogun's feet.

'You help the homeless in my city?' the Shogun asked, contempt clear in his voice.

'Yes, I seek to ease their suffering.'

Without warning, the Shogun's blade flashed, as his sword stabbed viciously through the young monk's throat, perforating his oesophagus. Blood drained from his victim's punctured neck, as his lifeless body fell to the ground, a pool of blood coagulating at the Shogun's feet.

'How dare these meddling monks prolong the lives of these disgusting vagrants!'

Immune to their leader's frequent displays of brutality, his samurai looked on with blank stares, revealing no emotion at the slaughter.

'Perhaps this is enough for one day, Lord,' one of his retainers suggested. 'We would not want to dull your blade.'

'One more,' the Shogun said, turning around and scanning the streets. 'I am still enraged by this priest's escape. Daimyo Shigemasa had better catch him!'

CHAPTER THIRTY-SEVEN

30 June 1626
Hizen Province

At the head of 1,500 samurai, Daimyo Shigemasa hurried to the Chikugo-gawa River region.

'In what direction are they moving?' he asked the regiment's commander.

They stood encircled by warriors and advisers, close to the still-raging waters.

'West, Lord.'

'What happened yesterday?'

'I'm sorry, Lord. They escaped us at the river.'

'They must be exhausted by now. How is it possible they escape a force of 300 samurai?'

'My men spotted four people, my Lord. They have help.'

'Three or four … what difference does it make? Your regiment has 300 warriors!'

'We don't know how they crossed the river, Lord.'

'Did they take a boat or swim?'

'We didn't see a boat, Lord, and it's not possible to swim, the river is too fast. Some of our samurai tried, but the river swept them downstream.'

'Then how did they cross?'

The commander sighed and shook his head, his shoulders hunched in acquiescence. 'I cannot say, Lord. Our horsemen chased them across the plain, but an expert bowman ambushed them.'

'Their helper is a ronin?'

'He must be a former samurai because our horsemen suffered terrible wounds. Some believe it was the Christian priest who wielded the bow.'

'A foreign priest wielding a bow? That's ridiculous!'

'It's what several reported, Lord.'

'Then they are imbeciles. Now tell me how they crossed the river.'

'The samurai who arrived first thought he saw them walk across, Lord.'

'Have your men been drinking, commander?'

'No, Lord. They do not drink on duty.'

'Then why is their judgement impaired?'

'I don't know, Lord. It all happened quickly.'

The Daimyo huffed. 'Now that *I* have arrived, we *will* get them. With almost 3,000 samurai on their heels, there will be nowhere for them to hide.'

'What is our plan, Lord?'

'We will use our great numbers, spread out, and circle in on them. We will scour every piece of land westward, leaving no stone unturned.'

'Yes, Lord.'

'And we will not rest until these runaway dogs are back on their leash. Then we will drag them to the Shogun.'

* * *

'They are closing in on us, aren't they?' Miguel asked. He wrung his hands, failing to notice the magnificent, deep-hued sunset over the distant Pacific Ocean.

'Have no fear, Miguel,' Father Joaquim answered as the quartet plodded on. 'If God be for us, who can be against us?'

'But there are so many, Father.'

'Believe, Miguel. He released us like Daniel from the lion's den, and helped us cross a raging river. He will not abandon us now.'

'Yes, Father.'

'Master Watanabe, I would like to thank you again for your help,' Father Joaquim said. 'Without you, we would not have made it this far.'

'In time, you will not need me.'

'I wish that were true.'

'Do not wish, Father. *Know.*'

Joaquim chuckled. 'Yes, you're right.' He smiled at his new friend. 'I remember what you said: Knowing completes the circle.'

'Good,' Watanabe replied, nodding his head. 'Do not underestimate yourself. Your skill as a warrior is impressive. If it were not for *you*, we would not have made it this far.'

'I sought only to slow them down. Thank God, I do not think I killed any of them.'

'Yet they seek to destroy you.'

'It is of no matter,' Father Joaquim answered. 'Their actions will determine their own fate. If they live by the sword, they will suffer the consequences.'

'And while they live by the sword, you live by the Cross?'

'Yes, but I have given my life to serve our Lord Jesus Christ and to carry the Word of God.'

'Perhaps the Way of the Cross is not so different from the way of the sword. Both involve a life of service.'

'Master Yamaguchi and I spoke of this sometimes.'

'Both involve absolute devotion. A samurai serves his warlord unconditionally. A Christian serves his Lord Jesus Christ without condition and would die for his faith.'

'Agreed, there are similarities,' Father Joaquim said. 'But there are telling differences.'

'Oh?'

'Samurai kill on orders from their daimyo. God does not allow Christians to kill.'

'But Christians *do* kill.'

'Only in self-defence or to protect the innocent. In no other way would I seek to kill another.'

'I make no judgement, Father.'

'I simply emphasize that Christians are different from samurai.'

'I prefer to focus on the similarities, not the differences,' Master Watanabe said. 'Focusing on similarities brings us together.'

'It is a wise philosophy—'

'Look!' Miguel's sudden shout interrupted the conversation. He was pointing to columns of wispy smoke rising above the woods before them. The young catechist cried, 'The forest is on fire! We have to turn back!'

But Tonia had already turned to observe the forested hill from which they'd emerged a few minutes before. 'We can't go back. Look there!' she cried.

Daimyo Shigemasa and his company of samurai emerged from the thick trees behind them. The soldiers had them cornered.

The pungent odour of the dry burning wood wafted towards them.

'What shall we do?' Miguel yelled.

'We will escape them in the fire,' Master Watanabe said.

'We can't run into that fire!' Miguel yelled. His eyes bulged. 'It will burn us alive!'

'Calm yourself, Miguel,' Master Watanabe answered.

'We have a fire and samurai in front of us and Shigemasa and his hordes behind us. We have nowhere to go! Why would I be calm?'

'Trust me, Miguel. As before, just follow me.' Watanabe stepped towards the forest, which was now engulfed in roaring flames.

'We *will* survive, Miguel,' Father Joaquim asserted.

As he spoke hundreds of Shigemasa's samurai began a rush down the hill to capture their prey.

Miguel backed away from the heat of the burning trees. 'Nothing can survive that fire!'

'We *will* make it, Miguel. You must believe. Raise your consciousness to a higher level.'

'I don't understand,' Miguel answered. 'I can't do it.'

Watanabe said, 'We *will* pass through unharmed. Again, let us hold hands and I will guide you.'

The wood popped and spat as the heat of the flames grew stronger. Going towards it was madness! Miguel stared in horror as flames fanned in all directions, prompting endless sparks to crackle and ignite. In the distance, Miguel saw crashing trees, thick black smoke, and animals fleeing in desperation. Wide-eyed himself, Joaquim saw Miguel's hands shake and realized his own shook as well.

'When I was a young man sailing in the Indies,' Joaquim said urgently, 'I saw naked men walk on beds of fire unharmed. I swear to you. I am frightened too, but it happened. I saw it! We must *believe* He is with us. This is God's test. You must embrace it.'

Turning back to face the hill, they saw Shigemasa's samurai charging at full speed towards them, encompassing most of the immediate horizon. As they charged, they raised their weapons in the air and roared.

Watanabe said, 'Miguel, we have run out of time. I can only offer you my hand, but it must be *you* who grabs it and takes the first step.'

'I cannot. Fire terrifies me. I was burned as a child. I cannot!'

Father Joaquim made the sign of the cross and grabbed Miguel's shoulders, facing him. 'What do you fear more, Miguel? The certainty of endless pain and torment, alone at the hands of the Shogun, or believing the Lord *will* save us and walking into that forest with your friends by your side?'

The charging samurai were closing in. The thundering of hundreds of stamping feet drew closer. Through the flames was the only way forward.

'Quick, let us hold hands,' Master Watanabe called out.

'Do as he says.' Joaquim took the lead by grabbing Master Watanabe's hand. Tonia followed and Miguel hesitated, then joined at the rear.

The flames had now reached the tops of the trees. As the fire intensified, the heat increased, sparking more trees as burning branches tumbled to the ground, scattering the wildlife. The smell of smoke blew in their direction, causing the group to cough.

Master Watanabe led them into the flaming forest. Entire trees raged in flames. Burning splinters blew in all directions, creating black smoke and ash that covered their faces. The heat was scorching, yet despite the almost overpowering heat they remained untouched by the flames. Miguel was terrified, making whimpering sounds with every step. He suddenly cried aloud in terror, dropped Tonia's hand to escape the flames, and ran straight towards Shigemasa's forces.

'What happened?' Father Joaquim asked, trying to see through the heavy smoke.

'He let go of my hand,' Tonia cried.

'We have to go back for him,' Joaquim yelled.

'They will take us, Father,' Watanabe replied. 'Is that what you want?'

'We can't leave him!'

'What about your plan to rescue the others?'

'God will show us another way. We *must* go back.'

'Are you sure?'

'What God has set His hand to do must triumph – even with setbacks.'

'Fine. I will lead us out.'

* * *

Miguel shook and squeezed his eyes shut as he lay in a pool of blood, captured by the samurai, who had beaten him savagely.

He covered his head with his hands as he continued to receive blows, but somehow it was still a relief from the choking smoke, heat, and soul-gripping terror of being burned to death. But the moment he glimpsed Father Joaquim and the other members of his group coming back for him, Miguel felt shame and guilt.

'There are the others,' a samurai yelled. A bloodcurdling cheer rose from their ranks.

CHAPTER THIRTY-EIGHT

Shigemasa's samurai beat Father Joaquim and his companions almost senseless. Blood oozed from a hundred wounds over their battered and bruised bodies. Dazed and almost unconscious, the quartet lay on the ground with their eyes closed as the enormous forest fire burned in the background.

'Get these canines up! It's time to put them back on their leash and rejoin the others,' Shigemasa commanded.

As samurai yanked Father Joaquim to his feet, Shigemasa walked over to face him. 'Did you really think you could escape me?'

Joaquim squinted at Shigemasa through the pain of his beating. The warlord stared back at him with contempt.

'There is nothing to escape from,' the priest said. 'Our faith is our freedom. You have no power over us.'

'Your words are empty,' the Daimyo replied as he struck Father Joaquim with his fist, knocking him to the ground.

Father Joaquim tasted blood and spat it away.

'You run because you're afraid. But no force in the world could prevent us from capturing you.'

'You underestimate the power of God.'

'And you underestimate me!' the Daimyo roared as he kicked Father Joaquim again. 'You will regret your escape, priest. I promise you.'

'I'm not worried. Our fate rests with God.'

'He does not exist. Where is your Jesus now?'

'Your sword may break me, but it cannot break the Word of our Father.'

'Watch your tongue, Christian dog. I am the daimyo of these lands. No force here is stronger than mine!'

'There has always been a force stronger than you, Daimyo. You're just not aware of it,' Father Joaquim answered.

'You live in the past, priest. There are no Christian daimyo any longer.'

'That is not the force I speak of.'

'Then who? These troublemaking ronin?' Shigemasa sneered at Master Watanabe. 'You filthy ronin. Have you been helping these Christians?'

'Yes.'

'Then we will crucify you alongside them. The Shogun despises ronin in league with Christians.'

Unperturbed, Master Watanabe returned Daimyo Shigemasa's gaze.

'Too much talking.' The Daimyo's son placed his hands on his hips. 'We need to punish them. Their escape has caused us great embarrassment.'

'We will punish them, Katsuie-san, rest assured,' the Daimyo replied.

'How?'

'For each escapee, we will kill a woman and a child from their village. They need to understand we will repay any escape by killing their dearest ones.'

'Please, no, Daimyo!' Father Joaquim cried out in distress. 'They have done nothing wrong. Take my life instead.'

'Silence, or I will cut out your tongue!'

'A clever idea, Father,' Katsuie added as he leaned forward. 'Let *them* feel the consequences.'

'These dogs almost cost me my lands. It is only fitting their beloved should die.'

'I want to be the one to deliver the message to Nagasaki,' Katsuie announced. 'Let me be the one to choose the women and children to perish.'

'I approve your request, son,' the Daimyo answered, smiling. 'Speed your way to Nagasaki, and deliver the message. Choose your victims well.'

CHAPTER THIRTY-NINE

1 July 1626
Suetsugu's Warehouse, Port of Nagasaki

'I don't think I can take much more,' Chinatsu confessed to her long-time friend Etsuko as samurai forced the women outside their warehouse prison.

Etsuko took Chinatsu's hand in hers. 'Stay strong. Maintain your faith. We can get through this.'

'But I'm so hungry, and I can't sleep.' Tears flowed down Chinatsu's cheeks. 'And my head hurts so much.'

Over the previous two days Deputy Suetsugu had chosen several women for exceptionally brutal torture in his effort to get them to recant. To achieve this goal, Suetsugu had set fire to Chinatsu's hair. Etsuko studied Chinatsu's blistered, hairless skull.

'Stay strong,' Etsuko answered. 'Remember what Father said: "They cannot do more to us than God permits."'

'But why does God permit so much torture? They even scorched my eyeballs. I can barely see.'

'Remember, our faith will get us through this storm. Our Lord is with—'

Chinatsu cried out in agony as a pole thumped both women on top of their heads. 'I told you whores to shut up! No speaking.' The guard rapped them once more.

As several women and most of the children cried, Deputy Suetsugu spoke up from the front of the courtyard, next to the water's edge: 'Welcome to another day of hell.'

Etsuko looked around at her fellow villagers. The psychological terrors they were suffering as they drifted in and out of sleep were every bit as horrible as the physical tortures they had endured over the last few days.

'Yesterday, I set hair on fire,' the Deputy declared. 'Who has had enough? Who would like to recant this useless faith?'

None of the women or children spoke.

'We can keep going until I have mutilated every one of you. I can remove your hands, your feet, your legs, your arms. I can cut off anything I want!'

Still no one spoke.

'Or I can burn or puncture you. Whom shall we start with today?' Suetsugu walked back and forth, sending fearful chills through each of the crouching women before him.

'What about her?' a senior guard asked as he pointed at Hatsumi, the prettiest woman among the villagers. 'I think we have ignored her so far because of her good looks.'

'You like her?' the Deputy asked with a chilling smile as he recalled forcing himself on her in private. Several other samurai smirked.

'Perhaps we can enjoy more private time with her,' another guard smirked.

'She's pretty, is she not?' He paused. 'Perhaps she is *too* pretty,' the deputy leered. 'Perhaps we should make her less attractive.'

'But, Lord Deputy, the guards enjoy spending time with her.'

'Nothing lasts forever. Bring her here.'

Guards dragged a weeping Hatsumi before the deputy.

The deputy withdrew a wooden cross from a bag and threw it on the ground before her. Suetsugu stared at Hatsumi with cold eyes. 'Step on it.'

'No, I will not.'

'Step on it or I will disfigure you,' the deputy shrieked.

Hatsumi cried but said nothing.

'Grab her and hold her tight,' Suetsugu said to his guards. 'Give me a knife.' The Deputy-Lieutenant grabbed Hatsumi and in one motion cut off her nose.

She screamed in shock and pain and then fainted, falling to the ground face-first, where she lay motionless as blood pooled beneath her.

Suetsugu wiped blood from his knife and pointed it towards the faces of the other women and children. 'This is what you get when you embrace this useless faith. Christianity will bring you nothing good. Recant this worthless faith before it brings you death!' The Deputy then threw Hatsumi's nose on top of her limp body. 'From this moment forward, the torture will get worse. I promise, you will all break soon.'

Leaving the warehouse compound, Deputy Suetsugu

commanded, 'Put these bitches back in their cage.'

As the doors slammed shut and several women rushed to aid Hatsumi, Etsuko stepped forward to address the group: 'Do you remember Father Joaquim's sermon last month from the book of Matthew?'

'Which one?' Ayame asked, holding her two small children close.

'Father Joaquim said, "Go to Jesus with your troubles."'

'I'm sorry, Etsuko. I'm too distraught to remember anything from last month.'

'Jesus said: "Come to me, all you who are weary and burdened, and I will give you rest."'

'Yes, I remember now.'

'I have prayed for the Lord to give us rest,' Etsuko said with a soft voice. 'I pray for our survival.'

CHAPTER FORTY

2 July 1626
Chikuzen Province, Kyushu

Shigemasa pushed his men and his prisoners without mercy on their return. So long as there was daylight and they could see, the Daimyo pushed forward with no rest for anyone.

Under most circumstances, the fastest route to the capital from the southern part of Kyushu took eleven days. But Shigemasa insisted on getting there faster, no doubt to impress the Shogun.

When they arrived in Kokura in the far north, they met up with the rest of the Christian prisoners and Father Joaquim discovered that all the men in his village were still alive. For that he was grateful. With slouching, emaciated bodies, the men looked exhausted. Pale white in complexion, they coughed non-stop; some spat blood. But despite their poor health, it pleased them that Father Joaquim and the catechists had also survived. As they viewed their friends again, they smiled with upturned faces and gleaming eyes.

Joaquim reminded himself of a passage from the Bible: *When you pass through the rivers, they will not sweep over you. When you walk through the fire, you will not be burned.*

As Joaquim reflected on its relevance, Miguel sidled up to him. Since Shigemasa had recaptured them, they had been forbidden to speak on pain of being beaten.

'I'm sorry, Father – for everything.'

'I know you are, Miguel, but you do not have to be.'

'We could have escaped, but I ruined everything.'

'Our village will survive. God has a plan for us. He will find another way.'

'How? Daimyo Shigemasa caught us.'

'I don't know, Miguel.'

'Soon, we will be in the Shogun's hands, and then it will be over for us.'

'These are tumultuous times, and your faith could well save your life.'

'I will try, Father.'

'Do not try, Miguel. Remember, faith *is* or it is not. Set your resolve and be unfailing about it.'

* * *

'Are the vessels ready?' Shigemasa asked, impatience clear in his question.

'We only have one large ship, Lord,' a retainer answered. 'We could not locate any more.'

'Our clan is travelling to the capital to see the Shogun, so fill the vessel with our most senior and experienced samurai and let us leave as soon as possible.'

'Yes, Lord.'

'How are our supplies? Do we have enough for the journey?'

'Yes, Lord. We raided several villages and took their food and water. Shall we load the Christians onto the vessel?'

Shigemasa contemplated the design and construction of a standard coast-hugging junk and considered where to stow the prisoners. Most shipbuilders in the region built junks of soft wood with multiple internal compartments, and bulkheads accessed by separate hatches and ladders. This would slow any flooding that might occur if the vessel was scuttled or damaged below the waterline; each compartment would be watertight.

'Yes, put them below deck.'

'At the bottom of the vessel, Lord?'

'Yes, I don't want them trying to escape by jumping overboard.' Nodding as he contemplated his reward, the Daimyo added, 'We need to keep these dogs alive. They are the Shogun's property to slaughter now.'

CHAPTER FORTY-ONE

2 July 1626
North Coast of Kyushu

Crammed into one of the junk's dark bulkheads, Father Joaquim and his three friends had no way of knowing the time of day.

Despite the darkness, one thing the prisoners could sense was that they were in rough waters, and despite its solid build, the junk pitched with great force.

In the past, Father Joaquim had travelled over this portion of water, from the north of Kyushu Island towards the capital city, albeit under more pleasant circumstances. The sea stretched 300 miles from Kyushu to Osaka, and comprised five distinct basins linked by channels. The waters of the Seto-Naikai were a beautiful emerald-green colour, their irregular coastline dotted with hundreds of small islands. To the west, the Inland Sea connected to the Sea of Japan. To the east, three straits connected the Inland Sea to the Pacific Ocean.

Despite being below deck, Joaquim recalled the Inland Sea as one of the most beautiful parts of Japan, affording breathtaking views of coastal scenery, small fishing villages, and hundreds of small volcanic and granite islands.

But Father Joaquim suspected it was not the scenery that drew Shigemasa to travel via the Inland Sea, it was speed. It was clear the Daimyo wanted to travel the 300-mile distance as quickly as possible, and it was equally clear Shigemasa had no desire to treat them well while he did it.

'This is despicable,' Tonia wailed, as samurai dumped waste into their compartment.

'I have no space to move. This is hell!' Miguel lamented. 'Why did I let my panic take over? I should have followed you through the fire.'

Watanabe said, 'People make choices, Miguel.'

'But why did I make such a bad choice?'

'Choices based on fear are seldom the best choice. *Love* is the key, Miguel, and then you must trust.'

'Words are easy,' Miguel answered, frustrated. 'It's easy to talk about trust out of harm's way. It is another thing to live it and walk into an open fire.'

'I agree, Miguel,' Father Joaquim replied as he nodded. 'It is when the fire is strongest that you need to trust the Lord the most.'

'I don't need to be saved. Someone needs to kill those damned samurai!'

'Revenge has no place in Christianity,' Joaquim said. Trying to empathize with him, the Jesuit thought, perhaps Miguel would have been better off if he'd stayed in Portugal. He just didn't seem strong enough for the mission in Japan.

* * *

Katsuie Shigemasa approached the edge of Nagasaki. Through the dark, he pushed his horse to its limits, desperate to deliver his father's instructions to Deputy-Lieutenant Suetsugu as soon as possible. With feverish impatience, he forced his horse forward in the dark with fast jerky movements. With cloudy skies and no moonlight, young Katsuie could not locate the correct path up the mountain. Impetuously he decided not to wait until daylight, but to make his own path, knowing Nagasaki lay just on the opposite side.

Those damned Christians! We should just kill them all! Why stop at a few women and children? Katsuie thought. His horse resisted his forward commands, making the young man irritable and causing him additional frustration. He urged him on with kicks.

Again, Katsuie's horse refused to climb the steep track. 'Get up there, you stupid beast!' Katsuie yelled. 'Get up there!'

The horse attempted to turn around.

With all his strength, Katsuie lashed the horse with his whip as he kicked its side, forcing it up over the steep ground. As the horse and its rider reached the summit the animal lost its balance, and, along with Katsuie, fell onto the jagged rocks at the base of the path. The horse died at once. Katsuie, meanwhile, landed on top of the animal, bounced off, then smashed his head against more rocks. He lay unconscious and hidden on the dark side of the mountain.

CHAPTER FORTY-TWO

7 July 1626
Osaka, Settsu Province, Honshu

'Come on, get up and move, worthless beasts!'

Father Joaquim forced his stiff muscles to move and reached over to give Master Watanabe a helping hand, imagining the difficulty older villagers might experience as they, too, sought to move their aching bodies.

'Don't make us wait! Get up and move, dogs!'

The prisoners made their way to the top deck, squinting at the harshness of the bright morning sunlight for the first time in five days. Father Joaquim's eyes began to adjust and he tried to verify that all the men of the village were still present and accounted for.

'March them to the main town square and wait for me there,'

the Daimyo commanded. 'From the town square, we will prepare them for their death march.'

Dozens of samurai tied the Christians with ropes and shackles as Shigemasa strode with a triumphant gait into the heart of the city, followed by his highest-ranking retainers. The march through the streets of Osaka towards the main town square began, punctuated by whippings and beatings.

The sight of the Christian procession shocked Osaka's residents. Christianity had been outlawed in Japan more than a decade earlier and most of the city's children had never seen a foreigner before, their surprise evident by their open mouths and bulging eyes. Some toddlers ran to their mothers out of fear. In every direction, residents gasped at the march and stared in astonishment. Others shuffled back a step or two as the procession approached, not wanting to get caught up in what was happening. But Father Joaquim thought he saw empathy on the faces of many.

Among the crowd were dozens of what the priest thought were fellow Christians who seemed to bow to them discreetly, or gaze at them with sympathy. But most of the residents, either out of fear for their own safety or feigned disguise, threw waste at the Christians as they shuffled past.

When they arrived in the main town square, samurai herded them into a small circle and instructed them to await the Daimyo, who was visiting Osaka's city hall.

Shigemasa, with his senior retainers and samurai carrying buckets of red paint, soon arrived, accompanied by high-ranking Osaka officials.

'Stand them up!' Shigemasa bellowed.

Osaka's governor entered the square, surrounded by high-ranking Bakufu officials.

'These Christians are criminals of the Empire,' Shigemasa shouted to the growing crowd. 'I will escort them to Edo, but first we will paint them red so all Osaka and all Japan will see them as criminals of the Empire.'

Dozens of samurai grabbed large paint brushes and slopped red paint onto the Christians, splashing it into their eyes, noses, ears, and mouths.

'I paint them red so all can see that death and torture await them in the capital!' the Daimyo roared.

'Let this be a warning to any Christians among you,' Osaka's governor added as he stepped forward. 'Recant your wretched faith before it is too late! Daimyo Matsukura Shigemasa will march these Christians to Edo, where the Shogun will torture and kill them. Who among you would like to join them?' The Governor gazed at the gathered residents. 'Who among you would like to own the belongings of any Christians in your midst? If you alert us to Christians, you may have their homes and their belongings. The Shogun will also pay in silver to those who inform us of hidden Christians. Who wants to become rich?'

Despite the mounting fear, no one spoke. Frustrated, the Governor approached a poor resident. 'You! Would you like to become wealthy?'

'Yes, Governor, I would,' the old man replied, 'but I do not know of any Christians in Osaka. It has been many years since I have heard of any.'

'What about you?' the Governor pointed to a woman standing nearby.

'Christians disappeared long ago, Governor. If there are any left, they live in secret.'

Father Joaquim watched as the Governor walked back to face the Daimyo. The Governor said a few words to Shigemasa, bowed, and then walked away.

'Let the death march to Edo begin!' Shigemasa yelled. He signalled to his samurai. 'Let this be the last day Osaka sees these mutts alive!'

The samurai grabbed the Christians by their ropes and dragged them down the street, causing some to fall in the process.

'Get up!' Shigemasa shouted. 'You cannot stall your fate. You will all experience the most painful crucifixion known to man, and nothing can stop it.'

'What will they do to us in Edo, Father?' Miguel's hands shook and his shoulders tightened.

'I don't know, Miguel. But the Lord walks with us.'

'How can God allow this to happen?' Tonia asked, as tears ran down her cheeks.

'You must have faith during life's storms, Tonia. That is how you know it is real.'

CHAPTER FORTY-THREE

13 July 1626
Edo, Musashi Province

Shigemasa enjoyed showcasing his importance as he led his procession of samurai and prisoners along the Tokaido Road and past a myriad of other travellers. From well-connected government officials to the poorest peasants, they lined the busy gateway to the grand capital city.

Shigemasa puffed out his chest and raised his head high, marching with a macho strut, proud to be an important daimyo from the south. As his swagger continued, more and more people along the road took notice of him. *Let them admire and revere me,* he thought, as though he were the Emperor.

The procession eventually arrived at the main *seki* on the city's outskirt. These checkpoints, set up at key strategic locations, were barriers on the city's periphery, where guards stopped all travellers for interrogation. By law, samurai or other individuals with special privileges were the only people allowed to carry weapons into the capital. In part, the *seki* checkpoints ensured no armed ronin entered the city.

Daimyo Shigemasa had a great deal of autonomy to govern his lands as he wished. However, once he entered the Kanto region – the area surrounding the capital of Edo – his activities were under the Shogun's firm control.

As the procession approached the main *seki*, Shigemasa moved to the front of the party. His flag bearer proudly displayed the Daimyo's family crest, his *mon*, denoting the prominence of his clan.

At the sight of the flag, several guards left their post to greet them. 'Daimyo Shigemasa, welcome to Edo,' the senior guard said. 'We have been expecting you for some time.'

'We encountered delays in our journey, but thank you. I present these Christian criminals as a gift to the Shogun, to do with as he sees fit.'

The senior guard inspected the prisoners, still painted red and standing in a long line. Following their arduous journey from Osaka, they looked haggard, with sagging postures and bent necks. Standing with his arms crossed and head tilted, the senior guard stared at Father Joaquim and his catechists. 'One of our riders will speed word to the Shogun of their arrival.'

'And where shall we take these dogs?'

'Two guards will escort your procession to the prison.'

'When does the Shogun wish to view them?'

'Soon,' the guard answered. 'Perhaps you may wish to visit the pleasure quarters and enjoy *yūjo* while you wait, Daimyo?'

'I will,' Shigemasa replied with a smile.

The two promised guards led the group through the checkpoint and towards the Tama River, which they needed to cross to reach the city. The Tama flowed from the mountains in the west down into Edo Bay. Although not a large river, it was too deep to cross on foot or horseback, so they had to take the half-dozen ferries ready to shuttle the prisoners into the capital.

The journey across gave them a few moments to rest and anticipate the hell they knew awaited them.

Joaquim marvelled at the city's grandeur. Everywhere he looked, he saw thousands of people. This was the biggest city in the world, he thought – much larger than any European city he'd been to. Large buildings appeared modern in design and were located everywhere. As he observed his fellow prisoners, it was apparent they had the same conflicted feelings: facing imminent death, they could not help but admire the magnificent city. Joaquim and most of the prisoners knew that while Kyoto, home to Japan's imperial family, remained the nation's formal capital, Edo was the centre of political and military power.

The trip did not take long. The guards and their prisoners stepped off the ferries and made their way past citizens who stopped to jeer and insult them, including Buddhist monks in Ikegami Honmonji on Edo's southern limit. The Shogun's checkpoint guards led Shigemasa's procession towards the centre of the city. All the while, the Daimyo's samurai continued to insult and beat the prisoners.

Joaquim observed the many houses of prostitution lining the main road they travelled. Many of the official lodgings along the road had been turned into brothels, catering to government officials and merchants.

As the group reached the Shitamachi area of the city, Joaquim and his companions were amazed at the sheer number of buildings and people. Because of general Shogun paranoia, massive ramparts and moats surrounded his castle grounds. This area, known as the Yamanote, also consisted of sizeable mansions of the feudal daimyo. The Shogun required these daimyos' families to live in Edo as part of the *sankin kōtai* system, which mandated that all Japan's feudal daimyo made annual journeys to Edo. The purpose was for the Shogun to keep watch over the daimyo and prevent any of them plotting against him. In addition, the *sankin kōtai* system also required the daimyos' families to live in Edo year-round. Should any daimyo consider raising arms against the Shogun, the Shogun could seize their families as hostages.

Finally, the lengthy and distressing parade through the city arrived in the Eta district.

'Straight ahead!' one guard yelled, commanding the group to make their way down a filthy narrow street. 'Do you see that building at the end?'

None of the exhausted Christians responded as they beheld an abominable, decrepit structure before them.

'That will be your last home before your execution.'

CHAPTER FORTY-FOUR

13 July 1626
Shogun's North-eastern Prison, Edo,
Musashi Province

The prison chamber smelled even more rank than the prison in Omura. Dead and near-dead bodies were strewn about, while healthier prisoners fought each other, often to the death, for food and more space.

It was not long before the newcomers settled themselves into nooks and crannies, by walls if possible, and alongside familiar companions if not.

Despite the misery, a few prisoners exhibited kindness amid the horror. One such, Akihiko, was a young man who lay motionless on the floor. Despite his extreme pain and loss, he often offered his limited water and food to anyone who needed either, including Tonia, Miguel, and Master Watanabe, who sat beside him, giving him aid.

'I see the misery in your eyes,' Father Joaquim said. He spoke to those around him, but his remarks were addressed to anyone who would hear. 'You think this is the end, do you not? All of you?'

A few weak mumbles and groans answered his trenchant question.

'Well, let me tell you,' Father Joaquim continued, 'you are wrong!'

An old farmer from the village spoke up: 'Why? Why are we wrong? What hope do we have now?'

Joaquim said, 'Man's frailty is God's opportunity.'

'Your words are empty!' an angry young man shouted. 'Only death awaits us now. Every person in this prison will die!'

'Who are you?' Joaquim asked. He squinted, trying to see through the dark towards the back of the prison. 'Why are you here?'

'My name is Susumu,' answered the agitated young man. 'I am a thief.'

'Why do you steal?'

'To survive.'

'Confess your sins, Susumu-san. Give your life to Jesus, and He will save you.'

'Don't waste your breath on me, foreign priest. I don't believe in your God.'

'Do you feel death is on our doorstep and things cannot get worse?'

'Yes. Only death awaits me now.'

'Then believe. Belief will set you free.'

'Are you insane, priest? Do you have any idea where you are? You need to wake up. We're all in a cell, condemned to death in the Shogun's prison!'

'Then you have no reason not to believe,' Father Joaquim repeated. 'Believe the Lord will help us, and see what happens.'

'Why?'

'Because you risk nothing and might gain the world.'

With those last words, the prison sat in silence.

* * *

Inside the small meeting room, Shogun Iemitsu knelt atop a plush golden pillow as he awaited the Daimyo. Owing to the formal nature of the meeting, he was accompanied by members of the Roju cabinet, who knelt in a short perpendicular line off to one side of him.

As Daimyo Shigemasa entered, the room became silent. He dropped to his knees and bowed deeply to the Shogun. Next, he crawled to the centre of the room to face the Shogun.

'Your arrival pleases us,' the Shogun declared, with no great conviction. Iemitsu glared at Shigemasa, who looked sheepish, sprawled out before him. 'We have been expecting you for quite some time.'

'Thank you, Lord. I know I should have arrived earlier.'

'And why are you late, Daimyo?'

'I am sorry, Lord. We had a problem. The priest escaped. It took a short while to recapture him.'

'You captured a priest on your fief and then lost him days later?'

'I am sorry, Lord. He escaped from Omura prison while I was collecting more gifts for you.'

'That is sloppy and negligent. Is this how you conduct your affairs?'

'No, Lord. We tend to our duties with great care. It will never happen again. I executed the negligent prison master myself.'

'I am divided on this issue,' the Shogun declared. His eyes were hard and expressionless as he viewed the Daimyo.

'What do you mean, Lord Shogun?'

'On the one hand, it pleases me you have captured a hidden Christian village. I will enjoy crucifying them. However, I am displeased that such a village still existed on your lands.'

'Yes, Lord. Their discovery surprised me as well.'

'This makes me wonder whether you are fit to govern your lands, Daimyo.'

'It will never happen again.'

'I will tell you what worries me, Daimyo.'

'What, Lord?'

'If there is one hidden Christian village on your lands, there may be more.'

'No, Lord. We do all we can to catch Christian mongrels on my lands.'

'It is not enough. Their cult remains. You will not stay in Edo. You will return home to unearth more Christians!'

'But Lord, is it not customary for daimyo to spend time in Edo before returning home?'

'You have humiliated yourself, Daimyo Shigemasa. We need to rebuke you.'

'I am sorry, Lord.'

'When you return to your lands, I want you to consider one thing – whether you are fit to remain as daimyo of your domain. We will evaluate you with greater scrutiny now.'

'Yes, Lord.'

'Remember, I am not averse to giving your lands to someone else.'

'That will not be necessary, Lord Shogun. I will annihilate Christianity from my lands.'

'A vessel is waiting for you now. Return home at once, and do not fail me again!'

With a flushed face, Shigemasa stared at the floor. Once more, he bowed to the Shogun and crawled backwards out of the grand chamber. After he exited the room, he was consumed by anger as he frowned and thrust his chest out. Nostrils flaring and grinding his teeth, he stormed down the hall, bent on hunting down and destroying more Christians on his lands.

CHAPTER FORTY-FIVE

14 July 1626

In a trance-like state, Father Joaquim saw a surreal apparition of his Jesuit hero, Saint Francis Xavier. The saint handed him a sword that looked like Master Yamaguchi's and in the background he saw the Shogun's *mon* fall to the ground.

Joaquim blinked open his eyes and as he sought to focus them he saw Master Watanabe looking at him curiously.

'You appear confused, Father, or perhaps unsure. What is it? Did you have a strange dream?'

'I did, my friend. And it was a powerful one.' The Jesuit shook his head to help clear it, and rubbed his eyes.

'What was it about, Father?'

He hesitated for a moment and scratched his head before

answering. 'I dreamed that I am supposed to challenge the Shogun.'

'How?'

'I don't know.' Father Joaquim shrugged and shook his head again. 'Perhaps it was just nonsense, or fantasy.'

'Do not disregard it, Father. Dreams are a way the Source speaks to us.'

'You mean a way that *God* speaks to us.'

'I can call Him God if doing so helps our conversation.'

Father Joaquim looked around the cell at the other prisoners, most still asleep. 'But what am I supposed to challenge the Shogun about?'

'I don't know, Father. It's your dream. But God has spoken to you through it.'

'Perhaps God wants me to challenge the Shogun's closest Buddhists monks to refute their faith.'

'I'm not sure, Father, but the Creator does not favour one faith over another.'

'That is a point about which we will have to disagree, my friend. Jesus told His followers He was the only way to the Father. If I believed that all faiths were the same, I would have had no reason to bring my faith in Christ here.'

'Hmm …' Master Watanabe leaned on his elbow, pondering Father Joaquim's words. 'One day we will have to discuss that thought in more detail. But for now, let's examine your dream and what you should do about it.'

'What do you think I should do?'

'You must trust your intuition on the matter.'

'But this is critical, Master Watanabe. All our lives are at stake. An entire village depends on me.'

'It matters not. The principles are the same.'

'What makes you so sure?'

'Did you not ask God for help, Father?'

'Yes.'

'Well, perhaps he sent me to help you. We are all part of His plan, are we not?'

Father Joaquim took a moment to consider. 'And what about your role in this, my friend? I have seen your abilities. Why can you not use your powers to free us?'

'I am only a guide, nothing more, to help remind you of who you are.'

'And who is that?'

'A small, but powerful part of Almighty God,' responded Master Watanabe. 'Does your Bible not say God created man in his own image?'

'Yes.'

'And elsewhere, does it not say, "The Lord thy God in the midst of thee is mighty; He will save?"'

'Yes, the Book of Zephaniah says that.'

'Then it is time for you to *know* that God lives in you, and that because of this, you have *His* powers.'

The rhythmic thud of footfalls interrupted the men's conversation. A key loudly opened a lock and the prison door flew open.

'The Shogun wants to interrogate the priest, his foreign aides, and the ronin who helped them escape,' a prison guard shouted. 'Come out at once.'

Father Joaquim emerged through the prison door, followed by Master Watanabe, Tonia, and Miguel.

'Prepare for the end,' the prison guard declared. 'You are about to meet the Shogun.'

CHAPTER FORTY-SIX

14 July 1626
Shogun's Castle

'Strip the mongrels and scrub them down. Don't stop until you get rid of their stench,' a senior retainer ordered several samurai.

'Including the woman?'

'She stinks too.'

'I'm sorry, Tonia,' Father Joaquim called out. Dozens of samurai descended on them, ripping their clothes off. As soon as samurai undressed the three men, they made them stand a few feet apart from one another. The samurai who stripped Tonia took longer, laughing as they moved her towards the three male prisoners. The men watched helplessly as guards pinned them against a wall.

Samurai poured cold water over each of the naked prisoners.

All but Master Watanabe shook from the shock of the icy water. Then servants used brooms to scrub the prisoners, from head to toe, before they splashed them again with water to rinse their bodies.

Each was then tossed a towel and their clothes.

Once dressed, Joaquim and his companions were dragged at knife-point to a guarded side room next to the grand chamber, to wait. The spiky knives scratched their necks. They sat on the floor in silence as a half-dozen samurai stared contemptuously at them.

The order came soon enough. 'Rise, canines. It is time.'

Miguel and Tonia blinked and fidgeted as they arose. Miguel's eyes shifted in panic and his breathing became rapid and shallow. The pair had little time to compose themselves as samurai shoved them down a long hallway towards the main entrance of the grand chamber. The doors were flung open and they were pushed inside.

'Bow, you dogs. Bow before my presence!' the Shogun shouted as they entered the room. Before they could obey, the blunt edges of samurai swords pounded them from behind, forcing them to kneel.

Joaquim was awestruck at the grandeur of the chamber. The Shogun had filled the large hall with high-ranking officials, samurai, retainers, and other prominent members of his regime. From the edge of the floor, the priest looked up at the Shogun. He was shocked by his youth, and then he noted dark eyes that were abnormally small and sunken into his skull. He only looked for a moment.

'Place them in the centre of the room!' Samurai obeyed the Shogun's command. 'So you are the one who has who caused all this trouble.' The ruler glowered at Father Joaquim.

'I do not know of what you speak,' Joaquim replied.

'The priest who escaped,' the Shogun sneered. 'Your escape caused our Kyushu authorities great embarrassment.'

Neither Father Joaquim nor the other prisoners responded.

'We will not make this long,' the Shogun avowed. 'You are all criminals of the Empire and we will torture and execute you for your crimes.'

'Of what crimes do you speak?' Joaquim asked.

'Do not mock me, priest. We banished Christians and your stupid beliefs more than a decade ago. You have defied our laws by hiding here and spreading your filth. You can reduce your torture, however ...' – the Shogun stopped to glance at his Roju cabinet members before resuming – '*if* you tell us where other Christians and priests are hiding.'

Again, no one responded.

'You can also reduce your torture by telling us which factions of ronin helped you escape Omura prison.'

'I think we differ about who is committing crimes in Japan,' Joaquim said. 'It's *you* who have committed a crime.'

The Shogun was taken by surprise. 'Against whom?'

'Against God.' Joaquim dared to look into the Shogun's eyes as he answered. '*You* have deprived the people of Japan of His Word and the ministry of His servants. *You* have denied the people the freedom to know God. And *you* have done so for greater power, control, and self-glorification.'

'How dare you speak out against me? I am the Shogun of all Japan! Beat him now!' Iemitsu's samurai complied.

'Of all the Christians in my possession,' the Shogun declared when the samurai had finished, '*you* shall suffer the most. You will *beg* me to kill you.' Iemitsu's nostrils flared as his eyes narrowed into his head.

'I have no fear,' Joaquim replied as he wiped blood from his nose. 'You should be more worried than me.'

'I should worry?' the Shogun roared. 'Of what?'

'"For the Lord knoweth the way of the righteous: but the way of the ungodly shall perish."'

'Do not preach your Christian filth here, priest! This is *my* castle!'

'I'm not afraid.' Joaquim stood with shoulders back, staring defiantly at the Shogun.

'Then why did you run away like a coward on Kyushu?'

'You misunderstand our intentions. We will never leave Japan. Our mission *will* survive here.'

'How dare you speak to me in such a tone? Give this priest another beating!'

Samurai again mercilessly pounded Father Joaquim. As he lay on the floor, gathering his wits, despite the blood in his eyes Joaquim stared up at the ceiling and saw the Shogun's family crest hanging from the rafters. He pulled himself upright and wiped his face with a sleeve. 'Your samurai have given me a thrashing,' Father Joaquim said.

'Do you wish another?'

'They can deliver a beating to captives, but how brave are they facing a man with a sword?'

'Tokugawa samurai are the bravest in all Japan. It was through battle my grandfather became Shogun.'

'Good,' Father Joaquim replied. 'Then perhaps you will accept a challenge.'

'What kind of challenge?'

Father Joaquim stood. 'A fighting contest.'

At first only the Shogun laughed, but soon the room was cackling along with him.

Joaquim interrupted the laughter: 'Are you not interested in discovering the locations of more hidden Christians?'

'What?'

'I hold the master list of all Christians in Japan, including foreign priests and clergy.'

The Shogun held up a hand and the chamber fell silent. 'What did you say?'

'I said, I offer you the whereabouts of all hidden Christians.'

'In exchange for what?'

'In exchange for our freedom: the four of us and all Christian prisoners in Edo prison.'

For a moment, Father Joaquim thought of the village's women and children in Nagasaki, but knew their release required an enormous amount of unlikely coordination on the Shogun's behalf. In his heart, he knew an opportunity would present itself later to effect their liberation.

'Why should I agree to such a contest? Now that I know you have this list, I can torture it out of you.'

'I suspect you already know that torture will not make me speak. And if I die under torture, the master list and your opportunity will die with me.'

'Perhaps we will put your bravado to the test and dismember you slowly.'

'Do you have so little confidence in your samurai?' Joaquim made direct eye contact, goading the Shogun. 'Are you really afraid your samurai can not defeat a *gaijin* Christian?'

Samurai murmured loudly at the impertinence of the suggestion. The Shogun glanced around the room and saw that many of his samurai looked unsettled. 'What kind of honour is there in trying to squeeze information from me that I will give freely if I am defeated? Are the samurai of the Tokugawa so afraid?'

A small tic began near the Shogun's left eye. He raised his hand to quell his samurai's agitated grumbles. 'Silence!'

Turning to face Joaquim, he declared, 'You *will* die, priest. No one challenges the Tokugawa clan and lives. But your master list of hidden Christians interests me, if you can be trusted.'

'We all die. It is how that counts.'

The Shogun turned aside to quietly consult with his council.

'Shall we accept the challenge?' he asked, gritting his teeth.

'I think we must, Lord,' whispered Inaba Masakatsu, one of the Roju cabinet members. 'The priest challenged you in front of your men. I think you *must* accept the challenge for the honour of your samurai and for the Tokugawa name.'

'I agree,' added Naito Tadashige, another cabinet member. 'The men will feel dishonoured and shamed if we do not accept.'

'But it's ludicrous!' the Shogun replied. 'The foreign priest and his aides stand no chance.'

'Why does he wish to fight?' another member asked. 'He would challenge us only if he thinks he can win.'

'Perhaps he believes the ronin will fight *for* him. Perhaps the ronin is very skilled,' Naito said.

'Then we will not let the ronin fight. We can control the rules of the contest. So shall we accept?' the Shogun repeated.

'What could be greater than the master list, Lord?'

'What if he is killed before he has a chance to tell us, Lord?'

'We will extract it from him before he takes his last breath in battle,' the Shogun said.

One after the other, each Roju cabinet member nodded in agreement.

The Shogun turned to Father Joaquim: 'It will be a pleasure to watch my samurai dismember your body, moments before you surrender the master list. We accept your pathetic challenge.'

Throughout the chamber samurai roared their approval.

Father Joaquim challenged the Shogun, his gaze direct and unflinching. 'If I win, how do I know you will keep your word? How do I know we will gain our freedom?'

The Shogun's face reddened as he clenched his fists. 'Do not insult me, priest. A samurai's word is stronger than metal.'

'Then we agree to the contest?' Joaquim answered.

'Consider this your death, priest.'

Joaquim nodded and bowed. 'Daimyo Shigemasa took a valuable sword from us on Kyushu. We request the return of this sword for our contest.' Joaquim banked on their former teacher's sword helping his catechists recall their training, and channel the spirit of Master Yamaguchi.

'Do you think a sword can save you, Christian dog?'

'If your samurai can choose their weapons, so should we.'

'If you knew anything about *budo*, priest, you would know that battles are not won by swords, but by the skill of the samurai who hold them.'

'So you do not object?'

'Use your sword,' the Shogun said. 'It will make no difference.'

The Shogun stood to address his retainers. 'Prepare the Budokan at once. We will slaughter these Christians tonight!'

CHAPTER FORTY-SEVEN

14 July 1626
Shogun's Budokan

Miguel said, 'The Shogun will bring his best warriors. Do you think we can win?'

Father Joaquim inched towards the nervous young man. 'Look at me, Miguel. I do not *think* we can. I *know* we can.'

Miguel sighed. 'Why are you so sure?'

'Because we are fighting for something important – our lives and those of our friends. We were trained by the best, Miguel. Master Yamaguchi was one of the finest warriors in Japan, and a great teacher.'

'But that was training. This is real life – life or death!'

'You're right. That was only training. But let us not forget the most important thing.'

'What?'

'Faith that the Lord is with us.' Joaquim sat down next to Miguel. 'We asked for His help, and He has answered. Just *believe*.'

'I do believe, Father.'

'If you believed, Miguel, you would not doubt the outcome. You would *know* He will answer.'

Miguel clutched his arms and stopped paying attention as he focused on the thunderous sounds that boomed from the main hall of the Budokan. Although he could not be sure, he thought he heard the Shogun's samurai chanting and stomping their feet.

'The end is near. Listen to the ominous noise coming from the hall next door. Others are being tortured and killed even as we sit here.'

'But *we* are not. Do you expect the Lord to solve your problems for you, Miguel, or give *you* the opportunity to solve them? Don't let fear prevent you from trusting God, Miguel. Have the courage to trust Him.'

'I will do my best, Father.

'When you feel weak or doubtful, rely on God for your st—'

The door swung open and a dozen samurai entered the room. 'Get up!' the lead samurai shouted.

As soon as they arose, the samurai beat them to the ground. As they beat Tonia and Miguel, the catechists cried out in distress. All of a sudden, Miguel shrieked as a samurai hammered his hand repeatedly with a sword handle. Worried about his young catechists, Father Joaquim tried to absorb most of the blows himself, on their behalf, but his efforts only seemed to attract additional rounds of beatings. As the wounded prisoners lay on the floor, the warriors stomped first on their bodies, and then their hands and feet. 'Now you are ready to meet the Shogun's fighters.' The lead samurai grinned.

'Get up!' he shouted. 'Don't worry. We will not beat you again. This time, the Shogun's warriors will do it.' Giving Father Joaquim one more kick to his back, the samurai repeated, 'Get up, I said!'

But the prisoners could not rise. Losing patience, the samurai hauled them to their feet.

'We must make you look pretty,' said the lead samurai. He wiped the blood from their faces. 'We cannot have you look unsightly before you leave this world.'

Father Joaquim looked at his young aides. 'Are you okay, my friends?'

'My hand, Father,' Miguel replied. 'I think it's broken.'

As the four were shoved into the main hall of the Shogun's Budokan, the noise was thunderous. Hundreds of Shogun Iemitsu's samurai stomped on floorboards and clapped their hands. As he looked around, Joaquim felt intimidated as the entire hall stared at their group, willing their demise. His heart pounded as the vibrating floors under the samurais' stomping feet caused his body to shake and tremble. The noise was deafening.

Up at the front of the Budokan the Shogun, his father, Hidetada, and the entire Roju cabinet sat on an elevated platform from which the Shogun would run the contest. Adjacent to the front podium and running along both sides of the training mats, Joaquim observed large spectator stands holding hundreds of samurai, keen to witness the bloodshed.

As he gazed around the massive hall, he and his friends were pulled over to the left side of the room, where the Shogun forced them to kneel. As the Shogun raised his right hand, the hall became silent.

'Welcome to the Budokan, where you will die!' the Shogun

shouted from the front.

Straightaway, the hall again erupted with cheers, yells, and loud rhythmic foot stomps.

'Silence!' the Shogun ordered. 'I will now read the rules of the contest.' He surveyed the hall before resting his eyes on Joaquim. 'One: There will be three fights, one for each Christian dog. Two: Each fight will be to the death, but in the priest's case, not until he has divulged the information. Three: I choose the order and the adversaries for the fights. Four: The winning side of the overall contest will have at least two victories, although I doubt the foreign mongrels will win even one.'

Again, the roar of hundreds of samurai resounded through the hall.

'Give them their sword,' the Shogun instructed a retainer before turning his attention back to Joaquim. 'After your deaths, your beautiful sword will look splendid in my collection. Now, prepare to be gutted!'

Inspired by the Shogun, the Budokan erupted once more in an exhilarated fury, no doubt intended to provoke and taunt the small group. Everywhere the priest looked, he could see Iemitsu's samurai gesturing obscenities and threats.

The samurai stomped their feet enthusiastically and clapped loudly.

Joaquim reassured his young aides. '*Know* that our freedom is at hand.'

'Yes, Father,' Tonia answered.

'Do you see this sword?' the padre asked. 'It belonged to our *sensei* and dear friend, Master Yamaguchi. Let this sword remind you of our training with him. When you use it, remember him.'

Tonia nodded.

'And remember the most important thing – the Lord stands with you.'

CHAPTER FORTY-EIGHT

14 July 1626

'The first death shall be your woman!' the Shogun roared from the podium.

Tonia spoke to Father Joaquim. 'Any final advice, Father?'

'Remain calm and trust in God. Let Him inspire your movements. What technique do you see in your mind's eye, Tonia?'

For a moment, Tonia closed her eyes and visualized the predominant technique she would use to defeat her opponent. It was a technique she had practised over and again under the patient instruction of Master Yamaguchi. Now all she had to do was hope an opportunity would arise to use it.

'I see defence followed by a counter-attack.'

'Good. There is wisdom in that. Follow your intuition. Your opponent will try to impress the Budokan and will come out strong. Focus on defence in the beginning, and protect yourself. When an opening comes, strike!'

'Do not waste our time, woman!' the Shogun shouted. 'Get on the mat!'

Father Joaquim extended Master Yamaguchi's sword to Tonia as she stepped onto the mat, where she bowed with respect to receive it before jogging to the centre of the mat to face the glare of hundreds of ruthless samurai.

'I call Akane-san!' the Shogun bellowed.

The noise level rose at once, deafening in its intensity. A large, barbaric figure emerged from the corner of the Budokan. At a distance, Father Joaquim thought the samurai was a huge man, but as the figure moved closer he saw it was a woman – by far the largest and most powerful woman he had ever seen.

Joaquim saw that Tonia was praying as she scrutinized her opponent.

'You will bow to the Shogun and then to each other,' the official on the mat announced. 'Then you will fight … until one of you is dead.'

The second the formalities were over, Akane charged at Tonia, taking massive swings with her razor-sharp sword. Tonia felt the rush of air on her cheek as the blade searched for its target. Within seconds, Akane backed Tonia into the corner of the mat, where she defended with quick jerky movements against the flurry of attacks. With each aggressive strike, Tonia raised her sword and blocked the attack, creating a fusillade of clacking sounds as the blades clashed. As she defended, Joaquim saw signs of weakness in

Tonia's enormous opponent and he became frustrated she was not doing more to counter-attack.

Akane took another rumbling charge at Tonia, this time forcing her to the opposite side of the mat. Once more, Tonia eluded the series of strikes by a thin margin, two of which missed her throat by inches. But suddenly Tonia seemed to relax and start to take control, as Joaquim noted that she was getting a measure of her opponent's technique. Now feeling more confident in her defence, Tonia allowed her training to kick in as she gathered her strength and refocused on her own abilities.

Surprised that Tonia had not died yet and could fend off her attacks, Akane seemed perplexed as she shook her head, glancing at the Shogun in bewilderment. The momentary lapse of attention was all Tonia needed. She slashed at Akane, cutting her wrist deeply and drawing a great deal of blood.

Akane shrieked in pain and almost dropped her sword. The Budokan went silent.

'Slaughter that mutt!' the Shogun yelled at Akane, as she tried to refocus. Akane raised her sword for a third round of strikes at Tonia, but her deep wound weakened her technique and everyone in the Budokan could see it. As she tried to raise her sword again, Tonia deflected it and slashed open her opponent's right arm, causing her opponent to drop her sword.

Akane screamed as blood spurted from her bicep. Tonia seized the moment and raised her sword. With a decisive sideways movement, she slashed it through Akane's exposed throat, severing her oesophagus. Blood spurted in all directions as the huge woman's shriek was cut short. The mountain of a woman teetered, then she fell to the mat with a thud.

The hall was silent. The shocked Shogun pounded his fist on the floor in frustration, baring his teeth and breathing heavily. 'Remove her!' he roared. 'I have never seen such luck.'

As samurai dragged Akane's corpse off the mat it left a red smear behind it. They threw the body into a corner. The Shogun yelled, 'Young foreign boy, get on the mat! I promise you will not have such luck.'

'What do I do, Father?' Miguel asked. 'I cannot fight with a broken hand. What can I do?'

'Do you remember the sword-removal technique Master Yamaguchi taught us?'

'I think so.'

'Don't *think*, Miguel. Look at me! *Know*. Remember the sword-removal technique! You must remove his sword and then defeat him with your hands.'

'Get on the mat, boy!' the Shogun roared.

'But what about my hand, Father?' With an ashen face and a trembling chin, Miguel remained motionless, laden with uncertainty.

The Shogun's samurai shoved him to the centre of the mat.

'Suzuki-san!' the Shogun shouted.

An athletic, dangerous-looking samurai emerged from the back of the Budokan and walked forward.

The Budokan erupted as the samurai in attendance chanted: 'Su-zu-ki! Su-zu-ki! Su-zu-ki!'

Suzuki strode powerfully towards the mat. As he arrived, he bowed twice to the Shogun, who returned the gesture with a nod and a grin. Next, Suzuki turned and bowed to Miguel, whom he gazed at with a cold, dark stare.

As they watched the way Suzuki moved, Joaquim and Watanabe knew at once that Miguel was outmatched by a considerable margin. As they looked at one another, the priest felt guilty for getting Miguel involved in the contest. If he died today at least it would be quick, rather than a lingering and painful end in a stinking, cold, dark dungeon.

Miguel returned the bow, his nerves on edge, evidenced by the shaking of his hands as he gripped his sword. Then, to Joaquim's dismay, Miguel ignored his suggestions and charged at Suzuki. Miguel used up his energy in a short period of time, and exhausted himself by swinging his sword from side to side with little purpose and skill. Suzuki defended the attacks effortlessly as though he were playing with a child, blocking each attack with perfect poise and precision.

With feverish, over-bright eyes, Miguel charged again, striking wildly at his opponent with large, jerky body blows, but to no avail. As Miguel raised his sword again and thrust down, Suzuki moved out of the way and countered with a tremendous blow to Miguel's wrist, slicing through the bone and severing his hand.

Miguel screamed as his hand dropped to the mat along with his sword, blood spurting from his arm.

Grinning, Suzuki chased Miguel to the opposite side of the mat, where Miguel tried to retreat, but a group of unsympathetic samurai threw him back on to the mat. Trapped in the corner, Miguel had nowhere to go. He tried frantically to locate his sword, feeling around him with his remaining hand, his eyes never leaving his opponent's face. Suzuki kicked the sword out of reach and laughed, before delivering a thrust deep into Miguel's chest. Bleeding copiously, Miguel stumbled to the centre of the mat, where he quivered and fell to his knees.

'Help me, Father!' he cried, and reached out his remaining hand.

Suzuki stood behind Miguel. With a decisive nod from the Shogun, the samurai brought his sword down fast on Miguel's neck, decapitating him in one smooth action.

Tonia and Joaquim watched in silence, their despair meriting no sound. But victory was not enough for Suzuki. He walked over to Miguel's head and kicked it off the mat towards Joaquim, who could only stare, horrified at the shocking display of disrespect.

'Your head is next,' the Shogun laughed. He guzzled a shot of sake.

Samurai gathered Miguel's body parts and threw them into a garbage container.

Joaquim could no longer control himself. 'The book of Psalms says, "the wicked are ensnared by the work of their hands". The Lord has judged you, Shogun Iemitsu!'

'Shut your mouth, priest, and get on the mat. Today your poisonous words die with you!'

Joaquim leaped onto the mat as he repeated a passage to himself. '"Let my soul live, and it shall praise thee! Let thy judgements help me!"'

'I again call Suzuki-san!' the Shogun shouted.

'Su-zu-ki! Su-zu-ki! Su-zu-ki!' the crowd chanted, louder this time, emboldened by their warrior's swift dismissal of his previous Christian opponent. Everywhere Joaquim looked, he saw angry samurai yelling and jeering at him. Some spat in his direction.

Interrupting their chant, however, the Shogun raised his hand, and the Budokan fell silent. 'And ... Daisuke-san!'

'Dai-su-ke! Dai-su-ke! Dai-su-ke!'

An imposing figure surfaced from the rear of the Budokan and approached the mat. Standing almost seven feet tall, Daisuke was an ogre, and by far the largest samurai within the Shogun's forces.

Watanabe jumped onto the mat in protest.

'Get off the mat, ronin!' the Shogun yelled. 'This battle does not involve you!'

'You have called two fighters,' Watanabe replied. 'I will be our second fighter.'

'You will get off the mat or I will end the contest!'

'How is this fair? How can you send two fighters against one?'

'This is my Budokan and these are *my* rules! Get off the mat or I will have you both executed!'

Reluctantly, Watanabe stepped off the pad and Joaquim approached the centre of the mat to face his two adversaries as he measured up his opponents. The priest knew defeating two of the Shogun's top warriors would not be easy, but he had to remain focused; the lives of all the villagers and Christians in Edo prison depended on it.

Joaquim asked himself what he knew about his opponents. He knew Suzuki was fast, skilled, and dangerous. He also knew Daisuke was large and powerful but, he could see, slower.

The parties bowed and the fight began.

Suzuki and Daisuke charged at Joaquim, but the priest made himself a target for Daisuke, forcing the smaller Suzuki behind the larger man. After years in the *dojo*, the priest knew to fight two at once he must use one attacker to block the other.

Keeping Daisuke between himself and Suzuki he thrust and parried until an opportunity presented itself. He slashed Daisuke's enormous legs with precision, drawing a copious amount of blood and a yell of pain.

Joaquim now positioned himself between Suzuki and Daisuke, making sure that while he watched the larger man, he could see

Suzuki sidle around to attack him from a blind side when Daisuke struck. Daisuke growled in anger, and hobbled in to deliver a devastating blow to Joaquim. As Daisuke cut down with his sword, the Jesuit sensed Suzuki moving in for the kill. Instead of parrying Daisuke's blow, Joaquim slipped out of the way. Daisuke's sword slashed the fast-approaching Suzuki who was watching Joaquim, not Daisuke. The blow cut his shoulder deeply before he had a chance to defend against it.

The Budokan fell silent. None had ever seen Suzuki suffer any kind of injury. Capitalizing on the confusion on the mat, Joaquim cut Daisuke's Achilles tendons from behind, causing him to crash to his knees.

As Daisuke fell, Father Joaquim also lowered himself, continuing to use Daisuke's enormous size as a shield. From his cover behind the giant samurai, Joaquim changed the grip on his sword and threw it like a spear at Suzuki, piercing his stomach. He reached forward and found a pressure point on the inside of Daisuke's wrist. The huge samurai resisted briefly, but in his weakened state, the bolt of pain that shot through his grip proved unbearable and his sword dropped, useless, to the mat. Picking up the larger man's weapon, Joaquim walked towards the mortally injured Suzuki. Beads of sweat had formed on Suzuki's face. He was sitting on the *tatami* in a kneeling *seiza* position, holding Master Yamaguchi's sword with one hand as it protruded from his stomach. His body trembled as shock set in, and his face was filled with confusion and disbelief.

The priest kicked his sword deeper into Suzuki's body, forcing the blade out through his lower back. Dropping Daisuke's sword, Joaquim disarmed Suzuki and decapitated him with his own sword in a devastating blow. The Budokan was silent.

Using his foot, Joaquim withdrew his sword from Suzuki's lifeless body. The priest then picked up Daisuke's sword and approached him. On his knees and unable to stand, Daisuke roared, ready to fight hand to hand if the chance came. Joaquim walked behind him as the giant struggled to follow him. He sliced through Daisuke's jugular vein with the giant's sword then threw it down in disgust as a fountain of arterial blood splattered far across the room, anointing the Shogun and his aides in a baptism of red.

CHAPTER FORTY-NINE

Shogun Iemitsu pounded his fists on the floor in fury. Three of his most venerated warriors were dead, and he'd lost the contest. Unsure how to respond, he turned to his cabinet members.

'We cannot let these dogs escape.'

'I do not think we have a choice, Lord,' replied Abe, the oldest member of his Roju cabinet. 'You declared that your "word is stronger than metal".'

'For the honour of the clan you must abide by the terms of the contest, Lord,' Sakai, a second member, added. 'We can avenge ourselves on this priest later.'

Veins protruded and pulsed in Iemetsu's forehead and neck as he battled with the urge to break his word and kill the priest. But he reminded himself that doing so would undermine his authority with his retainers, and lose the opportunity to get the list of Christians. He thought about the young man, Akihiko. Despite all that he had done to him, the cursed Christian still would not submit to his will. He knew this *gaijin* would be just as strong. The Shogun finally convinced himself that the Jesuit's destruction could come at a later time. 'We will not tarnish our word, but I will have my vengeance on this priest and his flock!'

Joaquim huddled with Tonia and Master Watanabe, mourning the loss of Miguel. The Shogun spoke. 'It seems, priest, you have done more than just spread your poisonous cult in Japan. It appears you have also learned the Way of our Sword.'

Joaquim remained silent.

'You and your band of Christians are free to leave.'

Joaquim bowed in acknowledgement.

'Return to Europe or go to the Philippines. If you stay in Japan, I will hunt you down and kill you!'

'We request the return of our friend's body so we may bury him.'

His anger barely contained, the Shogun replied, 'Do not try my patience, priest! We will incinerate his body; not an ash of him will remain. Soon there will be no trace or memory of your kind in Japan!' At his sign, samurai opened the doors. 'There is your freedom. Take it. The other prisoners will join you soon.'

* * *

'I command all Christians to stand up,' the lead guard yelled.

Following his earlier outburst, Susumu, the thief, had kept an eye on his new Christian cellmates. Their concern for one another seemed genuine. In silence, he'd listened to their discussions – and their prayers. Although part of him wanted to hate them for their weakness, another part of him recognized that their weakness – their unwillingness to fight their way to dominance – was, in fact, their strength. Leaning forward, his body language showed that the Christians impressed him, although he would not admit it. When the prison guards opened the door, startling the prisoners trapped inside, and commanded the Christians to arise, Susumu was not sure how to respond.

Most of the prisoners were slow to move, others incapable of obeying, owing to their weakened state.

'Did you hear me?' the guard shouted. 'I command all Christians to stand up!'

The Christians rose, including everyone from the village.

'If you cannot stand, raise a hand or a limb!' the guard yelled with impatience in his voice.

Several hands and feet rose, and the main prison guard counted. 'Are there any others?'

Again he looked around the jail for any motion, but saw none.

'One more time!' the main guard bellowed as his face tightened. 'Are there any more prisoners who believe in this Christ?'

One final prisoner rose in the far corner of the dark prison. Susumu.

* * *

Waiting for their friends to join them, Father Joaquim, Tonia, and Master Watanabe stood in a street next to the prison with their arms around each other, grieving for Miguel.

'Father,' a young man from the village cried out as he ran down the street, 'is it true? Are we truly free?'

'We are free,' Joaquim nodded. 'But we must leave Edo at once. I do not trust the Shogun.'

With an upturned face, Joaquim looked around at all the

familiar faces of his village, but struggled to see *all* the Christians previously incarcerated in the Shogun's prison. As the priest looked down the road and rubbed the back of his neck, a deep sense of anxiety pervaded his mind. He knew that any freedom they had won was short-lived.

As many of the villagers kissed the ground and praised God, Shinobu asked, 'Where's Miguel?'

'He is with God now.'

'Where are the others?' Joaquim asked Shinobu.

'They are coming. The prison guard has released all Christians, but some are ill or cannot walk.'

'We must help them.'

'They just released thirty Christians from the prison.'

'Thirty? A new one?'

The words were no sooner out of his mouth than Father Joaquim spotted feisty Susumu coming down the path, helping to carry the crippled Akihiko.

* * *

'I want them all slain, at once!' the Shogun shouted with curled lips and a reddened face.

'Yes, Lord,' Sakai, a cabinet member answered. 'We will execute them the moment they leave the city.'

'Why not before?'

'Because Edo needs to know that you keep your word, Lord,' Abe replied.

'That's ridiculous! They are filthy exiled Christians! How can we let them go?'

'This is a problem *you* created,' the Shogun's father said. 'Now you must live with it and hold your end of the agreement.'

'That's preposterous.' The Shogun paced back and forth. Unable to contain his frustration, he made a fist and punched a beam of wood.

'You should not have accepted the priest's ridiculous challenge in front of everyone,' Hidetada interjected. 'The Christian baited you and you fell into his trap.'

'How was to I know the priest and the girl had mastered the art of bushido? Who could know this?'

'What does it matter?' Hidetada replied. 'It is now up to you to uphold the honour of the Tokugawa name.'

'This is one more reason I abhor these foreigners. They deceive us. They come here under the guise of commercial trading, but learn our ways of battle in secret, then defeat us with it!'

For a moment, Iemitsu conjured up an alarming vision of the Spanish and Portuguese armadas invading his country, using the Way of the Sword in battle against them. He grimaced as his eyes narrowed.

'But how did they learn it?' a retainer asked. 'Who would teach them?'

'Ronin,' the Shogun spat. 'Dissenting ronin, who roam the land and have nothing better to do than to plot against me. Can you imagine an invading Spanish army trained with such skills? They could teach our techniques throughout Europe and conquer us!'

'I agree, Lord,' the retainer said. 'This is a threat. Perhaps it would be wise to expel *all* foreigners from Japan, including all foreign traders and merchants.'

'Perhaps we should seal off the country from the entire

outside world. I will not tolerate any faction that could challenge my authority.' Iemitsu pondered this idea, seeming to reach a conclusion.

'Let us be careful,' Hidetada interjected. 'Your grandfather, great Shogun Ieyasu, believed international trade benefits Japan. I do not think we should rush to cut it off.'

'I revere Grandfather Ieyasu, Father. He is our deity, but we must crush these Christians.'

'Agreed. Their cult remains a threat and we must complete their annihilation.'

'So, let us decapitate this band of Christians and hang the priest's skull in my castle.'

'How shall we proceed, Lord?' a retainer asked.

Iemitsu contemplated ways in his mind to massacre the Christians after they left the city without being seen to break his word and lose face.

'Place bands of samurai at all roads leaving Edo. Our spies will follow them through the streets. Once they have left the perimeter of Edo and are out of sight, we will massacre them.'

'What shall we do with their corpses?'

'Burn them and throw their ashes into the sea. But place their heads in a sack and bring the sack to me.'

CHAPTER FIFTY

14 July 1626
Streets of Edo, Musashi Province

'Well, my friend, you and Tonia have won our freedom,' Watanabe said. 'Now we must see if we can keep it. Can we escape the Shogun's grip before he changes his mind?'

'I suspect we still have some testing experiences ahead of us,' the priest answered. Father Joaquim thought of the immense task they faced, not least because of the appalling physical condition of many in the group. The priest could see that all were malnourished and few had had a good night's sleep in weeks. Some exhibited signs of illness, and many had recent, crude amputations, including hands or feet. Among the worst was young Akihiko. Because of his physical condition, others had to carry him. Joaquim knew these things would be limiting factors in terms of what options they had in pursuit of their freedom.

'What is our plan, Father?' Shinobu asked. 'Shall we walk towards the main *seki* to leave the city?'

'No, Shinobu.' Joaquim frowned. 'That would be too risky.'

'Why? I thought the Shogun promised us freedom.'

The priest answered. 'We cannot trust the Shogun. He is like Pharaoh and the Israelites. The moment we try to leave he will give chase.'

'Why?'

'Because he hates Christians and foreigners.'

'So, what should we do?'

'We must leave Edo immediately, but not on foot.'

'How then?'

'By boat. It will be harder for the Shogun's men to ambush us at sea.'

'But where will we get a boat?'

Joaquim looked at Watanabe and sighed before answering Shinobu. 'I don't know. We will need to pray for it.'

Master Watanabe nodded. The two of them moved towards a group of huddled men. Two of the men, Kenta and Jiro, had finished rewrapping Akihiko's stumps and were ready to carry him.

'Thank you, Father,' Akihiko said. He cupped his hands to the sides of his head to funnel the voices.

'For what?'

'For liberating us, for our freedom.'

'Don't thank me, Akihiko-san. Thank our Lord.'

'But I am told it was *you* who defeated two of the Shogun's top samurai in battle.'

'I can do nothing on my own. It was the hand of God that struck down those men.'

'Without doubt, you have great skill to defeat such venerated warriors. I did not know the Jesuits possessed such martial skills.'

Father Joaquim sat next to Akihiko. 'The founder of the Jesuits, Saint Ignatius of Loyola, was a knight before he repented and chose to lead his brothers as a priest.'

'Then warfare is good?'

'No, it is not.' Grimacing and shaking his head, Father Joaquim looked with soft eyes at the young man who would never walk again. 'The Society is bound by a different set of vows now, of poverty, chastity, obedience, and love. We will never conquer by the sword. That is not God's will.'

'But this time the sword bought our freedom.'

'Yes, Akihiko-san, but the sword must be a last resort. Isaiah tells us, "And they shall beat their swords into ploughshares, and their spears into pruning hooks." Our Lord Jesus told the apostle Peter that those who take up the sword will perish by the sword.'

'I understand, Father.' Akihiko looked at his stumps, no doubt recalling the sharp, cruel saw that had removed his feet. 'So what do we do now?'

'We make our way to Edo harbour.'

Several villagers joined the conversation. 'Then what, Father?'

'We find a boat and set sail.'

'Where will we go?'

'Nagasaki.'

'Nagasaki?'

'Yes. To rescue our women and children.'

Joaquim looked around and saw simultaneous looks of relief

on the faces of the villagers. Several stared speechless at the priest, mouths wide open, as they contemplated the daring mission ahead. He said for all to hear: 'I know many of you have many questions, and I regret I do not have all the answers. But God *does*, and nothing is impossible for Him.'

CHAPTER FIFTY-ONE

14 July 1626
Suetsugu's Warehouse, Port of Nagasaki

Deputy-Lieutenant Suetsugu and Governor Kawachi walked purposefully towards the Deputy's warehouse. 'I invited you to join us, Governor, because I want you to bear witness as the first of these vile Christians breaks and recants.'

'What makes you so confident that today will be the day? You have had two weeks, with no results yet.'

'They have been resilient, it is true, but when you see their broken state, you will be impressed.' Suetsugu was almost giddy over his plans and his confidence.

'Good. The Shogun expects results.'

'I am sure we will see results this afternoon. You will tell the

Shogun of my mutilation of the Christians, will you not?'

'I am sure the Shogun will reward you even more if you can get apostates,' the Governor replied.

To protect his warehouse from theft and damage, Suetsugu had built a fence along three sides of its perimeter. The open side faced the water of Nagasaki harbour, allowing trading ships to dock, so the Deputy could load and unload his riches. To prevent escape, a dozen guards watched the perimeter throughout the night.

As the Deputy and Governor arrived at the gate, the guards bowed before admitting them. Then, as they approached the entrance, two more samurai slid open the large doors.

Inside, everyone remained still – not out of fear, but because none had the strength to move. Without exception, the women and children looked ghost-pale with deep dark circles under their eyes. They gazed at the authorities in silent rebuke as they were scrutinized like animals in an unholy experiment.

'I have allowed them *just* enough food to remain alive,' Suetsugu chuckled. 'Just about,' he added.

'They look appalling,' Governor Kawachi added. 'You have done well, Deputy. Now let us see these recantations you promised.'

'Bring them to the yard!' Suetsugu shouted. 'This afternoon someone will recant. I am tired of being merciful to you mutts.' He turned to address the guards: 'Is the water boiling yet?'

The guards nodded their affirmation.

'Who shall we mutilate this afternoon?' Suetsugu gazed at the emaciated women and children.

All tried to avoid eye contact with the Deputy as he gazed at the women before making his choice. 'You, young girl, we have ignored you this week. Get over here.'

The young woman, Hatsumi, broke down in tears, unable to move. Kawachi scrutinized the woman, perceiving her sense of fear and terror.

'I remember this girl,' Governor Kawachi interjected as he examined her. 'Was she not the good-looking one?'

'She was,' Suetsugu chuckled, 'when she had a nose. Bring her here.'

Several guards rushed over to Hatsumi and grabbed her.

'No more! No more!' Hatsumi cried as samurai dragged her towards the pot of boiling water.

'I will not waste time,' the deputy declared. 'One simple question: Do you recant?'

Hatsumi said nothing.

'Do you recant?'

Her terrified sobs formed her only response.

The deputy nodded to four guards, who dragged her towards the pot. As two of the guards restrained her, the other two grabbed her arm, twisted it behind her and forced it into the boiling water, holding it there. Suetsugu and Kawachi watched with blank faces as her arm boiled, turning red, then dark purple. She collapsed from the pain with her arm still in the pot.

The guards released their hold on her and let her collapse onto the ground. At a sign from Suetsugu, a samurai threw cold water on her face and slapped her to revive her.

Suetsugu then approached Hatsumi, who was curled up over her injured arm, sobbing with pain. He stood above her. 'Do you recant?'

Hatsumi did not respond.

'Do not test me, girl! Boil her other arm.'

Hatsumi screamed, 'I recant! I can't take any more. I recant!'

'Magnificent!' Suetsugu turned to the Governor, smiling as though he had won a game. 'I told you someone would recant today.'

'Good, Deputy-Lieutenant. You are achieving results; this will please the Shogun.'

'The rest will recant within the next five days.'

'How can you be so sure?'

'The first one is always the hardest. In five days, if the rest of them have not recanted through torture, I will kill them, starting with their youngest and working my way to the oldest.'

Suetsugu glanced towards the mother of a newborn. Her startled eyes, and tightened hold on her infant, revealed that she understood his message.

'Good, Deputy. I leave you in charge.'

Suetsugu walked over to the new mother, snatched her baby from her, and held the infant up in the air, his fist around its neck. 'Do you see this baby?' he shrieked. 'If you have not *all* recanted within the next five days, you will all be responsible for this baby's death!'

CHAPTER FIFTY-TWO

14 July 1626
Edo Harbour, Musashi Province

The sight of thirty emaciated, mangled strangers stumbling through the streets of Edo in the early evening attracted an audience. The tall European man and what appeared to be an old ronin leading them created an even more intriguing spectacle.

Looking around the bay, Father Joaquim struggled to discern how they would get back to Nagasaki. The southern trading port was far away from Edo and the group had no money to pay someone. More importantly, the Christians were outlaws and no one would want to risk themselves, or their boat, to transport fugitives from the regime to the other end of Japan.

Tonia inspected the boats in the harbour. Anchored together

in the centre part of the bay, large craft with tall sails wallowed together in choppy waters, surrounded by a plethora of smaller vessels. She perused the distinctive flags that hung from the larger boats as they blew in the wind. 'I see only the Shogun's official red-seal ships, and small fishing boats. I don't see anything in between.'

'Neither do I.' They continued to look at the choices without success.

'There is one boat that would serve us well,' Master Watanabe said. The old ronin pointed to a mid-sized boat at the end of the harbour partially hidden by a couple of larger ships. It floated at anchor below a small hill on which a Buddhist temple sat. Joaquim looked at the brownish-grey boat. It looked old and leaky, and far from seaworthy. By choice he wouldn't have used it as a ferry.

'Who do you think that ship belongs to?' Tonia asked.

'I think the temple monks,' said Master Watanabe.

'There must be something else,' Father Joaquim said. The seagoing instincts of his youth warned him this ship would likely drown them all as soon as they were out of sight of land. He pinched his lips together and rubbed the back of his neck. 'How can there be only one possible boat for us?'

'Because the others are out at sea now. Their owners are making a living. What's wrong with the monks' boat?' Master Watanabe asked. He was hurrying to keep stride beside the longer-legged padre while looking unhurried himself.

'It belongs to the Buddhists!'

'So?'

'Since Buddhists have hated Christians for over a century now, why would they help us?'

'Did you pray for a boat, Father?'

'Yes, I did.'

'Well, there it is. In the entire harbour it is the *only* boat that fits your needs.'

'I find it difficult to believe God would have Buddhists help us.'

'Do you believe God has greater wisdom than you?'

'Of course.'

'Then put away your prejudices. They are clouding your mind. *That* is your boat.'

'We have no money to offer,' Father Joaquim said, as though that fact would settle the debate.

'Ask them for help.'

'Perhaps it would be better if you ask for us. You are not a Christian priest. Perhaps they will be more receptive to you.'

'You must not become dependent on me, Father.' Master Watanabe stopped walking and turned his gaze from the boat back to Father Joaquim. 'I am only a guide showing you the way.' He placed his hands on the Father's shoulders and gave him a reassuring smile. '*You* must do these things. I cannot do them for you.'

The priest nodded. 'Very well.'

'Are you sure, Master Watanabe?' Tonia asked. 'If you're wrong, they might turn Father Joaquim over to the Shogun ... or kill him. Most Buddhist monks are skilled warriors.'

'There is but one way to find out, Tonia.'

CHAPTER FIFTY-THREE

14 July 1626
Buddhist Temple, Edo Harbour, Musashi Province

Joaquim knew he had no other option. He owed the villagers the chance to reunite with their families in Nagasaki.

As he made his way up the seeming endless stairs cut into the steep hill, he noticed several colourful flags, long and vertical, affixed to long wooden poles and cemented into the ground. They displayed a variety of Buddhist phrases and bore the prayers used by the Amidist Buddhist sect in Japan. *Namu Amida Butsu*, read the first flag – *Hail to the Buddha Amida*. A little further up the hill another flag read, 'He who advances is sure of salvation, but he who retreats will go to hell.' Reading the mantras, Joaquim shook his head and thought, *I must be out of my mind*. As he passed more flags he felt relieved he could read kanji, an essential skill for all Jesuits in Japan. He bit his lip and shook his head as he read some of their warnings.

The Japanese warrior monks emerged when Buddhism was introduced to Japan. It came to Japan through China, and when it reached Japan it complemented rather than threatened the existing religion, Shinto, known as 'The Way of the Gods'. Shinto involved the worship of thousands of *kami*, regarded by Buddhists as manifestations of the Buddha himself. So the creeds of Buddhism from China and Shintoism from Japan coexisted well.

However, this was not the case with Christianity. Christian doctrine contrasted with Buddhism, and conflicts always arose when the two religions came into contact. A major obstacle for the priest was that Buddhism was aligned with the Shogun, and the Bakufu regime all but enforced Buddhism as a matter of law. Now that the Shogun had banned Christianity from Japan, Father Joaquim couldn't imagine a Buddhist warrior monk contradicting the Shogun's edict and helping a Christian. Yet he had to try. To convey his peaceful intentions, he came alone and unarmed.

Joaquim was surprised that he reached the top of the stairs without being challenged. Surely they must have seen him climbing for a while now.

'Halt where you are.' A bald monk confronted him at the top of the stairs. He pointed a sharp blade at the priest as a warning. Father Joaquim raised his hands above his head. Monks surrounded him and one ran to a nearby structure and rang the temple bell to alert the remaining members of the community. Another ran to a lookout at the top of the hill to see if other trespassers were approaching.

Within a few minutes, dozens more warrior monks joined

the crowd surrounding the priest. All had shaved heads and wore beige kimonos and trousers, with lightweight black jackets. The bulkiness of their clothes informed the Jesuit of the lacquered plates of armour underneath their robes. Some carried weapons, including knives, bows, spears, and swords.

Joaquim stood before them with his hands raised. The shouting intensified. A sharp pain to the back of the head put the priest on his knees on hard stone ground.

He found himself surrounded by a horde of yelling, aggressive warrior monks, all wielding sharp *naginata* spears pointing at him from all directions. At a moment's notice, he could be sliced into pieces. He bit his lip and waited for what came next, believing his demise was imminent.

A voice said, 'Who are you? A merchant? A trader?'

'I am a Christian priest.'

'Kill him!' someone in the crowd yelled.

'No, let us collect a reward for him. His capture is worth money.'

A quarrel broke out among the monks, who continued to point their spears at Joaquim's head. The quarrel subsided when the temple's grey-haired elder and head monk arrived. His presence noticeably calmed the atmosphere, though Joaquim's heart still pounded in his chest.

'Quiet, I said!' As the last of the younger monks stopped arguing, the elder said, 'What is the problem?'

'This *gaijin* is a Christian priest. We caught him on our grounds, approaching the temple.'

'Is it true, stranger? Are you a Christian priest?'

Joaquim studied the old man, wondering if what he saw was mercy towards his disposition.

'Yes, I am.'

With that admission, the yelling and shouting flared up again. 'We should kill him!'

'Quiet!' the old monk ordered. He raised his hands again. 'Control yourselves. We will not have another outburst like this.'

The rambunctious younger monks relaxed their posture further, lightening their aggressive posture towards the priest.

Looking again at the intruder lying on the ground, the elder asked, 'Why are you here?'

'I am here to ask for help.'

'He came to the wrong place,' one monk replied as he jabbed Father Joaquim in his side with his pommel.

'Lower your weapons and be silent,' the elder monk ordered again. '*I* am conducting this interrogation.' Looking down again at the priest, he continued, 'It is strange that you are asking us for help, Christian priest. We are a Buddhist community. Are you aware of this?'

Father Joaquim nodded. 'I am.'

'And yet still you come here. Who needs help?'

'My village, a farming community from Kyushu: women, children, husbands, fathers, elders, everyone. Unless we can get a ship to Nagasaki, the Shogun will slaughter us all.'

'The Shogun wishes to annihilate you because your village is Christian and you are their patriarch?'

'Yes, he wishes to destroy us because we are Christian.'

'The Shogun is fierce,' the elder monk added. 'He crushes anyone he dislikes.'

'He is a tyrant.'

'The priest is an enemy of the regime,' interjected one of the younger monks. 'Let us collect a reward for him!'

'Let us kill him!' another shouted.

'That's enough!' the elder monk scolded. He turned his attention back to Joaquim. 'You are brave to come here alone. What inspired such boldness?'

'We will all die if I do not. The samurai has already burned the village to the ground and murdered our village elder.' As he spoke, he relived the pain of Master Yamaguchi's needless death.

The elderly monk studied the priest for a moment, then reached down to help Joaquim to his feet. 'My name is Kansuke,' he said. 'We will help you. My apprentices and I will take you to Nagasaki.'

The younger monks immediately expressed their dissatisfaction, but the elder quieted them.

'Thank you, Kansuke-san. I am Father Joaquim Martinez, and on behalf of my village, I thank you.'

'Why should we help them?' a monk fumed. 'Christians are our enemies.'

'Enemies of yesterday can become friends of tomorrow,' Kansuke answered. 'The teachings of the Buddha require compassion towards all beings, not just other Buddhists. Here is an opportunity, a chance to express that compassion. Remember, every situation allows us to experience a different part of ourselves.'

Only partly convinced, a young monk asked, 'What shall we do, Kansuke-san?'

'Get the vessel ready. We sail at sunset.'

CHAPTER FIFTY-FOUR

14 July 1626
Edo Harbour, Musashi Province

To smuggle more than fifty people undetected aboard a boat was a formidable task, particularly when those people comprised two factions who distrusted each other. The early-evening darkness aided their secrecy but, try as they might to be quiet, making noise was inevitable. To aid their clandestine activities, several of the monks staged a boisterous mock argument as a diversion in another part of the harbour.

The situation became even more complicated when the diversion failed, and a pair of government soldiers ran over to the Buddhists' boat, demanding that they cease all activity until a larger squadron of soldiers arrived to investigate.

An altercation resulted and before the two soldiers could reach the main shoreline to get help, Kansuke's monks tied them up and gagged them before hiding them in the dark brush next to the shore.

Joaquim had travelled on many different types of ships in his lifetime. One thing about junks was their battened sails, which made the vessels fast and easy to sail. This boat looked old, and Joaquim noticed much of the wood was decaying. But the Buddhists still used it to earn a marginal income. Like most traditional junks, the hull of the vessel had a horseshoe-shaped stern, supporting a high watch deck where several Buddhist flags fluttered, with the largest that of Amida Buddha, at the top. The Buddhists congregated next to their flags as they boarded. The Christians moved to the bow. Having boarded everyone, apparently without detection, the monks set sail for the open ocean.

As Father Joaquim raised his head after a prayer of thanks, he spotted several of the monks glaring at him. He thanked the Lord that Kansuke was travelling with them.

* * *

'Approach,' the Shogun commanded the four Buddhist warrior monks. The monks crawled, in deference to their great dictator. 'My servants tell me you have valuable information. Speak.'

'We have information regarding a foreign Christian priest and a group of Christians.'

'What?' the Shogun demanded.

'A foreign priest approached our community seeking our help.'

'And where is your community?'

'Edo harbour, Lord Shogun.'

'What did the priest seek?'

'Use of our shipping vessel, Lord.'

Flushed with fury, the Shogun said, 'Where did he wish to go? The Philippines?'

'No, Lord. He asked to go to Nagasaki.'

'And are they still at the temple?'

'No, Lord. Our elder temple leader agreed to take them.'

'Why would your temple leader betray me and the laws I have commanded?'

'He said he would help them on grounds of compassion, but our loyalties lie with *you*, Lord Shogun. We serve only you and your regime.'

The Shogun pounded his fist on the mat in front of him before responding to the monks.

'You are wise to serve me and to act as informants. In reward, you shall live and receive a small gift of silver. But your temple leader will not be so fortunate. He will die along with anyone else in league with him. Are you sure they went to Nagasaki?'

'Yes, Lord. It is what the foreign priest requested.'

'Collect your silver as you leave my castle.' The Shogun snorted and huffed as he envisioned flaying the leader of the monks for daring to defy him.

'This priest is far too unruly,' the Shogun declared. 'He should retreat to the Philippines, but has the audacity to return to southern Japan!'

'They are an insolent group,' responded Sakai. 'They insult you with each act of defiance.'

'But why return to Nagasaki?' the Shogun pondered aloud. 'Surely he knows they will face re-arrest.'

'Their families are still in Nagasaki, Lord.'

'You think they will try to rescue their families?'

'It is possible, Lord. They are renowned for their brazenness.'

'Never!' The Shogun stood and thundered. 'They could never be that bold!'

'What would you like to do, Lord?'

'Prepare our greatest red-seal ships. We will destroy them at sea!'

'Yes, Lord. We will coordinate this at once.'

The red-seal ships were armed merchant sailing vessels bound for other Asian ports, with a red-sealed patent issued by the Shogun. Such patents were valuable because the regime limited them in number, and the Shogun sanctioned every red-seal ship, which protected them from pirates.

More often than not, the Shogun granted these coveted red-seal permits to his favourite daimyo and merchants in return for gifts, benefits, and other favours. The Shogun knew these were the safest and most reliable ships in Japan because no pirate or foreign nation dared to interfere with them.

Five minutes later, a senior administrator named Tadao hurried into the grand chamber to speak with the Shogun and his Roju cabinet. Well-known in the Shogun's administration, he had administered more red-seal patents than anyone, and thus knew everything there was to know about vessels and the sea. The Bakufu regime considered Tadao the foremost expert on red-seal ships.

'We need to destroy a Buddhist ship,' the Shogun informed him. 'The vessel is carrying a large group of runaway Christian criminals. We must catch them at once and destroy them.'

'Yes, Lord Shogun.'

'What do you advise?'

'Send larger, faster vessels than the enemy's, Lord.'

'How many large ships do I have at my disposal?'

'There are five large red-seal ships in Edo harbour at present, but you will not need five.'

'Good, we will use all five.'

'But, Lord, you will not need that many. I know the Buddhist vessel you seek. It is small and of no significance. You will need only two red-seal ships to catch and destroy it.'

'I will not take any chances. I want those Christian criminals dead!'

'But, Lord, daimyo have already loaded some of these red-seal ships with expensive goods and merchandise. There is no time to unload them for such an unexpected military mission.'

'Then set sail with the goods aboard.'

'But the goods and merchandise could be lost or damaged, Lord.'

'I don't care about goods and merchandise. I care about exterminating Christians!'

As Iemitsu shouted, members of his Roju cabinet cast anxious glances at one another. They knew the Shogun despised Christians, but perhaps these latest demands bordered on hysteria and obsession. They also knew full well that ships loaded with cargo were always a sensitive and contentious issue, given the amount of money involved and the number of people who could lose money. Any problems with lost cargo would be an administrative nightmare. The Roju cabinet members scratched the backs of their necks as they continued to glare at one another, though none dared raise objections given Iemitsu's visible fury.

'But what about the daimyo and head merchants, Lord? These vessels and cargo belong to them.'

'I don't care about the daimyo or merchants. They exist to

serve me. Without me, they would not have their lands or red-seal patents!'

'Yes, Lord.'

'Prepare the vessels at once!'

'And what about men, Lord Shogun? How many men should we send?'

'How many can we load per ship?'

'About 200 per vessel.'

'Then put the maximum on each. We will send 1,000 men after them. And make sure they load all the cannons. I don't want any excuses.'

'Are you sure we require such a large force to destroy such a small, decrepit Buddhist vessel, Lord?'

'I want this ship obliterated!'

CHAPTER FIFTY-FIVE

15 July 1626
Pacific Ocean

With only a couple of monks tending to the boat's navigation nearby, Joaquim and Tonia sat towards the bow, gazing out over the port side, watching the contrast of orange, peach and yellow colours emerging on the horizon.

Sensing Tonia's grief, Father Joaquim sought to bring her some comfort. 'You miss Miguel, Tonia?'

'I do, Father, a great deal. He had a good heart.'

Glancing now at the Buddhist monks on the opposite side of the vessel, Tonia changed the conversation. 'To be honest, Father, I'm surprised we *have* made it this far.'

'Oh? Why's that?'

'Because the Shogun wants to destroy us, and the odds are against us. I am very surprised we found a boat.'

'I'm surprised ... and not surprised.' The priest rubbed his chin.

'What do you mean?'

'I'm surprised the Buddhists are helping us, but I'm not surprised the Lord has answered us.'

'I thought the odds were against us.' Tonia's stomach grumbled. The monks had given the Christians some rice and a little dried fish, but they did not have much to spare.

'Jesus said, "*Ask and it will be given to you; seek and you will find.*"'

'I like that passage, Father.'

'All prayers are answered, Tonia, no matter how big or small.'

'It is odd, but it almost seems like this boat was waiting for us.' Tonia continued.

'In a large harbour filled with ships, who can say? I *do* believe in God's providence. And I *do* believe He has a plan for us. The Lord sometimes answers before we have even asked.'

For a few minutes, Father Joaquim and Tonia closed their eyes and sat in silence, facing the rising sun and praying.

'I saw you were awake,' Kansuke said as he approached them. 'May I join you?'

'Please, Kansuke-san.' Joaquim made room for their benefactor. 'Please, sit down with us.'

'It is a beautiful morning, is it not?'

'Very beautiful,' Joaquim and Tonia answered in unison as they gazed at the brightening sky.

'We would like to thank you again for your help, Kansuke-san,' Father Joaquim said. 'Without you, we would not have survived. How can we ever repay you?'

'The survival of your village is more than enough.'

'I am confused,' Tonia stated. 'Will the Shogun and his regime not make you suffer for helping us?

'Yes.' Kansuke smiled, revealing creases beside his eyes that reminded Joaquim of Master Yamaguchi. For a moment, he almost forgot to whom he was speaking.

Joaquim asked, 'Why do you help us?'

'The Shogun killed my son.'

Father Joaquim's heart contracted with empathy. 'I am sorry, Kansuke-san.'

'He murdered him personally for helping a homeless man in Edo. He was slain for bringing him food when the Shogun was conducting one of his murderous sword-swinging expeditions in the city. The Shogun despises the homeless, and killed my son for helping the destitute.'

'The Shogun is evil.'

'And that is why I stand up to him now. I should have confronted him then, but I did not, and I have regretted it ever since.'

'Living under an oppressor is never easy,' replied Joaquim. He empathized with the Buddhist elder. On countless occasions, the priest could recall himself wanting to use his long-acquired martial skills to raise arms against his oppressors in Arima. But his deep Christian faith had inspired him to act otherwise.

'I believe the strong should protect the weak. The Shogun is a dictator and, in time, all dictators fall.'

'You are brave to oppose him,' Joaquim said.

'What about you, Father? The Shogun expelled Christianity from Japan over ten years ago. And yet you stay, at risk of losing your life.'

'It is God's will.'

'But it is dangerous for Christians. Why do you do it, Father? What do you want to accomplish?'

'Our Bible says, "Go into all the world and preach the gospel to all creation. Whoever believes and is baptized will be saved."'

'And what does that mean?'

'I am but a servant in this world. In this life, I seek nothing more than to spread the Word of God and to save the souls of many.'

'Even if it means your own life?'

'Our holy book assures us that even if we take on serpents, or drink that which is deadly, it will not hurt us.'

'And, like me, you defy the Shogun.'

'Then it looks as if we are both brave men.' Father Joaquim chuckled.

Tonia jumped from her seat and pointed into the distance. 'Look at that!' she shouted as she ran to the edge of the boat to get a better view. 'Do you see?'

Joaquim and Kansuke followed her. Behind them, a gargantuan wall of grey-black clouds moved towards the coast. This terrifying force of nature brightened briefly as bursts of lightning exploded within, then it rolled inexorably forwards, driven by a rising wind.

CHAPTER FIFTY-SIX

The commander of the fifth and last of the five red-seal ships brought up the rear as the flotilla travelled in single file, enjoying a moment of calm on tranquil seas. The stout, five-masted ships were gaining on the smaller Buddhist boat, despite the calm winds.

Besides their cannons, the Shogun's soldiers had armed the red-seal ships with many European arquebuses, whose round lead bullets would cut right through the Buddhist ship.

Joined by some of his men, the commander declared, 'I feel sorry for those pathetic Christians. They don't stand a chance.'

'But why send so many of us?' a samurai asked. 'It's as if we're going to war.'

'Because the Shogun despises them,' the commander answered as he leaned against a railing.

'I heard a rumour that the Christians embarrassed the Shogun with their superior fighting skills,' another samurai added.

'That's not possible,' the commander laughed at the idea.

'It's true. I was there,' another samurai interjected. 'The foreign priest and his female aide killed three of our samurai, including the great Suzuki-san and Daisuke-san. The priest and his aide were very skilled with the sword.'

'It was luck,' the commander huffed. 'Only luck could allow them to accomplish such things. I can guarantee they will not be so lucky at sea.'

'It will be a pleasure to blast holes through them,' another samurai declared. 'Then we can jump on their crumbling vessel and cut off their heads.'

The commander frowned and looked away, distracted from the conversation. He stared at the weather around him and at the way the sea was behaving.

A shout from a samurai lookout seemed to confirm his fears. He stared up at the man in the mast, and then in the direction he was pointing. 'Look!' the lookout yelled.

In the distance, the commander could see a massive black cloud mass appearing along the horizon. The bright day seemed to change in a moment, as though a candle had been snuffed out in a dim room. The dark clouds rolled forward with a speed that surprised the experienced commander, and a tremendous gust of wind slammed into the vessel, causing the sails to flap and billow with loud snaps and cracks. The ship began to heave and pitch as the sea developed ever-deeper peaks and troughs. Around him men ran to untie and luff the sails.

Ignoring his samurai companions, the commander barked out orders. 'Lock down everything that can move. Guard the battens! Furl the sails!' His hat flew into the sky as another powerful gust hit them.

In every direction the samurai looked, they could see roiling waters. The storm winds slammed their boat as if it were a toy. Rocked by the churning waters under their feet and the wind against their bodies, the soldiers, many wearing full body armour, stumbled, crashing to the deck.

'Where did this storm come from?' a samurai asked.

'How can this be?' the second mate shouted above the wind's fury. 'How can a storm rise from nowhere?'

'I don't know!' the commander yelled. 'Watch that mast!'

The mast bent as though it were a bamboo bow. *A little more force*, he thought, *and it will snap.*

Another gust smashed into the ship, stronger than the last. Junks have no keel, but nevertheless, the boat heeled over as a massive wave raised up one side and then broke over the deck. The surging wave swept three samurai into the raging water before the ship righted itself.

Darkness enveloped the ship as the storm hit them squarely. Rain lashed the deck, stinging anyone exposed to it. Huge waves crashed over the decks, meeting torrential rain driven almost horizontal by the furious winds. As the men looked for a place to escape the winds and water, a huge wall of water rose in front of the prow. The commander tried desperately to steer the ship along the wave and ride it. The green water curled towards them, and then struck the ship hard, releasing an enormous surge of water over the deck. As it washed along the decks the sea claimed more men as they lost their footing and were swept away.

Before anyone could recover, a fourth wall of water towered over the vessel, a giant fist of green and white foam that seemed to hit them amidships as though in slow motion. It snapped the masts and washed yet more samurai who had not tied themselves down into the foaming depths.

'Look!' the second mate yelled.

Through the pounding rain and black rain clouds, the sailors could barely see the ships ahead of them. A massive wave, unlike anything they had yet experienced, rose from the sea beneath the black cloud. As it rose, a huge trough appeared beneath it, pulling the ships back towards it, sucking up everything in its path until it could hold no more. The wave crashed down onto the lead vessel, cracking it in half, and sending debris in all directions.

Seconds later, another behemoth destroyed the second ship.

The commander of the fifth ship ran to the stairway leading below deck, but lost his balance as the vessel shifted under a huge wave. Falling to the level below, he regained his footing and dashed into his cabin, where he grabbed a pencil and wrote one line on a tag. He turned as fast as he could, to seize a carrier pigeon out of a cage that lined the wall, and affixed the tag to its leg.

When he reached the deck again, pigeon in hand, he could not see the Shogun's other two ships anywhere. The full fury of the storm was now upon his own vessel.

'Fly!' he shouted and released the carrier pigeon into the air, watching it fight against the wind, its wings struggling to contend with the swirling air. A vicious squall threw him against the stern of the vessel. The sharp pain in his back was fleeting. He realized he could no longer feel his limbs, nor move as he wished. As he lay helpless, a mountainous wave swelled above his ship. It paused, and the water curled, seeming to lose its momentum. The commander stared at its beauty and power. It was the last thing he saw as it fell on him, as the last of the red-seal ships, its crew, and samurai sank to the bottom of the ocean.

CHAPTER FIFTY-SEVEN

15 July 1626
Shogun's Castle, Edo

Accompanied by three attractive young men, the Shogun had been drinking non-stop in his private chamber for several hours. As was typical, he had ordered that no adults enter his chamber and that no one disturb him.

'Who would like to have a bath?' the drunken Shogun asked as he gulped another shot of sake before stumbling towards his companions.

'I already had a bath today,' Eiji answered.

'Who will have sake with me?' Iemetsu lined up cups on the table and filled them, spilling rice wine all over the table.

A knock at the door interrupted them. 'What is that?' the intoxicated Shogun rumbled.

'It's the door, Lord. Someone is knocking.'

'I left orders that no one disturb us!' The Shogun stomped to the door and threw it open. Several petrified retainers stood before him.

'Do you wish to die?' the Shogun screamed. 'I told you not to disturb us!'

'We are sorry, Lord, but we have an urgent message. A messenger pigeon from the commander of one of your red-seal ships.'

The retainer handed the small tag to the Shogun.

Hurricane and tsunami. Fleet destroyed.

With flushed skin, the Shogun grabbed his sake bottles with a roar and smashed them on the ground, sending wet glass all over the chamber. He stormed over to a tall elegant cabinet and kicked it over, shattering the exotic chinaware that rested on top. Baring his teeth with shaking extremities, he turned to his male consorts. 'Get out before I smash *you*.'

Within an hour, Iemitsu had convened with his Roju cabinet and a small group of his most senior retainers in one of his castle's meeting rooms.

'I don't understand how this priest can be so lucky!' the Shogun raged, still drunk from his sake binge.

'I am confused by the message,' Inaba, one of the Roju cabinet members, commented. 'Why would the commander write hurricane *and* tsunami?'

'What do you mean?'

'A hurricane results from violent wind, and a tsunami is the result of an earthquake. How could both hit them at the same time?'

'And why such a short message?' asked Sakai. 'Why only five words?'

'Maybe he did not have time for more.'

'In my entire life, I've never heard anything like this,' declared Abe, the eldest of the cabinet. 'A storm of this magnitude would for sure destroy our coastline and Edo. And yet we have received no reports of damage.'

'The scenario is most unusual,' the others agreed.

'It's *not* unusual!' the Shogun roared. 'It's luck, pure luck! Well, his luck is about to run out. We will annihilate the priest and his followers!'

'What would you like to do, Lord?' asked Sakai.

'This time, we will send *twenty-five* ships after them!'

Wide-eyed and jittery, Iemitsu appeared increasingly paranoid, glaring at his Roju cabinet for support.

'But, Lord, there are no more red-seal ships left in Edo, and you'll have to pay a fortune for the daimyos' destroyed fleet and lost cargo,' responded Abe.

'I do not have to pay anyone anything. I am Shogun of Japan, and this is *my* country! If any daimyo is not happy, let him *dare* come to me with his complaint!'

'We need to make alternative arrangements, Lord,' Inaba interjected.

'What do you mean?'

'The Christians have already travelled too far. Even if we procure more vessels, we cannot catch them before they reach Nagasaki.'

'How do we even know they are alive?' Naito asked. 'If the hurricane or tsunami destroyed our ships, how would they have survived?'

'I don't care!' the Shogun screamed. His wild eyes and unkempt hair showed a lack of control. He wiped the spittle from his lips with his sleeve. 'We will assume they are alive and not stop until I have their skulls in a sack.' He breathed in, then looked at each cabinet member, signalling his demand for agreement. 'Does everyone understand?'

'Yes, Lord,' the cabinet members and retainers said in unison.

'Good. Now what is our plan?'

'We need to mobilize forces in the south, Lord.'

'How do we do that?'

'Send carrier pigeons.'

'Wait,' Abe, the eldest cabinet member, interrupted. 'I thought we intended our activities to be covert. We need to be careful to protect the Tokugawa name. Remember, Lord, you gave the priest your word that you would assure his freedom. You said before all your word is stronger than metal.'

'So what do you suggest?'

'We engage assassins and mercenaries,' Abe answered. 'Forces that are not *official*.'

The Shogun raised his eyebrows as he lifted his head and leaned forward. 'Who?'

'Tanaka-san. He is from the old province of Iga, and the most ruthless of all mercenaries.'

'I do not know this man. Who is this Tanaka-san?'

'He is from before your time, Lord. Your grandfather, Ieyasu, was familiar with him,' Abe answered. 'He is an invincible assassin, Lord, and his posse consists of ninja and other mercenaries,' he added. 'They are discrete killers ... but very expensive.'

'Hire them and kill the Christians.' The Shogun nodded, his volume increasing. 'I don't care how much it costs. Just bring me their heads.'

CHAPTER FIFTY-EIGHT

18 July 1626
South Coast of Kyushu, Kagoshima Area

The waters had at times been rough with large swells, but after four days at sea, the monks' vessel and its unusual passengers approached southern Kyushu and Nagasaki. To arrive undetected, Kansuke decided, the vessel should land in secret in thick brush along the coast, some distance away from Nagasaki.

Despite their time together – or perhaps because of it – the mutual distrust between the Buddhists and Christians continued. Unperturbed by any antagonism, Joaquim was helping Akihiko by cleaning the infected wounds around his ankles when Kansuke approached him. A short while before, one of the younger and more aggressive Buddhist warrior monks had lashed out at a

Christian for eating the last of the food on board. The incident had led to some shouting and shoving, yet before Joaquim could intervene, Kansuke had ended it by scolding his younger apprentices, threatening to increase their manual labour if they did not collaborate with the Christians.

'Do you have a moment, Father?' Kansuke asked.

'Of course, Kansuke-san. I always have time for you.'

'I want to apologize on behalf of my young and impetuous monk.'

'It is of no consequence.' Father Joaquim looked up from his work on Akihiko's ankles and smiled at his rescuer. 'Young men are ... well, *young* men. Without doubt, your apprentice is hungry too.'

'I regret to say some of my acolytes are self-centred.' Kansuke sat down beside Father Joaquim and Akihiko. 'I think some of them could benefit from a lesson in altruism.'

'A lesson that could benefit us all.'

'I am reminded of a Buddhist mantra on which we meditate. It says, "The source of all misery in this world lies in thinking of oneself. The source of all happiness lies in thinking of others."'

'That is a delightful sentiment,' Joaquim replied. 'We have a similar passage in the Bible: "Love thy neighbour as thyself."'

'Inspiring, Father. It appears we are not that different after all.'

'Similarities bring us together. Differences set us apart,' Master Watanabe said, joining the conversation. 'Do you imagine there is more than one God?'

'What do you mean, Master Watanabe?' Joaquim looked around at his surroundings, staring at the sea.

'Is there a Christian God and a Buddhist god?' The old ronin answered his own question. 'There is only one God – the Creator of us all. One way is not better than another. It is just different.'

Before Father Joaquim could respond, a shout distracted him. 'Look!' A monk pointed far off into the distance behind them.

'Let's hope it is a cargo vessel,' Noboru, a villager, said.

'It is not,' Master Watanabe stated with a stern look. 'Its passengers have hostile intentions.'

'How do you know?' Noboru asked.

'I can sense it.'

As the ship approached, it became clear it was far larger and faster than the little junk, and carried significant manpower.

'Look at the size of that craft!' a Buddhist monk shouted from the observation deck. 'It's enormous!'

'It's Tanaka-san,' Watanabe declared, as he recognized the symbols displayed on the mast flag. 'He was a very powerful warrior in the old days. Now he's a ruthless mercenary who kills for money and glory.'

Everyone on board ceased what they were doing and stared at the fast-approaching vessel. With wide eyes and open mouths, they watched in silence as the ship closed the gap between them. Many of the villagers muttered among themselves, their fear rising with the volume of their chatter.

'Can we defeat him?' Tonia asked with a trembling voice.

'Light always defeats dark.'

'How many are they?'

'I would guess about two hundred ninja and other mercenaries,' Master Watanabe answered.

'But we are only a small village of unarmed Christians,' Noboru fretted. 'And many of us are too ill and frail to fight.'

'Perhaps they won't catch us.' Tonia voiced her hope, her expression contradicting her words. 'They are still far away.'

'It's only a matter of time,' Watanabe answered.

'Is there no way to avoid them?' Father Joaquim asked. He tried to gauge their distance from land relative to their distance from their pursuers. Studying the large approaching ship in greater detail, his face showed signs of worry.

'Yes, there is a way, if we can make it ashore before they take us at sea.'

'Then let us land early,' Father Joaquim suggested.

'But what about when *they* land?' Noboru asked with bulging eyes as his hands shook. 'How will we evade them then? How can we defeat a force of 200 mercenaries?'

'We will help you,' Kansuke declared.

'We cannot ask you to risk your lives a second time, Kansuke-san,' Joaquim said. He placed his hand on the old Buddhist's shoulder. 'You have already done more for us than we could have hoped.'

'Nonsense. We have not done enough.'

'They are a formidable force. You will be in great danger,' Tonia said.

The old Buddhist smiled at her. 'Perhaps, but we will *not* live in fear.'

'Are you truly prepared to die for us?' Joaquim looked into the serene face of the monk, and saw fortitude, strength, and resolve.

'Compassion knows no boundaries, Father,' the old man said.

Kansuke commanded his crew to land their vessel in the part of the coastline where thick green trees and foliage lined the shore. The Buddhist vessel changed course and steered towards a thickly forested area of the coast. Close behind, their pursuers trailed them, closing the gap.

'There are so many of them, and they are heavily armed!' a

monk shouted. As they bit their lips, the Buddhists observed dozens of moving bodies on the advancing enemy ship, preparing for their lethal assault.

'This is not our fight, Kansuke-san,' another asserted. 'Why are we helping these Christians?'

'Agreed,' another monk added. 'They are our enemies; we should not help them.'

'Do we have to go through this again?' Kansuke appeared to be losing his temper. 'Will we be cowards and run away?' The old monk held up his hands, commanding attention. 'Listen! Do you want to attain enlightenment? If so, you must abandon the thought of *us versus them*. Remember the Buddha's teachings: We are all *One*.'

'I don't need to help Christians to achieve enlightenment,' a young monk declared.

Looking first irritated then empathetic, Kansuke continued: 'Compassion is the root of the Buddha's entire teachings. You must cultivate the aspiration to help others *before* the aspiration for enlightenment. In the name of Buddha, I command all of you to treat our new companions as the dearest of brothers.'

'Yes, Kansuke-san.' Some of the monks appeared to have understood their master, while others still struggled. But before anyone could reply, a thunderous boom jolted them out of their contemplation. A spout of water appeared just ahead of them. A moment later a second boom shot smoke and wood splinters into the air, as a cannonball found its mark on the junk's side.

Tonia screamed as a sharp piece of wood pierced her stomach.

'Guns!' one of the Buddhist monks shouted. 'Ready your guns!'

'Prepare for landing!' Kansuke yelled.

Manoeuvring the batten sails with skill, the warrior monks steered the junk to shore.

Another cannonball slammed into the stern, killing several monks on impact. Fire engulfed the rear of the craft.

The Buddhists steadied their guns and fired their arquebuses at the approaching ship. Black gunpowder filled the air.

'Retreat to the bow! Man the battens! Prepare for landing!' Kansuke shouted.

CHAPTER FIFTY-NINE

18 July 1626
Outskirts of Nagasaki

The boat was listing badly now as terrified villagers jumped into the shallow water under a continuous flow of lethal musket balls from the mercenaries. They waded quickly for the shore, some pausing to help the sick and wounded abandon the ship. Many of the younger Buddhist warrior monks leaped for their lives as well. People stumbled and called for help only to disappear under the water, which was slowly turning orange from the blood of those now floating face-down. Father Joaquim carried Akihiko from the boat and called over his shoulder, 'Are you sure, Kansuke-san? You should flee with your people. Save yourselves.'

'Go!' Kansuke shouted back. 'We will give you cover. Run!'

Joaquim staggered through the surf with Akihiko on his back, appalled at the carnage around him. He glanced back just long enough to see a monk standing next to Kansuke fall, no doubt hit by a ball from an arquebus.

* * *

The arquebuses themselves were not very accurate, but the sheer power and number of them was devastating. A broadside of musket balls pitted the Buddhists' ship, splitting off equally dangerous splinters of wood, and two more monks near Kansuke fell.

'Gather all the ammunition!' the old monk shouted. 'Disembark. Hurry!'

The scene on the slowly sinking ship was chaotic. Warrior monks who could jumped into the shallows and waded for shore as more cannon fire obliterated the main deck in two massive explosions. Monks were flung into the water, or were impaled on the fractured wood of the deck. Men cried and hauled themselves ineffectually to some sort of safety, leaving severed limbs and smears of blood behind them. Others collapsed into the water. The Buddhists who survived ran up the short beach, some helping their wounded brothers despite the fusillade of musket balls peppering the beach in little spouts of sand.

Once behind the thick tree line of the forest's edge, they paused to regroup.

'Form a perimeter and fire as they disembark!' Kansuke shouted. Where they could, monks found makeshift stands on tree branches, or if they had the time cut rudimentary ones, to balance the heavy weapons as they readied their remaining arquebuses.

Tanaka's boat cast a long, ominous shadow over the beach as it neared the shore. A flash from the gunwales and a delayed boom uprooted a clump of young trees as an incoming cannonball exploded near the left edge of the monks' perimeter, sending dangerous shards of flying wood around them. Through the drifting smoke and jungle debris, the monks saw dozens of screaming mercenaries standing on the deck, ready to jump into the shallows. The air resounded with their fearsome chanting. The monks readied themselves from the tree line. They had gained a small advantage.

The beach sloped down to the water so the monks now had the high ground, such as it was. As soon as Tanaka's mercenaries began their descent on the long rope ladders from the huge vessel, Kansuke and his men fired their arquebuses. Ninja fell into the blood-stained water washing against the sand, joining the floating bodies that now impeded their ability to gain the shore. The ninja on board the ship gave covering fire to their comrades by firing into the forest.

Still, plenty of mercenaries made it to the beach, and soon a fearsome onslaught of well-paid soldiers of fortune charged the forest. The monks fired in volleys, displaying shooting skills that dropped more of their attackers into the sand.

'Retreat and reload!' Kansuke shouted. The monks turned and ran deeper into the forest, repositioning themselves behind tree trunks. Partially shielded from return fire, the monks fired again at the mercenaries who had gained the forest edges.

The black smoke of the arquebuses provided the mercenaries enough cover to take control of the beach. The monks fired their last remaining rounds into the smoke, hoping to kill a few more of their attackers. Then they dropped their firearms and charged the mercenaries with their *naginatas*, short swords on poles. The clash of metal and shrieks of combat and dying soon filled the forest.

* * *

Several miles inland, the Christians had stopped in a clearing in the forest for a brief rest. Father Joaquim accounted for everyone in their group. So why, Noboru asked, could he – and then many others – hear people approaching?

Joaquim set Akihiko on the ground and faced the forest behind them. He withdrew Master Yamaguchi's sword from a brown canvas sack and tracked back towards the sounds. The priest listened and took stock, but the sounds of rustling grass, cracking twigs and foliage persisted. Barely breathing, the villagers waited in silence.

Just as Joaquim prepared to strike, a lone Kansuke emerged from the forest, setting everyone's fears at ease.

'Kansuke-san, thank heaven it's you. Where are the others?' Joaquim asked. He lowered his sword and stared at Kansuke. The old monk was sooty, sweaty, and blood-streaked, and clearly exhausted and traumatized from the fighting.

'Only a few remain,' Kansuke answered. He approached, out of breath and bleeding from his shoulder.

'We are forever indebted to you and your men. How can we repay you?'

'Help a Buddhist one day, Father. That's all I ask.'

'Without question, Kansuke-san.'

'Now I must return. My remaining brothers have suffered

great injuries, and I must attend to them.'

'You should have stayed with them.'

'I wanted to see you one last time to tell you you're safe to continue your escape.'

'We will not forget you.'

'We are forever brothers in spirit, Father.'

'What about your men, and Tanaka and his mercenaries?'

'Almost all dead … on both sides.' Kansuke sighed. 'Save your village. Let the death of my brothers not be in vain.'

'Yes, Kansuke-san. With your help, we'll survive.'

After embracing Father Joaquim, then Master Watanabe, Kansuke disappeared back into the forest.

'What now?' Noboru asked. 'Shall we continue?'

'First, we catch our breath and pray for our fallen Buddhist friends.' He pulled out his little hidden Bible and read. '"My command is this: Love each other as I have loved you. Greater love has no one than this: to lay down one's life for one's friends."'

CHAPTER SIXTY

18 July 1626

The forest contained massive *sugi* trees, their gnarled trunks creating huge pillars topped by evergreen foliage, while at their feet grew smaller deciduous trees and brush. Joaquim was sharing the burden of carrying Akihiko with Master Watanabe when he heard a commotion at the back of the procession. As he looked, he saw several villagers gathered around something. 'What's happened?' he yelled, concerned that the slowest had fallen far behind.

'It's Tonia, Father. She's fallen. Come quickly!'

Joaquim left Akihiko with Watanabe and ran back to Tonia.

'She's lost a great deal of blood, Father,' Noboru said. He lifted the cloth covering her injury, and Joaquim winced at its severity. The stomach wound, with the stub of a protruding piece of wood still present, was severe and oozing significant blood. Tonia looked ashen.

'Why did someone not tell me about her wound?' Joaquim asked, frustrated.

'She kept it to herself,' Noboru answered.

'Leave me, Father,' Tonia moaned. 'I cannot go on.'

'You can, and you *will*.' Joaquim knelt beside her, brushing her black hair away from her face.

Kazuo, an old villager who had seen many wounds in his time, inspected Tonia. He looked up at Joaquim and shook his head. 'I don't think she'll survive, Father. Her wound is great, and she continues to lose much blood.'

'She will be all right,' Joaquim insisted, tears stinging his eyes.

'I'm sorry, Father.' Tonia shivered, her words struggling to be heard. 'I feel so cold and tired.' Closing her eyes, she drifted into unconsciousness.

Watanabe stepped forward. 'There is a way to save her. You could heal her.'

The priest's heart skipped a beat, and he frowned. 'What do you mean?'

'The healing power of God.'

'Our Lord Jesus could heal through miracles, but I am not He.'

'But His power is also in you.'

'I wish that were true, but *He* is the Lord; I am only His servant.'

Watanabe quickly removed the wood splinter and soaked up the fresh bleeding it caused.

Then he told Joaquim, 'Let us both place our hands on her wound. Close your eyes, Father, and give me your hand.'

Father Joaquim grabbed the man's hand. Together, Father

Joaquim and Master Watanabe closed their eyes and pressed firmly on Tonia's wound.

'Do you believe God can heal her, Father?'

'Yes, I do.'

'But do you truly *believe,* Father?'

'*Yes.*'

'I want you to *know* God *will* heal her.'

'Yes, Master Watanabe. *I know He will.*'

'It's not enough. You must *feel* He will heal her. Can you feel it, Father? Can you?'

'I feel it,' said Father Joaquim. He felt flushed and warm, and somehow slightly dizzy and outside his own body while still partly in it.

'Thank God for healing her, Joaquim. I want you to thank God from the bottom of your heart for bringing her back to you.'

'Yes.'

'*Feel* this thankfulness for God's mercy.'

'I feel it!' Joaquim replied, tears of joy streaming down his face, as a sense of warmth emanated around her wound and his own strength appeared to diminish. 'Thank you, God, thank you, for bringing this woman back to us!'

'In the name of our Creator, the Source of our Spirit, we pronounce the healing of Tonia, and so it is!' Watanabe declared.

'*And so it is,*' Joaquim echoed.

But despite the successful transfer of energy, it wasn't that easy. After doing their best to stitch and bind her wound, blood continued to seep from it. They had to change the bandages frequently and she fluctuated in and out of consciousness, as her temperature rose. At one point, Tonia stopped breathing and everyone thought she was dead. But then life suddenly returned, and she gasped and moaned and started to breathe again.

It took two days for her to noticeably start to heal, but gradually the wound closed, her temperature lessened, and the bleeding stopped. Joaquim, Watanabe, and the villagers huddled around the young catechist as she slept. Several of the villagers also took advantage of this pause in their travels to take a much-needed rest. In the evening of the second day Tonia's eyes flickered. Father Joaquim, whose gaze had never moved from observing her, was changing her dressing. He noticed at once. He touched her cheek. 'Welcome back,' he whispered.

Tonia rubbed her eyes. Looking at Father Joaquim, she said, 'I had the strangest dream ... and I feel ...' She placed her other hand on her stomach. 'I feel better.'

As she looked closer, she saw that her wound, although still raw and purple, was healing, and the bleeding appeared to have stopped.

Father Joaquim lifted Tonia and embraced her, repeating, 'Thank You, Lord. Thank You.'

Watanabe placed his hand on the priest's shoulder. 'We need to move on now, Father. We are still being hunted.'

In their concern for Tonia, they had almost forgotten the Shogun and his army. But now, rested, they needed to continue their journey. Their lives still hung in the balance.

CHAPTER SIXTY-ONE

19 July 1626

After marching all night through thick mountainous forest, the villagers approached the edge of Nagasaki with caution.

Three men, appearing to be guards, sat washing their feet in a stream below.

'Tell Father Joaquim,' whispered Noboru to his companions. He volunteered to remain as a lookout.

'Did they see you?' Joaquim asked when he slid next to Noboru.

'No.'

'Show me.'

Moments later, hiding behind a boxwood shrub with Noboru, Joaquim peered down the mountainside, observing the three officials below. The officials sat on large rocks, chatting and watching the gentle running waters of a small stream. For sure, Joaquim thought, these soldiers had been posted to this remote location to crack down on clandestine travel in and out of the city.

'What shall we do, Father? Shall we head in another direction?'

'No. We'll capture them.'

'Capture them?' Noboru's wide eyes revealed his surprise. 'But what if more are down there, out of our sight? Or what if they escape? They could amass an army to pursue us!'

Joaquim said confidently, 'They won't escape.'

* * *

Ten minutes later, Father Joaquim carried Akihiko down the mountain, towards the creek, making no effort at stealth, crashing along the path, talking in a loud voice. When they reached the spot where the officials had been washing their feet, the area was empty.

'Halt where you are!' An official shouted, and he and his companions burst from their cover.

Leaving Akihiko on the ground, Joaquim turned and fled up the side of the mountain.

'I said, don't move!' the official yelled. He chased Joaquim and hauled him back to his companions guarding Akihiko at the creek side. 'You, *gaijin*, are under arrest. Wait until the Governor sees what we have captured.'

'Are you sure you captured us?' the priest asked. He pointed over the guard's shoulder.

'What?' The guards spun around, scanning their surroundings. A group of ragged-looking peasants ran down the side of the creek, charging towards them. Confused by their greater numbers, the guards turned to flee, only to see another group running at them from the other side. Then from a third direction came several more, all armed with thick branches, large rocks, and other makeshift weapons.

'Drop your swords,' Joaquim said.

Overwhelmed by the futility of their situation, the officials surrendered. As the villagers grabbed them by their uniforms, they looked humiliated, and dipped their chins to their chests.

Noboru asked, 'Do we kill them?'

'There's no need,' Joaquim answered. 'God creates life; He does not destroy it. *We* will follow the same principles.'

'So we take them as prisoners?'

'Did you enjoy being a prisoner, Noboru-san?'

'No.'

'Then why would you subject them to captivity?'

Frustrated, Noboru said, 'Because *they* would do it to *us*!'

'We do not seek to avenge anyone. We seek only our freedom and to give that which we wish to receive.' Father Joaquim smiled.

'What do you mean?' Now Noboru looked puzzled.

'We let them go.'

'What? Why did we capture them only to let them go?'

'To deliver a message to the Governor and the authorities.' Father Joaquim scanned the villagers before speaking loud enough for all to hear. 'We will give the authorities what they want – a final confrontation. We will unite all hidden Christians on the island of Kyushu and win back our freedom. I'm tired of hiding. Don't you agree?'

Some in the village looked confused and fearful at the outrageous suggestion.

Taro, one of the captured guards, stepped forward.

'I will deliver your message to the Governor.'

'Tell him Father Joaquim will unite a colossal force and will meet his army in Omura at dawn, if he has the courage to come.'

* * *

'Governor! Governor Kawachi!'

'What is all the commotion?' Governor Kawachi answered. 'Now is not a good time. I'm meeting with the Deputy-Lieutenant.'

'But it's urgent, Governor,' Taro insisted, breathless. 'The Christians have challenged us to war!'

'What?'

'A foreign father and his band of Christians captured us.'

'You mean you captured them!'

'No, Governor, they captured us. They were forty in number, and we were but three.'

'How is it possible that forty Christians roam free?' the Governor asked, wide-eyed.

'I don't know, Governor, but I recognized some of them. I have seen them before.'

'Where?'

'Here, Governor, in Nagasaki. You declared them guilty and instructed Daimyo Shigemasa to take them to Edo. It was Father Joaquim, Governor.'

'That's impossible!'

'No, Governor, I spoke with him face to face.'

'How can that be?' the Governor repeated. 'How could that be the least bit possible?'

'Could the priest have escaped a second time?' Deputy Suetsugu asked in shock.

'No one could be that lucky,' the Governor said. 'How could anyone escape the Shogun's grip?'

'It was him, Governor,' Taro affirmed. 'And he challenges you to war.'

'How can a group of Christians wage war against the regime? It's ridiculous.'

'He says he's amassed a colossal force against us, Governor; that he has united all hidden Christians on Kyushu.'

'Is it possible, Deputy? Could he accomplish such a thing?'

'If he unites all the hidden Christians and the ronin together, it is possible. There have always been whispers that a rebellion could rise one day.'

'He said Christians are tired of hiding, Governor,' Taro added. 'He said it's time to reclaim their freedom. And he said he challenges your army to meet him in the fields of Omura next to the bay at dawn.' He paused as he cleared his throat: '… if you have enough courage to face him.'

'If *I* have enough courage? *Me*? He has the audacity to challenge *me*? And question *my* courage? I will bury this priest.'

For a moment, the Governor dreamed of his sweeping victory over the underground Christians. If they all came out of hiding, and he annihilated them in one broad military stroke, the Shogun would shower lavish incredible praise and rewards upon him for such a decisive victory so soon into his post. In the eyes of the regime, they would hail him as a hero.

'What shall we do, Governor?'

'We will utilize every force available to us. I will wipe this vermin from the face of the earth! Call on every samurai and official capable of bearing arms.' The Governor turned again to his deputy-lieutenant. 'Summon Daimyo Shigemasa at once. This war will take place on his lands. Command him to bring every samurai he has – no exceptions. Then summon anyone in the regime who can bear arms, but not our prison guards. Those incarcerated must remain so.'

'Is that it, Governor?'

'No. Make sure you communicate one thing to all our forces: *I* will be the one to cut off the priest's head in battle. *I* will finally put this dog to death!'

CHAPTER SIXTY-TWO

19 July 1626
Shimabara Castle

'Is this a joke?' Shigemasa asked as he read the letter from Governor Kawachi.

'No, Lord, it is not,' Taro confirmed.

'But I have just returned from delivering this priest to the Shogun.'

'It is real, Daimyo Shigemasa, and the Governor orders you to make preparations at once. Will you comply?'

'Of course, I will comply. Like the Shogun, I despise these Christians.' Still astonished at the news, Shigemasa added, 'I shall mobilize my entire clan right away. Every samurai under my command will present himself at dawn for battle. The Christians almost cost me my son when he rode to Nagasaki. I *will* see all of them dead.'

By some miracle, shepherds had found Katsuie wandering, grievously injured, in the remote mountains, his mount dead on the jagged rocks below. Recognized and returned to his father's house, he had yet to recall his identity, but was alive – for now.

By instinct, the hardened warlord gripped his sword next to his hip as he responded.

Taro nodded. 'The Governor and the Deputy-Lieutenant will join you on the battlefield.'

Taro and the other two officials bowed and left, leaving Shigemasa surrounded by his most senior retainers and samurai.

'How could that wretched priest escape the Shogun and get back to Nagasaki so fast?' Shigemasa asked as he paced. 'If this Christian army somehow took control of even a part of my domain, the Shogun will take *all* my lands.'

He nodded his head, as if affirming his own words. 'By dawn, I want my entire army on the battlefield, ready to obliterate these Christians once and for all. Tomorrow, this priest's luck runs out, and every Christian alongside him will perish!'

* * *

20 July 1626
Deputy Suetsugu's Warehouse, Port of Nagasaki

Hundreds of battle-experienced samurai either rode or marched hurriedly to join forces at Omura preparing for the battle with the Christians. The governor's entire legion had left Nagasaki at a forced march, and the city was now eerily quiet.

The evening peace was interrupted by a group of men cautiously approaching the prison warehouse, though they made no real effort at stealth. Several of the dozen men assigned to guard the warehouse came to investigate.

'What are you still doing in Nagasaki?' Noboru asked. Like the two men beside him, he was dressed in the uniform of an official of the Governor. 'Do you not know a war is about to begin?'

'We are guarding this warehouse, as the Governor ordered us to do.'

'What, are you cowards? Why have you not presented yourself for battle in Omura?'

'We told you: the Governor instructed us to watch over the warehouse.'

'The Governor ordered *twelve* men to look after a bunch of helpless women and children? What kind of men are you?'

'What is the purpose of your questioning?' asked the lead guard. He peered more closely at the new officials, whom he had never seen before.

'The Governor has ordered *us* to inspect the city for cowards hiding from battle. Where do you think the Governor needs you most?' Noboru pressed. 'On the battlefield facing the enemy, or standing in front of a locked warehouse full of crippled, harmless women? Which action carries greater honour?'

'To fight in battle,' one of the younger guards answered as he dropped his chin to his chest.

'We cannot all go,' another guard replied. 'Some of us have to remain to watch the warehouse. Three of us will stay. The rest will go to battle.'

'Good,' Noboru answered. 'The Governor needs every man available.'

'It must have been a miscommunication regarding our numbers,' the lead guard suggested. 'We are not cowards.'

'Show it with your actions. Show it on the battlefield.' Noboru nodded curtly and turned and walked away. His two companions followed him.

Two hours later a lone figure approached the three remaining guards.

'Halt,' the most senior guard yelled. 'Move and we will kill you.'

'I've come to offer you a chance to live,' Father Joaquim said matter-of-factly.

'What?' the senior guard said. He scrutinized the priest's rugged features. Recognition slowly dawned on him. 'Wait. I know you. You're the *gaijin* priest who's leading the rebellion.'

'I've come to offer you a chance to live.'

'You offer *the three of us* a chance to live? *You* should worry about *your life*, priest.'

'Do you see those men out there?' Father Joaquim asked. 'They are the fathers and brothers of the women and children in that warehouse.' In the dark, the guards could only see faint outlines, enough to reveal many men, but not enough to reveal their emaciated, weakened condition.

'They are Christians outlawed by the regime,' the senior guard said. 'They deserve death and torture.'

Ignoring the guard's rant, Joaquim continued: 'The Lord has mercy for those who repent – and so do I.'

'You were unwise to come here alone,' the senior guard said as he drew his sword.

'Apologize and ask the Lord for forgiveness and you may live,' Joaquim offered. 'Do it not and your fate rests with the fathers and brothers on the hill.'

'I will cut your head off, priest.'

Joaquim produced a sword from behind his back, swinging it with skill. 'Will you comply? Will you apologize and ask the Lord for forgiveness?'

In response, the senior guard charged at Joaquim.

The Jesuit blocked the attack with his sword, parrying and moving into a position where he sliced off the guard's head in one smooth action. Stunned by the priest's sword skills and the death of their senior guard, the junior guards froze, staring at their superior's lifeless head.

'I extend our offer of mercy one more time. Apologize for your crimes against these innocent families and ask the Lord for forgiveness.'

'Yes, yes, we apologize!'

'Leave your weapons and be on your way, young men. And may the Lord have mercy on your souls.'

The remaining guards dashed past the warehouse gates and down the street.

The village men emerged from the shadows and smashed open the warehouse lock. The gate swung wide, but instead of being joyous, the women hid in the back of the warehouse, ashamed of their disfigurements. The men entered behind Father Joaquim and stood silhouetted against the evening light. Cautiously one, then another, of the women and children emerged from the shadows.

After hugging their loved ones, the men quickly ushered them out of the dark confines of the sinister structure. But the deplorable condition of their mangled women and children shocked and appalled the men, causing many to weep at the effects of their torture. As families reacquainted themselves, Joaquim counted the women and children, pleased to discover that not a soul was missing.

Several of the most mangled women approached him timidly.

'Father, we must confess a heavy weight on our hearts,' said Hatsumi. Then she burst into tears.

'What is it, Hatsumi-chan?'

'Several of us recanted and apostatized in the deputy's warehouse.'

Joaquim replied, 'The Lord knows your heart. Have no fears.'

'What shall we do, Father?'

'Revoke your apostasy, and it shall be no more.'

Several other women and children gathered around. 'By the will of our hearts, we revoke our apostasy.'

'And so it is!' Father Joaquim exclaimed. 'And let us not forget that *all* of this is possible because of God Almighty.'

'Amen,' the crowd agreed.

He gave thanks to God. 'Let our joy here today also travel far, and serve as inspiration to all Christians here in Japan and abroad.'

'Amen,' the crowd responded.

'Come, let us leave now. The Governor will soon learn of our escape. We are not yet out of the darkness.'

CHAPTER SIXTY-THREE

20 July 1626
Fields of Omura, District of Nagasaki

Animals fled in all directions as a large army prepared for battle on the plain of Omura next to Omura Bay. Governor Kawachi, Deputy-Lieutenant Suetsugu, and Daimyo Shigemasa surveyed their legions of samurai and other warriors, arranged in well-defined units, almost 5,000 men in total. Although Governor Kawachi was the symbolic authority figure and representative of the Shogun's regime, Shigemasa was the most experienced in battle, so he would lead the forces in crushing the Christians and their ronin allies. The Daimyo had dispersed his army across the long field in 20 detachments of 250 each, to implement his battle plan.

First, seven heavy cannon and five massive catapults would unleash devastating carnage on the assembled Christians, no doubt sending them into panic. Then, on the front line of each detachment, *ashigaru* foot soldiers bore arquebus-style muskets. The samurai class considered *ashigaru* their social inferiors, but to be effective combatants. The Daimyo could not overstate the importance of his *ashigaru* troops in the grand scheme of his battle plans.

Behind the *ashigaru* stood their loaders, who would prepare and load the next rounds of musket balls into spare arquebuses as they fired. The Daimyo had also assembled a specialized group of expert bowmen who would fire on the enemy with unpredictable trajectories.

Following a devastating volley of lead and arrows, spearmen would advance on the opposing army.

Yet, despite the overwhelming power of the Daimyo's opening offensive, the real strength of his army was in the thousands of ruthless samurai forces, who would obliterate any remaining Christians with their razor-sharp swords in close hand-to-hand combat.

After his victory, Shigemasa pondered, would the Shogun reward him with even more lands? In his mind, the experienced warlord knew he would be victorious in slaughtering any force the Christians could muster. The only unanswered question was when the Christians would arrive. He had sent out multiple spies, but had not yet received word of the enemy's approach.

'Look!' the Deputy-Lieutenant shouted at that moment, as he pointed. 'Our spies.'

A few minutes later, the informants arrived. 'Have you spotted them?' Shigemasa asked.

'We have seen nothing, Lord. We inspected all the surrounding meadows and valleys.' The spy shrugged. 'Nothing. No sign of Christian soldiers.'

'They must be having difficulty coordinating their pathetic rebellion,' the Governor said. He was growing annoyed. Kawachi could not understand why their spies could not spot the insurgents' army.

'Perhaps it was a hoax,' one spy suggested.

'It is not a hoax!' the governor replied. 'The priest has escaped the Shogun somehow, gathered men, and captured our guards.'

'A Christian rebellion is overdue,' Suetsugu added. 'There have long been whispers of an uprising.'

'Then where are they?' the daimyo growled.

The Governor shook his head and huffed. 'The stupid priest obviously knows nothing of war. Without doubt, he is overwhelmed by our show of force.'

'So what do we do, Lord?' one spy asked.

'Keep looking.' Shigemasa spat on the ground from his elevated position in the saddle and continued to wait.

* * *

'What were you doing up there?' Tonia asked as Father Joaquim returned after an hour alone on the mountain.

'I was praying. Difficult decisions require quiet, contemplative prayer.'

'And what have you decided?'

'We head to the mountains.'

'I thought we were going to the fields of Omura?'

'No. The Holy Spirit told me we should head to the mountains.'

'Are you sure?' Noboru asked. 'Many cannot climb and we could get trapped in the mountains.'

'If your intuition tells you this, Father, you should follow it,' Master Watanabe interjected. 'This is how the Creator often speaks to us – with a still voice when your mind is quiet.'

'Will we hide in the mountains?' Shiro asked.

'I don't know, Shiro-kun,' Father Joaquim answered with a soft voice. 'I don't have all the answers yet.'

'But how will we escape, Father?'

'The Lord will show us the way. We need only to trust Him.'

'Are you certain, Father?' Noboru asked. 'The Governor and Deputy-Lieutenant are evil and strong in number.'

Father Joaquim stopped and turned to face the villagers and former prisoners before opening his Bible. 'Listen to this. Take it to heart.' He read: "Do not be afraid; do not be discouraged, for the Lord your God will be with you wherever you go."' He closed the book. 'That message God gave Joshua is also for us.'

'Yes, Father,' Noboru answered. 'I will try to have courage.'

'You need not try.' Father Joaquim smiled at him. 'You already *are* cour—'

Before he could finish speaking, a woman near him shrieked and grabbed her shoulder. An arrow protruded from it, and she clutched at it in agony. Another arrow struck a tree beside Father Joaquim's head. 'Protect the children!' Father Joaquim shouted. 'Get them on the ground! Where are the arquebuses we seized from the guards?'

After a few moments of confusion, and having spotted two horse-mounted samurai who had fired the arrows, the villagers fired the confiscated arquebuses, striking one rider. The other samurai rode away, with the injured rider's horse following.

* * *

Back on the battlefield, two guards ran past the Daimyo's army, towards the official flag bearers, where they knew they would find the generals. Moments later, they reached the Deputy-Lieutenant, breathing hard and struggling to speak.

'Why are you not watching my warehouse?' Suetsugu said.

'The Christian women and children …' – the guard stopped to catch his breath again – '… have escaped.'

'What do you mean? What happened?' the Governor shouted.

'The priest and his companions ambushed us, Governor.'

'How is that possible?' the governor roared. 'I instructed a dozen guards to stand watch!'

'They pretended to have orders from you that all but three of us should join you in the fight, and we believed them. So when the Christians arrived, they outnumbered us, Governor. The priest cut off the head of our senior guard.'

'So it *was* a hoax!' Shigemasa thundered. 'The priest tricked us, too. This whole war challenge was a diversion to carry out his rescue.'

Red in the face, Kawachi, Suetsugu, and Shigemasa felt flustered and infuriated amid the confusion.

'Look,' Suetsugu said as he pointed across the field. 'More spies are coming.'

Two horses galloped hard across the plain, only one with a visible rider. A limp body hung across the neck of the other mount.

'Lord Shigemasa,' the spy said, 'we spotted the enemy on the edge of Nagasaki.'

'Are they coming here?'

'No, Lord. They are heading towards the mountains.'

'How many men are they?'

'I do not know, Governor. Their force was hidden.'

'What happened to this samurai?' Shigemasa asked, nodding towards the dead man tied to his horse.

'They shot him.'

'So they have weapons.' Shigemasa felt pleased that armed conflict would finally proceed, and that his clan would have the opportunity and honour to annihilate the Christian sect once and for all.

'What do we do?' Suetsugu asked.

'We send our army into the mountains after them and finish this.'

'Our entire army?'

'Yes. This ends today,' said the Governor. 'It's time to kill this troublesome priest – and all the remaining Christians with him.'

CHAPTER SIXTY-FOUR

20 July 1626
Tara Mountains, District of Nagasaki

Shigemasa divided his forces into two units. By midday, the first unit, smaller and on horseback, had arrived at the location where the spies had spotted the fleeing Christians. The second unit was made up of samurai foot soldiers and other ground troops, along with those responsible for transporting the heavy cannons and catapults via oxen. For a large and bulky unit, they moved quickly.

'There they are,' the spy leading the first unit called back from the brow of a hill. The horsemen watched the Christians below make slow progress across the narrow valley. They were a bedraggled group struggling their way forward, most appearing to be in a weak and debilitated state, others hobbling at the rear, unable to walk unassisted.

'Where are the rest of them?' one of the horseman asked. 'I count fewer than fifty.'

'Maybe we should just take them,' another suggested.

'No,' their leader said. 'The Daimyo ordered that we only track and spot them, and then report their location back to him right away.'

'I don't understand. Why stop here?' said his companion.

'These Christians are deceptive. They could be a decoy, meant to lure us into a trap. We will not disobey the Daimyo's orders.'

* * *

'Look.' Noboru pointed to the samurai scouts sitting on their horses on the brow of a hill far behind them. 'Samurai. We're moving too slowly. They're going to catch us.'

'He's right, Father,' Master Watanabe agreed. 'We're too slow.'

'I know,' Joaquim replied, carrying Akihiko on his shoulders. 'But what can we do?'

'Leave me,' Akihiko answered. 'Leave me behind and save yourselves.'

'We will *not* leave you.' Joaquim adamantly shook his head.

'I can take Akihiko-san,' Master Watanabe offered. 'I know of a small cave nearby. It has just enough space for the two of us to hide.'

'I don't know, Master Watanabe.' Joaquim rubbed the back of his neck. 'You have given us so much help on this journey. We need your assistance.'

'No, you don't need me. Remember, Father, I told you, I'm only a guide.'

'But I can't perform miracles like you do.'

'What do you mean? I only guided and observed you, Father. You don't need me. You should not depend on me. The same spirit that lives in Jesus also lives in you. You have the same powers.' Master Watanabe paused. 'Believe and *know* that you can move mountains, and you will.'

Joaquim clutched his hands as he observed the legions of samurai approaching from a distance. As they advanced, their numbers appeared to swell. And as the army closed in on them, Joaquim noticed the increased nervousness of his village.

There was an awkward silence as Father Joaquim and Master Watanabe acknowledged it was time to go their separate ways.

'Thank you, my friend, for everything you've done for us.'

'You're most welcome. I wish you well on the rest of your journey.'

'Thank you, Master Watanabe,' Tonia added, her eyes brimming with tears. 'We will miss you.'

All the refugees bowed to honour him. Then Master Watanabe picked up Akihiko, placed him over his shoulders, and walked away.

'We will meet again,' Master Watanabe promised as he left. 'Now go, and remember – the Creator walks with you.'

CHAPTER SIXTY-FIVE

Without Akihiko, the villagers moved faster, and their quicker pace brought them to a spot known to many in the village.

'I know these mountains.' Noboru studied the area, his face registering increased concern. 'There is no exit along this path. We have trapped ourselves.'

'Should we go back, Father?' Tonia asked.

'No.' Joaquim shook his head, resolute. 'We will *not* go back.'

'Why not?' Noboru challenged the Jesuit. 'The mountains are too steep ahead. We can't get through.'

'The Lord tells me we must move forward.'

'How do you know that?'

'Because my intuition tells me so.'

'If you are wrong, we will *all* die,' Noboru declared, waving his hand towards the women and children.

An older villager added to the fear: 'Noboru is right. It's impossible. I know these mountains too.'

'It's impossible.' A growing murmur of dissent permeated the group.

'*Nothing* is impossible for the Lord!' Father Joaquim roared. His uncharacteristic fierceness quieted the crowd. Exasperated, the priest appeared finally fed up with the villagers' defeatism, observing hopelessness and futility in their body language. Once they were all silent, he jumped onto a rock to address them.

'Long ago a large group of God's people was held captive by harsh and cruel overlords. Through many powerful miracles, God convinced those overlords to release His people. But soon the overlords and their armies chased after the fleeing people, until the people came to a great sea. If they turned back they would encounter their pursuers. If they went forward they would drown. They protested to their leader, saying, "Did you lead us into the wilderness just to die?"'

'Does that sound familiar?' Father Joaquim saw signs of understanding emerge on the weary faces before him. Hope flared within him that his message would convince them that this path was possible, that they could overcome this obstacle, despite their weakness and injuries.

Noboru pursed his lips and placed his hands on his hips. He said, 'It's the story of the children of Israel fleeing Egypt. But that is not the same as our problem.'

'How is it different?' Joaquim challenged.

'*You* are not Moses.'

Joaquim spoke in a voice loud enough for all to hear. 'You are correct, Noboru. I am not Moses, nor do I pretend to be. But the same Spirit who spoke to Moses speaks to me. And you will hear Him speak to you, too, if you truly listen.'

'But how do we know for sure?' Noboru asked.

'Let me tell you another story.' Father Joaquim saw that he had their attention. 'A prophet was bold enough to speak out against an evil king and queen. As a result, the queen swore to have the prophet killed, so he ran into the wilderness, and sat under a tree, waiting for death. Then an angel came to him and told him he was not alone, and to go up on the mountain – much like this mountain. And when he was on the mountain, a great wind passed by, but the Lord was not in the wind. Then came an earthquake and a huge fire. But the Lord was not in the earthquake or the fire. But after the fire came a still, small voice that told the prophet what to do. He obeyed the still, small voice, and everything happened just as the still, small voice had told him. Do you know this story?'

The villagers looked puzzled until young Shiro spoke up. 'It is the story of the prophet Elijah fleeing from Queen Jezebel.'

'That's right, Shiro-kun. And how did the Lord speak to Elijah when his life was in danger?'

'Through the still, small voice!' Shiro shouted, with a wide grin and eyes that sparkled.

Joaquim jumped down from the rock and lifted Shiro into the air. 'That's correct, Shiro-kun. And the still, small voice – my intuition – is telling me we must go on, just as it told Moses the Israelites must walk into the sea. God parted the sea for them, and He will make a way for us.'

'Are you certain, Father?' Noboru asked, his expression betraying his doubt.

Joaquim hesitated for a moment, then said, 'I *believe* that God is walking with us. Have faith, and trust the Lord.'

'But in these mountains, there is no room for error. If your intuition is wrong, they will slaughter us.'

'Going ahead shows we trust in God. Where man is weak, God is strong. We were never meant to be alone and do everything on our own. Remember, man's extremity is God's greatest opportunity.'

'Yes, Father,' more villagers answered. In front of him, the people seemed to gather new hope. Tired limbs appeared to find new energy, and the villagers stretched and prepared themselves to march again. The priest and the villagers exchanged smiles. They offered support to one another.

'Let us not fear. Nothing in this world can harm us with God to protect us and provide for us, if we ask Him.' Silently, Father Joaquim reflected on one of his favourite Bible passages: "Yea, though I walk through the valley of the shadow of death, I will fear no evil: for thou art with me; thy rod and thy staff they comfort me."

The exhausted band of Christians carried on towards the end of the road. Before them stood the entrance to a small abandoned silver mine at the base of the mountain. It appeared closed, deserted many years before. And, as Noboru had warned, beyond the silver mine, the mountains appeared too steep to climb.

They were, as predicted, trapped.

The group approached the battered entrance to the mine with trepidation. The entrance was dark, shallow, and sealed-up. Joaquim gestured for some to investigate it further. Their search revealed that the mine comprised an extensive cave system buried within its tunnels.

With ashen faces, the entire village glanced back at an advancing company of samurai on horseback. Heavily armed, their body language revealed their confidence, poised for the pending slaughter. But they held back, merely watching.

'Why are they not attacking?' Noboru asked, clearly uncomfortable.

'They are waiting,' Joaquim answered.

'Waiting for what?'

'For their leaders.'

'But why not charge? They have us cornered.'

'Those in charge want to execute us with their own hands; they hope to gain political favour by it.'

Noboru fidgeted. 'What do we do?'

'We pray, and we wait.'

'Wait for what?'

'Their arrival.'

'And then what?'

'Then it is up to God.' Father Joaquim sat down on a large rock and everyone gathered around. 'Our lives are in His hands now.'

Beneath him he felt the ground vibrate. Small stones tumbled around. Birds startled into the sky. Then all was still again.

CHAPTER SIXTY-SIX

Less than an hour later, Shigemasa, the Governor, and the Deputy-Lieutenant arrived at the end of the path, dismounted from their horses, and laughed as they approached the shabby little band of Christians huddled together at the entrance to the mine.

A sudden flight of birds startled horses and warriors alike, as they headed towards the far mountains. The surrounding trees were eerily quiet. Nothing stirred. No wind. No creatures. No birdsong.

'Stay here,' Joaquim instructed. He approached the three officials.

The samurai's horses began to paw the ground and snort. Their riders patted their necks and calmed them, but one started to turn and its rider was forced to make the horse turn a complete circle in an attempt to gain control. Hooves jittered as riders struggled to contain their mounts. Horses snorted, their ears flicking nervously backwards and forwards, as they pulled on their bridles.

'So, we have finally caught the infamous Father Joaquim,' Shigemasa gloated. They stood no more than a few feet apart.

Feeling vindicated, the Daimyo cast a contemptuous gaze at the fatigued-looking priest, clearly thinking about imminent lethal revenge. 'You have caused us much trouble, priest. You were fortunate to escape twice, but your luck has run out.' Shigemasa looked back at the Governor and Deputy-Lieutenant and chuckled. 'I think his head will look good hanging in the Shogun's castle, do you not agree?'

'Where is your Christian army, priest?' the Governor asked. 'Your message suggested thousands of hidden Christians.'

'We are here now,' Joaquim answered. He pulled his shoulders back and looked Kawachi in the eyes.

'That pathetic group?' Shigemasa laughed again as he pointed to the bedraggled group behind the priest.

'Our greatest force is not visible to your eyes,' Joaquim said.

'What do you mean?' The Governor looked perplexed.

'God – God is with us in these mountains.'

'Your God does not exist,' the Governor answered. 'And each of you will learn this today when we behead you.'

'"The Lord knoweth the way of the righteous: but the way of the ungodly shall perish,"' Father Joaquim quoted.

'What?'

'It's from the Bible.'

'You are a fool for believing in that,' the Deputy-Lieutenant mocked. 'The Shogun is god in Japan.'

'Have your men drop their swords and ask the Lord for forgiveness, or I will pick up mine.' Joaquim lifted his chin and pulled back his shoulders.

'Grab your sword, priest,' the Daimyo shouted. 'It is time to end this.'

Joaquim turned and walked back to his group.

'Now what?' Noboru asked.

'Now we thank God for protecting us.'

'That's it?'

'No. Have enough faith in Him to believe in a miracle. Be ready to enter the caves in the mine as soon as you see my signal, all of you.'

'What signal?'

'You will know it when you see it.'

The priest closed his eyes and reflected on one of his favourite Bible passages: *If you have faith as small as a mustard seed, you can say to this mountain, 'Move from here to there,' and it will move.* As he reopened his eyes, he collected himself, making his peace with God and thanking Him for what would come next. Then he withdrew Master Yamaguchi's sword from its sack. Wielding it with his strong forearm, he walked back and confronted Shigemasa's army a short way away.

He scanned the valley. From left to right he saw thousands of battle-ready samurai, thirsty for their blood. He felt a gentle tremor beneath his feet. Looking up he saw wispy, rainbow-coloured clouds motionless in the sky above him. He smiled, absorbing their beauty, not comprehending their meaning.

'What is that fool doing?' said Shigemasa. He remounted his horse next to the Governor and Deputy-Lieutenant. 'Does he truly believe he has a chance against us?' His head pounded, pressure building behind his eyes. *The air was suffocating in these mountains, heavy, oppressive.*

They laughed at the Jesuit's audacity. Behind them, a number of the samurai shifted uncomfortably and their horses snorted, and pawed the ground once more. They had heard rumours of a *gaijin* warrior priest who had killed two of the Shogun's greatest fighters in one fight. They had not believed it, but seeing the courage of the priest before them – a man who dared challenge the might of a thousand samurai, unarmed and alone save for a magnificent katana in hand – they began to believe it was true.

A rattle of stones scuttled behind them. Horses skittered, their nervousness enhancing their riders' doubt.

'Turn to me and be saved,' Father Joaquim shouted, 'all you ends of the earth; for I am God, and there is no other!' With that he raised Master Yamaguchi's sword above his head. The afternoon light caught the blade, and it flashed like a celestial flame as he drove it into the rock beneath him.

As he did so the ground trembled again and shook. The horses neighed in panic and tried to retreat, crashing into each other. Trees swayed. The troops looked around in confusion and fear, staggering off balance as the earth beneath them began to ripple and shake more violently.

Leaving his sword lodged in the rock, Joaquim hurried back to the mine entrance. 'Into the mine,' he shouted, waving them inside. 'Now!'

The Christians hurried into the mine as quickly as they could, doing their best to hide in the various crevices.

Looking through the entrance, they saw the earth continue to erupt and split with growing power. Joaquim saw Shigemasa's samurai stumbling and falling to the ground. In every direction soldiers lost their balance as they braced themselves against the instability of the very ground they stood on. The Jesuit saw fear and confusion and wide-eyed wonder in the faces of samurai gathered to kill him and his people. The walls of the cave shuddered. The

Christians huddled together and held their breath, deafened by the cracks and groans of the earth as it strained around them.

'Take him!' Shigemasa shouted. He pointed at the cave, but as samurai struggled to cross the shaking earth, the ground split and rocks and boulders crashed down from the mountain above.

The leaders fled on horseback, terrified, just before the earthquake caused a landslide to bury the charging warriors. As Joaquim watched from the narrow entrance of the silver mine, the earthquake vented its fury on the samurai host. From neighbouring mountains, gigantic movements of soil, rock, and trees crashed down the sides of the cliffs, gathering speed and power; a tsunami of rock and earth that destroyed everything in its path.

In their cave sanctuary, the very foundations of the earth shook and wavered, the noise thunderous. The screams of animals and men reverberated through the tunnels, as Father Joaquim and his villagers readied themselves for their inevitable end.

Then the mountainous cul-de-sac collapsed in on itself, and became an unstoppable crushing force that filled the adjacent valley, engulfing everything beneath a huge deluge of earth and mud.

From outside, the entrance to the mine disappeared. No visible trace remained; removed from the face of the earth; lost to memory.

CHAPTER SIXTY-SEVEN

20 July 1626
Silver Mine

Hours later – or was it days? – when the tectonic earth movements ceased, the Christians found themselves completely sealed in the mine. In the darkness, everyone was overwhelmed with the raw smell of fresh earth and gravel, their lungs full of the swirling dust.

'Is everyone okay?' Father Joaquim called out. 'Check your family members. Check your neighbours.'

Chatter and commotion broke the silence as the dust began to finally settle and the earth again resembled something solid, to be trusted. After a while, someone called out, '"But I have chosen you, and ordained you, that ye should go and bring forth fruit, and that your fruit should remain."'

CHAPTER SIXTY-EIGHT

23 July 1626
Shogun's Castle

With a large crowd on hand to applaud his every move, Shogun Iemitsu practised his archery skills in the large courtyard of his castle. His practice had paid off. He had become skilful, and each time he hit the bull's-eye with great accuracy the crowd responded with applause and cheers. And each time, in response, he raised his arms in triumph as he swaggered around the yard.

Amid one such display a senior retainer approached him. 'Lord Shogun, you have a message from Nagasaki.'

'Give it to me.' Snatching the note, the Shogun read the piece of paper, his temper rising, his cheeks reddening, until he exploded in uncontrollable fury. Crumpling the paper, he threw it on the ground before grabbing his bow, with which he smashed a lantern that sat on top of a nearby post. Turning one way and another, looking for objects to help him vent his fury, he grabbed a handful of arrows and smashed them over his knee. He grabbed more arrows and was about to break them, but stopped and gazed around the courtyard, full of his samurai and scores of servants, each of whom sensed their vulnerability. Frozen with blinking eyes, everyone peered around, pondering who would be the victim of the Shogun's wrath.

Hell would be paid ...

EPILOGUE

24 July 1626
Kuchinotsu, Shimabara Peninsula, Kyushu

As dawn broke, a lone peasant crossed a muddy rice field towards a small village in Kuchinotsu at the southern tip of the Shimabara Peninsula. The peasant walked with purpose as he observed the natural beauty of the unique location surrounded by green hills, ample blossoming trees, and local fauna scurrying in all directions. In the centre of the village, the peasants were preparing to have their only paltry meal of the day. As the stranger approached, peasants arose to receive him.

'How may we help?' the village leader asked.

'I come to carry news to all villages in Shimabara and Amakusa,' the traveller answered.

'We are listening.'

'I carry news of a Christian Father who has evaded the forces of the regime. Empowered by God, he has overcome the Shogun, the Governor, and the Daimyo in one stroke. It is good news for all hidden Christians.'

'But we are not Christian,' the village leader replied, his voice shaking.

'I also come to recite an old poem about the divine revelation,' the visitor declared.

'Recite your poem,' the village leader said.

> *When five years shall have passed five times,*
> *All the dead trees shall bloom;*
> *Crimson clouds shall shine brightly in the western sky,*
> *And a boy of divine power shall make his appearance;*
> *These things shall usher in a Christian revival in Japan.*

'*Tachi-Aguru*,' the village leader replied. Rise up.

'*Tachi-Aguru* for sure,' the messenger responded. 'It is time for all Christians in Japan to rise!'

Acknowledgements

In completing this novel, I would like to thank my entire family and circle of friends, who supported me on this long journey of bringing this story to life.

In particular, I would like to thank my father David, my mother Heather, my sister Kristjana, and my grandmother Delores, for their tireless support and generosity, and for being the great listeners they are.

I would also like to extend a special thank you to Jelena and Xavier for their inspiration, patience, and support in bringing this endeavour to completion.

Last, I would like to thank my agent Peter, and my editors, Jerry and Jennifer, whose expertise, skill, and mentorship were invaluable in bringing this project to fruition.

Author's Note

Swords of Silence was inspired by real history and real characters in history, including the Shogun of Japan and other members of his regime. Among others, these included his cabinet members, the Daimyo ('warlord') of Shimabara, and the Governor and Deputy-Lieutenant of Nagasaki.

Not least, however, this novel was inspired by the real heroes of history, including all the brave missionaries of the Mission of the Society of Jesus – otherwise known as the Jesuits – along with their faithful converts.

Remaining true to events of the past, I ask myself: Who am I to soften the edges of history to create a more gentle story?

Shaun Curry